MW00617500

A laudable sci-fi yarn that's both irreverent and relevant.

- KIRKUS REVIEWS

Very symbolic of the fear that plagues many societies today. The first-person narrative voice is powerful... The writing is evocative, and at time, reads like poetry. This is a book that will appeal to fans of crime fiction and sci-fi. Star Rating: 4.5 / 5

- MANHATTAN BOOK REVIEW

Richter's fable is laugh-out-loud funny, but the humor is more like a hot stick in the eye than slapstick. Satire that cuts this close to the bone should carry a warning sticker.

- RABBIT HOLE REVIEWS

L.I.F.E. IN THE 23RD CENTURY

L.I.F.E. IN THE 23RD CENTURY

A DYSTOPIAN TALE OF CONSUMERISM, CORPORATE COFFEE, AND CROWBARS

JASON R. RICHTER

Dedicated to everyone that continues to support this type of behavior.

"A comfortable, smooth, reasonable, democratic unfreedom prevails in advanced industrial civilization, a token of technical progress. Indeed, what could be more rational than the suppression of individuality in the mechanization of socially necessary but painful performances..."

Herbert Marcuse

This is not a public service announcement.

Repeat, this is not a public service announcement, nor a threat-level upgrade.

An unidentified terrorist cell has not, repeat, not leveled the corner store with explosives made from easily attained household products.

Your life is not in danger.

You should not make your way in an orderly fashion—being mindful of children, the elderly, and the infirm—to the hardened concrete bunker in the basement of your apartment building. Prayers for protection sent up to the deity of your choice will go unheeded for many reasons, but mainly because they are unnecessary.

This is not the Emergency Broadcast System.

This is not even a test of the Emergency Broadcast System, which, in this instance, is not the same as saying that this is a genuine emergency. Had this been an actual emergency, you would have been instructed in what to do. But you won't, because this isn't.

The head of Homeland Security will not issue a statement regarding the current situation. Swift Terror Assessment and

Response teams will not be deployed to the scene. The Inquisitor Branch of Homeland Security will not launch a full-scale investigation into the incident.

There is no smoking crater to examine. No toppled building. No next of kin to notify. No one saying, "Is this your son/daughter/father/mother/brother/sister? We know it's hard, but we need to be sure, ma'am/sir."

Celebrities will not stage a telethon for the victims' families. Waiters will not ask you to donate toward building a memorial statue/reflecting pool/amusement park. Magnetic remembrance paraphernalia for your automobile will not be available at this store or any other patriotic retailer.

Suspected terrorists, accomplices of suspected terrorists, and all their relatives will not be shown wearing black hoods on every channel, while being led into a super-maximum federal detention center. Images of armed guards and thirty-foot electrified fences topped with razor wire around a squat building capable of withstanding ground zero nuclear assault will not be available for your viewing pleasure.

The President will not interrupt your must-watch, can't-miss sitcom. He will not give his rousing, "situation normal, there is nothing to fear" speech from the safety of Air Force One six miles above your apartment. He will neither plead with you to remain calm nor assure you that everything is fine, while they ferry members of Congress to an impregnable bunker inside a mountain until the dust settles.

Doomsayers will say that this is an apocalyptic event. The End of Days.

Religious fanatics—ours and theirs—are like the lottery. Eventually, someone will get the numbers right.

However, at this moment, all apocalyptic seals remain unbroken. The Choir Invisible is still rehearsing for the grand finale. The Horsemen are doing nothing more terrible than letting their mounts graze.

There is no threat.

No attack.

No telethon.

No Apocalypse.

No terrorists.

Not tonight.

NO TERRORISTS.

Not tomorrow, either.

Trust me.

This has not been a public service announcement. We now return to my life, already in progress.

L.I.F.E.

Noun

: an electronic machine implanted in citizens of the United States of America starting in the 23rd century.

Abbreviation for:

Life-force Input and Feedback Equipment

CHAPTER 1

This sort of thing does not happen. Manufacturers install fail-safes, politicians enact laws against the possibility of the giant box rolling toward me. The box is two lanes wide, double the height of my car, and spins chunks of asphalt into the air when a corner hits the road. Except for me, the highway is empty, my car's auto-drive rocketing me closer and closer to the corrugated steel container. Collision-avoidance software warns me of the imminent impact. Surely, there must be some program built into my car, and at the last instant, my car will swerve to safety. The car is calculating. Sizing up the box. Waiting for the precise moment. I keep my hands in my lap, watching the box spin closer and closer, chunks of pavement bouncing off my car's windshield. The last thing I want to do is touch the steering wheel, engage manual drive, and nullify all the processing the car requires to save me.

The container takes to the air, and I see nothing but empty road in front of me. I knew there had to be something that would keep me safe.

A shadow falls across my car.

Then the sun goes out, and everything stops.

Is that the last thing you remember?

The thought comes into my head, partly as a voice, partly text.

Yes, I reply in my head.

What do you remember before that?

Before that?

Before that?

I was at work.

No, I was leaving work, I believe.

Yes, I was in the parking lot at work. The lasers in each eyelid paint a new message icon on my eyes, as I near my car. Using the trackball in the roof of my mouth, I scroll over with my tongue and select the icon from the heads-up display. The message auto-plays.

Greetings, P. McGewan-X04.

I try to see my car through the spectral image playing on my eye.

Today's audit is sponsored by the Office of Homeland Security and will help to ensure proper levels of patriotism throughout these United States. Please make your way to your vehicle with haste and have a nice day. God bless you. The soft-spoken woman disappears. Lasers paint a green glow around my car, just when I thought my vehicle location Gizmo needs another update.

The Auditor stands at my car's bumper, waiting. His Sanitary Human Interface Terminal circles in a lazy holding pattern over his head, like an indifferent vulture. When I stop at the prescribed six paces from him, the flat screen breaks from its holding pattern and approaches me. The Auditor didn't speak, didn't even turn to look at me. The Interface Terminal hovers a foot from the tip of my nose. A recording of the Auditor appears on the screen. I can see the actual, real-time Auditor punching commands into his wrist.

"Is this your conveyance, citizen?" barks the face on the

screen, while the actual Auditor stares at the horizon, his face placid.

"Yes, sir." I click the button in the roof of my mouth, activating the heads-up display, and tongue the trackball of the mouth-mouse until I got to my car's title and registration. The documents display on the screen on my left wrist for the Auditor. The Terminal scans the title's barcode, and then the license plate.

By far, this was the easiest of Patriotism Audits. No historical trivia questions, no physical activity, no Bible verses to recite–just document production. Next, the face on the screen asks me about the magnetic memorabilia, and I'm already scrolling to those receipts.

"How many pieces of magnetic memorabilia are you displaying?"

"Seven, sir." I pull up the receipts on my wrist and hold them out for the Terminal's laser scanner. Once each magnet is scanned, I should be on my way.

"Why seven, citizen?"

The flesh-and-blood Auditor still does not glance in my direction, but his recorded face on the screen never breaks eye contact.

This is a new question.

"Four is the minimum required by law, but seven is suspicious. What are you hiding, citizen?"

Patriotism Rehab Prison, here I come. I swallow and try to think of an answer.

"And this one," a laser point jumps out of the Terminal and details a spot on one magnet, "is worn and discolored on the edge. Do you not respect the memory of the lives lost that this magnet commemorates?"

Your heartbeat is elevated, and you are perspiring. Would

you enjoy a mood stabilizer? Perhaps a muscle relaxant? Your
personal counselor is only a tongue-click away.

I tongue-click, No, to all these on my heads-up display and
try to think of a suitable answer for the Auditor.

"I hereby charge you with conduct unbecoming a Patriot
and inappropriate commemoration of lives lost in the War on
Terror. Fine of thirty-thousand credits or one year in Patriot
Rehabilitation. How would you like to repay society for your
negligence, citizen?"

A charge sheet appears on my heads-up with my bank
account next to it. Without looking over my shoulder, I knew a
pair of Homies was standing by to drag me away if I didn't
choose the fine. As soon as the hourglass turns back to a pointer,
I select the fine and watch the credits disappear.

The Homies slump off with the Auditor in trail, but his
Terminal remains for a moment. "A Patriot remembers," whispers the face before following its master.

I peel the offensive magnet off the bumper. Dozens of my
coworkers are being led to the hover buses that take them to
Patriotism Rehab. Tuesday will be rough, like always. The rest
of us, those who get to go home tonight, will have to pick up the
slack for the missing coworkers until they are rehabilitated or
replaced.

As I turn, a glint of silver catches my eye. At the distant
corner of the lot where the Auditors head, stands the sole
Inquisitor to rule them all. He's easy to spot. His obligatory
black leather trench coat shapes his body into a perfect
rectangle. His bald head pivots, his mirrored sunglasses reflect
the sunlight, like twin searchlights of a malicious lighthouse.
Watchful, patient, he waits for the next soul to splinter on his
reef. For a moment and from a safe distance, the Inquisitor
seems ridiculous. He looks like an upside-down exclamation
mark in front of the handful of contraband Spanish curse words

I know. Then, his gaze turns toward me, and I hustle to my car; auto-drive takes me away as soon as the door closes.

Very good. What happened before that?

The workday is ending. It's Monday. Monday means audits.

Even with twelve chipper reminders on the hour, every hour throughout the workday that Auditors would be coming, we still groan as a collective when we see them standing in the parking lot. The groan, per individual, equals only a bare whisper but multiply that by a thousand souls, it might as well have been a scream.

Patriots do not groan out loud at the sight of Auditors. Patriots look forward to proving their patriotism through weekly audits.

But there's still the groan. The groan that says, Really? Again? Couldn't you pack it in for one week? Just one?

The entire day shift dismounts the slidewalk and makes their way through the lot. Not too slow. Not too fast. Patriots neither try to outrun Auditors nor do they 'lollygag' which is the retro buzzword of the week. Last week, Patriots did not 'dilly-dally.'

The result of this unhurried rush looks like a drunken tornado. No one wants to lead; no one wants to bring up the rear. Everyone wants to be in the center. No one can see the entire group, no one can agree on the eye of the storm.

Coworkers parked closest to the building are met by Fitness Enforcement Agency Auditors, who always move the quickest because of their lack of auditing tools and body fat. The tan, muscular, and lightly oiled women in their bulletproof sports bras and spandex short-shorts go to work, shouting for squat thrusts.

"Jumping jacks, now move."

"On your back for Hello Dollies."

"On your feet, citizen. Run in place."

The rest of the lot is peppered with random Auditors from all branches of government. Besides FEA Auditors, the others use identical Terminals, and the only way to tell what sort of audit was to listen to the questions from the hovering screen. A Patriot knew every answer to every question that an Auditor might ask, but a smart Patriot eavesdrops, just in case they are asked the same questions in their audit.

"What is the Third Commandment?" shouts the face on the screen, while the thin strip of an Auditor checks her makeup in the mirror Gizmo on her L.I.F.E.

"Thou shalt have no other Gods before me," the citizen mumbles.

"Is that a question or a statement?" screams the Terminal.

"A statement, ma'am," says the citizen, this time louder and with more conviction, "thou shalt have no other Gods before me."

"Very good," says the Terminal. "Let's find out how well you know the Nicene Creed."

"What is the Seventeenth Amendment?" asks the next Auditor to a citizen standing at attention beside his vehicle.

"Congress shall have power to lay and collect taxes on incomes," the citizen says proudly to the screen, "from whatever source derived, without apportionment among the States, and without regard to any census or enumeration, sir."

"Very good," says the Patriotic History Auditor.

"Thank you, sir."

"Unfortunately, that's the Sixteenth Amendment," the disembodied head snaps, while the Auditor updates his status on his L.I.F.E. Two Homeland Security officers step up and grab the citizen. One Homie holds a gun to the citizen's head, while the other puts him in handcuffs.

"Wait," shouts the citizen, hands secured behind his back,

"I know it. It's the Terms for Senators. I can recite it. Please, let me recite it." One Homie hits the citizen in the neck with a stun gun. The citizen turns silent and limp, as the Homies drag him away.

The pack of employees thins as we progress. I parked at the far end of the lot, not the last car in the lot—that would arouse suspicion—but close to the last car.

Where do you work, citizen?

United States Cubicles.

What do you do at United States Cubicles, citizen?

I ensure we meet quality standards when the production line machinery installs drawer pulls.

What is your name, citizen?

P. McGewan-X04, cubicle production tech, fifth class.

Stand by. Stimulant dispensing.

My awareness deepens by a small increment as if transitioning from a vivid dream to a very drunken state of consciousness. The difference was subtle but noticeable. For a moment, I believe I am still in a dream state, floating weightless. Or I am dead. As I regain awareness, I notice my lips are stretched into an 'O' and a tube is taking up most of my mouth, heading down my throat.

I am neither dead nor dreaming. I am in a hospital. More specifically, I am floating in the thick gel of a sensory-deprivation tank; the tube in my mouth feeds, hydrates, and oxygenates my blood and body. I know my eyes are open, but only because of the resistance that the gel puts on my eyelashes when I blink. Blinking five times in a row activates my heads-up display. The lasers inside each eyelid wink and draw a grid directly onto my retinas. Working my tongue around the tube, I reach for the mouth-mouse. Each screen on the grid has the same message, "Your L.I.F.E. is temporarily suspended. Please stand by." The date/time screen is even shut off. Midnight flashes in the upper-left corner, 1 JAN 2203 flashes in the upper right. It might be midnight, but it's certainly not New Year's Day of the year I was born.

Instrumental music plays in my head. Then, a woman's voice.

Please stand by. All doctors are currently assisting other patients. A medical professional will be with you in the order you were revived. Your expected wait time is, the voice pauses, less than two minutes. We appreciate your patience. Your business is very important to us. Please remain calm, and a doctor will be with you shortly.

The music comes back. I can't remember why I am in a hospital or why the computer asked me the brain damage questions that everyone watches on television.

The woman's voice returns, the soft music plays in the background.

Did you know that since the inception of the Life-force Input and Feedback Equipment network, it has saved millions of lives? L.I.F.E. can alert paramedics in case of injury, heart attack, and stroke. L.I.F.E. can administer life-saving medication, while paramedics are in transit. And remember to visit the Gizmo store. Listen to your favorite radio stations, balance your checkbook, find showtimes, shop for groceries, or have a confidential chat with a personal counselor. The possibilities are endless. Ask your healthcare provider for authentic L.I.F.E. hardware and software. L.I.F.E., the one piece of equipment you cannot live without.

Every time I hear that commercial, I roll my eyes. When I had my annual service a few weeks ago, that commercial played on a loop in the lobby's Muzak system. We all have it installed at birth, I wanted to shout. Immigrants must be retrofitted with a L.I.F.E. rig before they can receive citizenship. The government insists that everyone gets the required upgrades, and as our bodies change, they resize the biometrics for ease of use and comfort. I went through ten different mouth-mice before they found one that didn't leave a callus the size of a squash on my tongue.

They might as well urge me to drive a Vague Automobile or drink Ishmael's Coffee. We don't have a choice. There is no competition. Well, the big corporations, like Ishmael's and Vague, prop up shadow competitors, companies that distribute coffee and cars that both taste and handle like they were made of the same material, namely used toilet paper. But it's cheaper for them than a monopoly lawsuit.

The life of a competitor is easy. Never waiting on customers, never worrying about inventory, just sitting in your shop watching videos on BluTube, and waiting for the monthly "profit" check to arrive from your "competitor." After retirement from the cubicle factory, when I've put in my forty years watching a machine install drawer hardware and am allowed to leave my X-class job, I intend to open a coffee shop as a competitor to Ishmael's.

There's a vibration in the tank, as the music stops. A screen the size of my palm warms up several inches in front of my face, and a recorded female voice plays in my ear. *All interactions are recorded for quality assurance and use in our training.*

Then, a real male voice says, "Thank you for your patience, I'm Doctor D. Kiefer-G55. I'm going to turn the monitor on so you can see me. Give me a thumbs up for 'yes' and a thumbs down for 'no.'"

I put the thumb on my left hand up, and the doctor's mustached face appears. The screen is high-impact plastic, no thicker than my fingernail, and floats freely in the gel.

"Try not to speak, or you may dislodge the tube and get a mouthful of gel. Just give me a thumbs up for good or thumbs down for bad. How are you feeling?"

Thumbs up.

"Good. I'm going to explain your injuries and do a few tests. If you do well, you'll be on your way home in no time. Okay?"

Thumbs up.

"Excellent. I'm going to override your L.I.F.E., so I can show you where you sustained injuries." The laser grid on my eyes shows a green outline of my body, parts flash red, as the doctor spoke. "You were dead for a few moments, as your skull was separated from your spine, eight of your vertebrae were crushed, likewise, your right arm and right leg were shattered entirely, your left shoulder was dislocated, your pelvis was fractured here, here, and here, and you had a pretty severe concussion. All that has been repaired, and we don't expect any complications. Okay?"

Thumbs up.

"Now, I'm going to test your reflexes. You may feel a slight prick, but just try to relax." An electrical impulse makes my right arm jerk, then my left, and then both legs. Likewise, each hand contracts, along with both feet, as the device, whatever it is, hovers through the tank. "Good. Reflexes are normal. I'm going to let some light into the tank now, so I can do a visual inspection. If you can't handle the light, just make a fist and I'll stop, okay?"

Thumbs up.

"Here we go."

Light slowly shines into the tank, and I can make out the room, full of similar tanks, some blackened, some empty. A few are transparent with doctors or nurses standing in front of them, holding clipboards, talking to floating patients contained therein. Dr. Kiefer-G55 is shorter than me, probably six-foot, with brown hair parted over his right ear and a bushy mustache. He doesn't look up at me, just maneuvers the screen around the tank using the trackball on his clipboard. Satisfied with what he sees, the doctor brings the screen back in front of my face.

"Everything looks good. Do you have questions?"

Thumbs up. The grid on my eye shows a list of questions, and I scroll down with my tongue to the first relevant one.

"An airborne container ship dropped a forty-ton Conex box on your conveyance," the doctor answers, after reading the question from his clipboard. "Fortunately, only one Conex box fell, and there was no one else on the road at the time."

I scroll to the next relevant question.

"You've been here for four days. We would have had you out in two days, but reattaching your skull to your spine was tricky, and we had to send for a specialist."

I absorb this information, then thought of one other question.

"Your attorney sued the company that owns the container ship. The negligent loadmaster was fired and faced civil and criminal charges. He had to pay you thirty-million credits, a sum matched by the company. Then the loadmaster was publicly executed two days ago. We hoped to have you at the execution for closure, but that was not possible. The execution is available to purchase on thumb drive in our gift shop if you'd like a copy. It's also streaming on BluTube for the next 90 days, I believe. The container ship company, as a peace offering, also provided you with a new conveyance." The doctor scrolls down on his clipboard. "A brand new Vague," the face on the screen says with a wink. "A real beauty. Any other questions?"

Thumbs down.

"Okay, I'll get the nurse, and we'll get you discharged and on your way. Have a nice day." The screen didn't shut off when he calls for the nurse. She was ten feet to the doctor's left, but he uses the clipboard's vid-link to summon her. Another screen moves into position in front of my face, this one filled by the blonde nurse. "Nurse," the doctor says into his vid-link, "sedate this man, and start his discharge paperwork."

"Yes, doctor," the nurse says, as she walks up to take the doctor's place in front of my tank. The doctor's screen shuts off and retreats as he walks to his next patient's tank. The nurse's screen centers itself in front of my face. "Good morning," she says, her smile taking up most of the screen. I give her a brief wave. "I'm going to give you a sedative, so we can get you out of this tank. Your record indicates that you are not allergic to any medication. Is that true?"

Thumbs up.

"Okay, read through the warning that pops up, and I'll be back in a few minutes." The nurse looks familiar. She seems friendly, but her eyes dart back and forth as she spoke, reading from the script scrolling across her clipboard. When the nurse leaves, the grid displays several hundred pages of warnings and disclaimers. I scroll to the bottom of the first page when I hear:

Doctor prescribed sedative, now dispensing.

My wrist vibrates as L.I.F.E. mixes different drugs into the sedative, then shoots the potent liquid into my artery. Just before consciousness leaves me, I realize that the nurse looks like my wife.

At Superior Patriotism, our specialty is making sure that you are driving the most patriotic car on the road. Custom bumper wraps and magnetic memorabilia to fit any vehicle and any budget. Ask about our subscription services. The look of your vehicle can be updated at your request or whenever new War on Terror commemorative designs become available. Remember, you aren't a Patriot until you visit Superior Patriotism.

Gravity and consciousness arrive at the same instant, and I jerk upright in the recovery room recliner. The grid appears in my vision.

Please stand by while your L.I.F.E. initializes.

The status bar reaches one hundred percent, and I scroll through each screen to make sure I still have all my Gizmos installed. The date/time is correct, according to the clock on the wall. My planner is back online, as well as my email and phone. I have several messages, text and voice, from various relatives wishing me well. One message is from my boss. He tells me to take a few days off and come back when I'm ready. My bank statement shows the deposit of the sixty million credits. The next item is the hospital's withdrawal of forty million credits for my stay, which put me at twenty million, and a Gizmo calculates that I can safely take three more days off from work before I get behind on my bills.

A button on my wrist deactivates the grid, and I pull my belongings from a box next to the chair. My jumpsuit looked like the hospital had cleaned or replaced it. The nametape over the left breast pocket looks new, P. McGewan-X04 stitched meticulously, along with my company's logo. The front of the jumpsuit closes automatically once my feet and hands go through the appropriate openings. My boots conform to my feet as I step into them. The only item remaining in the box is my universal identification card, which I place in my left breast pocket.

As I open the curtain to leave the recovery room, my wrist vibrates.

Please make your way to the Discharge desk on this floor.

After several wrong turns, I activate the map Gizmo, and the grid points me in the right direction.

The woman sitting at the glass-encased Discharge desk doesn't look up. Her Terminal drops from the ceiling on a retractable arm, causing a screeching sound in both of my ears.

"Name?" her image asks, as I take a step back.

"McGewan-X04." I expect some reaction when I say 'X04.' A knowing smile to let me know that she had started in a lowly

X-class job and worked her way up to administrative specialist, the O-class. Alternatively, a grimace would let me know that the X-class was beneath her contempt. Instead, her face is blank. She probably discharges people from every class, every day and has no opinion one way, or the other.

A document appears on the side of her screen. "Read this, thumbprint where appropriate, sign at the bottom." I oblige her with four thumbprints on the margin and a scribbled signature with the stylus dangling from a string. "Your doctor has issued a prescription," she says, as her Terminal tries to get closer to me and make eye contact. The shrieking noise increases as the Terminal moves nearer, so I keep bobbing and ducking to keep clear of it. "The pharmacy is on the first floor. I'll send you a map. Have a nice day." She pivots away and aims at the man standing behind and to the right of me. "Name?"

Once I am away from the desk, the ringing or feedback or whatever it is stopped, but every doctor and nurse I pass in the hallway with a clipboard brings it back. My head pounds on the elevator ride to the lobby. Three doctors stood between me and the door to the first fifty floors, but I am alone for the rest of the trip.

There's a short line at the pharmacy. I zone out, trying to relax enough to stop my headache. The pharmacist's Terminal drops from the ceiling, startling me visually and audibly, as a wave of static assaults me. I step around the screen and up to the counter.

"I have a prescription," I say directly to the man behind the counter. He looks down, sweat beading on his forehead, his hands shaking.

You are experiencing a panic attack. A mood stabilizer is being dispensed, and your personal counselor will be with you momentarily.

14

The med Gizmo on my wrist display shows that no medications are being administered.

The pharmacist's hands stop shaking after a moment, and he maneuvers his digital image in front of me again, the feedback screaming in my ears.

"Sanitary Terminals are for everyone's protection, sir," says the face, as I stumble back. The man behind the counter mumbles to himself, while his recording deals with me. "What was your name, sir?"

"McGewan-X04," I say, keeping my distance from the Terminal.

"Please place your left wrist in the prescription tube," the man's head tells me on the screen, as it leads me to the appropriate tube. I place my left arm up to the elbow into the clear plastic. The tube seals above my elbow, and the pharmacist's Terminal moves on to help someone else.

Nothing happens. I watch as three people step up to other prescription tubes, get their prescriptions updated, upgraded, and integrated into their L.I.F.E., and then they leave while I stand here.

I grow impatient, as nothing continues to happen at my particular tube. My headache intensifies the longer I stand in the pharmacy. Wave upon wave of pain erodes the shores of my good humor. My ears and neck crisp with the anger that wells up inside me.

"Excuse me," I say, finally.

The Terminal turns to me from across the pharmacy. "Yes, sir?" asks the pharmacist's face.

"I know you're busy," I say, trying to keep the fury out of my voice, "but I have been standing here for almost twenty seconds, and nothing has happened."

"Oh, my word, sir," the pharmacist gushes on the screen, but far enough away that the screaming in my ears has stopped.

The actual pharmacist quakes at the counter several paces away. The tremors seem to shrink him from the top down until he becomes a haircut hovering at counter level. "I am so sorry, sir," says his disembodied face. "Let me see what's the matter."

Everything will be fine. Your superiors will most certainly take pity on you for a minor error.

"You think?" mumbles the actual pharmacist from approximately floor level.

Though, there is always a shortage of souls at the Molybdenum Mines, so try to be more diligent.

The actual pharmacist whimpers from under the counter.

"Well," says the confident face on the screen, "here's the problem. Your L.I.F.E. operating system is obsolete. No wonder nothing happened."

"Obsolete?" I ask. "I updated it five days ago."

"Five days? There have been two updates, four builds, and sixteen service packs in the last five days, sir. I couldn't possibly give you a prescription with such an antiquated operating system. You must update or go without."

The prescription tube releases my arm to allow me to select the update on my wrist display. I scroll through the hundreds of pages of terms of service and end-user license agreements on my heads-up display, and at the bottom, agreed to the agreements by tonguing the 'Agree' button with my mouth-mouse. If I would have stood in the pharmacy for another full minute, I would have become most disagreeable.

"There," I say, as I jam my arm back into the prescription tube, until 'Download Complete' flashes on my heads-up display.

A mechanical arm releases my wrist display and I can see the mechanism imbedded in the working tissue of my arm. The delicate robot removes specific vials, adds different vials. In less than ten seconds, it fills my prescription. When the tube opens, the pharmacist's Terminal drops from the ceiling, right in front of me. "Would you like me to tell you the warnings for this prescription?"

"No," I say, as I attempt to leave the pharmacy. The noise in my ears continues, ebbing and surging, as I move away from the Terminal, while the pharmacist continues moving it toward me.

"Potential side effects?"

"No," I repeat.

"Drug interactions?"

"Just send it all to me. I have to go," I say, ducking under the Terminal.

Anti-depressant dispensing. As your personal counselor, I advise — but the voice trails off, as I run out onto the street.

CHAPTER 2

The hospital's doors whisper closed behind me and I freeze in my tracks. Four days of sensory-deprivation, whether conscious or not, changes a person and I am unprepared for the noise and motion of the world. My head still buzzed, but the street noise drowns out most of it.

Standing motionless on the slab of concrete by the hospital's entrance, people sweep in and out of the hospital, keeping an arm's length from me. Everybody is in a hurry, heads lowered, concentrating on the five feet of slidewalk in front of them, shouting at their wrists. Dictating memos into their word processors. Negotiating business deals over the phone. Programming reminders into their organizers. Punching make-believe zombies on their heads-up display. Podcasting about the reality show they watched last night. Shouting gibberish at themselves, the recipients of their tirades unseen.

The front of every building has a liquid billboard, giant television, or holographic image screaming advertisements down at the heedless masses. Ishmael's Coffee. The Flanery Defense. Vague Automotive.

My wrist vibrates after a few moments, followed by the grid and a whisper in my head:

Your heart rate has increased, and your palms are perspiring. Would you care for a mood stabilizer?

I select, 'No,' with my tongue.

Perhaps a chat with your personal counselor?

'No,' again.

I step forward and wait for an opening on the slidewalk. It only takes a moment before I see a woman get off to my left, and then her vacated set of yellow footprints are under the soles of my boots, whisking me down the street.

Please stand by, your consumer experience software is calibrating.

After a brief pause, the voice returns.

Based on recent activity, the following slidewalk ride is brought to you by the makers of prescription Chillaxafed.

A holo-cone shoots up around my feet, the world around me slightly opaque from the holographic images. Sweaty, shirtless men levering a railroad track into place, driving railway spikes into the ground in slow-mo.

War on Terror got you down?

The announcer's voice pipes directly into my head, but it screeches and hisses on my eardrums.

Constant fear of a fiery death wearing you out? Unable to focus at work because there might be a suicide bomb with your name on it? Ask your healthcare expert if prescription Chillaxafed is right for you. Physical alertness has never felt so mellow.

Calm.

Responsive.

Alert.

Productive.

Chillaxafed.

The Patriot's mood stabilizer.

Click 'Learn More' for more information.

Two buttons appear chest-high in front of me. My fist strikes 'Dismiss' and the holo-cone to dissipate.

On my right, liquid billboards take up the first-floor windows of every building I pass. The looping video clips play, and every spokesperson's voice goes directly into my head, trying to get my attention. To my left, the slidewalk going the opposite direction whips shouting people past me. Beyond them, vehicles weave back and forth through the constant press of traffic.

Something's wrong, but over the buzz, billboards, traffic, and all those voices, I can't put my finger on it. I look up, the muscles in the back of my neck protesting as I stare. The buildings appear to go on forever, bowing in toward one another across the street. A thin sliver of blue sky is barely visible, black dots—drones—circle in a constant holding pattern. One female voice makes its way to the front of my consciousness.

"You won't believe this. There's a guy just staring up at the sky."

What's he looking at? asks another woman.

"The sky, I guess."

Why?

"I don't know, but he isn't working or using a Gizmo. He's just riding the slidewalk in silence, staring at the sky. Like a psychopath."

That's creepy.

I look down, then to my left and right. Several people on the slidewalk are looking up, trying to see what I am looking at. I turn around to the woman behind me.

"Oh, no, he's looking at me now."

Call the police, the voice tells her.

"Are you talking to a woman on the phone?" I ask.

"He's talking to me," the woman says, looking at my feet. "To me. Directly."

Hang up and call the police, says the voice on the phone.

I stumble backward, off the slidewalk, and into the first door that appears.

The recorded voice in my head thanks me for choosing Ishmael's, but the buzz distorts the name. The 'S' at the end continues for several seconds.

A Terminal runs across its tracks to meet me at the door. "Welcome to Ishmael's," says the perky, young woman with a flourish of what I could see of her hair. "Would you care to try our new Mocha Monkey in a commemorative mug? All proceeds from the sale of the mugs go to the survivors and families of the victims of the tragedy." A picture of the drink rotates next to her face. The picture is small, but the mug appears to depict giant blocks crushing cars with the legend, "Forever Remembered."

"What tragedy?" I ask, gritting my teeth as the feedback buffets my eardrums.

She blinks several times, jerks her head side-to-side, moving the camera to stay centered on her face. "What tragedy? Where have you been? Terrorists hijacked a container ship last week and dropped dozens of forty-ton boxes onto people on the freeway. It's only been all over the news for the last four days."

"I've been in the hospital for the last... four..." I say, only to stop as the wheels in my head spin. The headline scrolling across the nearest newspaper states something about a sole survivor being released from the hospital that morning. When I look up, I stare at the back of the Terminal. The woman turns to look at the newspaper, as well. She pivots the screen until I can see her face again.

"You're him, aren't you?" she asks, her eyes wide. "You're the sole survivor!"

People turn their wrist cameras toward me, relaying an image to their eye, no doubt recording it for later.

"No, no," I say, "I'm the sole victim of an entirely different circumstance. Just came in for a coffee."

"No, you're him. I saw your picture on the one-hour special."

Without warning, two voices come into my head, one male, one female, but both say the same thing in un-synched stereo.

Talking to, looking at, or following someone, especially a person of celebrated status, is stalking and not allowed by law.

I glance around at all the wrists pointing at me and wonder who thought about stalking me, and more importantly, why I can hear their personal counselors. Then, the perky coffee employee's words sink in, so I turn my attention back to her.

"One-hour special? About what?"

"About your struggle to survive the vicious terrorist attack, your will to live despite insurmountable odds, your..."

"Wait," I say, waving my hands in front of her face, "my entire life wouldn't fill up an hour of television, let alone the minor car accident I got into. I'm sorry, but you've got the wrong guy."

"I know it's you," she says, her eyes red, tears dropping onto each cheek. "I know it's you. Excuse me." Her face shoots into the ceiling and vanishes. At the back of the room, I see a lone figure run through a door marked, Employees Only. I slowly turn and stare down each camera pointing at me until every-body goes back to their USA Tomorrows and Grande Mocha Monkeys in the Forever Remembered commemorative mugs. I stand there for a while, thinking, wondering if terrorists had, in fact, dropped the container onto my car.

A tone starts in my ears, as televisions drop from the ceil-ing. Each customer snaps their head up to stare at the flat screens.

The voice in my head, distorted by feedback, says, *The following Presidential Address is brought to you by Ishmael's.*

The Patriot's coffee. Now, an important message from the President of the United States, Matthias Jackson. The Ishmael's logo fades out, and the Presidential Seal comes on the screen, then fades out, to show the President sitting behind his desk in the Oval Office.

"My fellow Americans..."

I double over in agony at the sound of President Jackson's voice saying, "... eight minutes ago, Eastern Standard Time, excuse me..."

President Jackson clears his throat and takes a sip of water, his lips touching the water sounds like a tidal wave crashing into my skull. "Eight minutes ago, at 8:05 a.m., Eastern Standard Time, the Hermod shoe factory outside Knoxville, Tennessee, was bombed by terrorists."

Plugging my ears only makes the buzzing worse as President Jackson continues to speak.

"No survivors have been found at this time, but a terrorist organization in Madagascar has taken responsibility for this heinous attack against America. We cannot allow such attacks on American soil to go unpunished."

I try to induce hyperventilation, remembering a news blurb about terrorists surviving torture through this practice.

"As we speak, a bill is on the Congressional floor, which will allow us to carry out measures to defend this great country of ours. These measures will prevent such assaults against Americans from happening in the future. As good American citizens, we all must unite in this cause."

Practice is what I need, as the faux hyperventilation has no effect on the treble staff grinding through my eardrums.

"Every American, regardless of race, religion, or creed, must stand together as Christian Americans. I know that I speak for all Americans when I say to the survivors and families of the victims of this attack, America will never forget the price you paid today. Thank you, and may the Lord be with you." President Jackson's face is replaced by the Presidential Seal. After a moment, the seal fades into another room.

"No, thank you," I mumble, as the screaming pain recedes, and I can take a normal breath.

The President's press secretary stands behind a podium, an American flag to either side of him. "I will now answer questions about President Jackson's address."

I shake my head, hold my breath, and flex every muscle in my body, as my ears take another beating. The camera pulls back to show the press secretary standing in front of a six-foot square screen. The outlines of hundreds of small boxes fill the screen, tiny faces visible in each through my half-open, tense eyelids. "Yes," says the press secretary, touching one box to enlarge it and take up most of the screen space. A reporter's face is identifiable, though transparent for a moment. People in the control booth switch perspective to the reporter sitting behind a desk, taking up the entire television screen.

"T. DeVore-Y16, New York Times. Exactly what are these defensive measures President Jackson spoke of?"

The cameras cut back to the press secretary. "As Americans, we are protected by the Lord Jesus Christ..."

"Amen." Everyone in the coffee shop mumbles aloud.

"... and two hundred thousand modified B-1200 Stealth Velociraptor Unmanned Drone Bombers. These drones are equipped with scanners that detect any explosive materials throughout the country. If we detect explosives, the drones will engage and vaporize the terrorists with pinpoint accuracy, along with anyone within a half-mile radius of said terrorists. This is a temporary measure, under the Articles of War on Terror, until the law passes unanimously through both houses of Congress, making it a full-time defensive provision. Next question. Yes?"

The reporter's cube shrinks and is quickly replaced by another, a woman this time.

"J. Callen-Y25, San Francisco Chronicle. Isn't having B-1200 Stealth Velociraptor Unmanned Drone Bombers flying over our homes, twenty-four hours a day, an invasion of privacy?"

The press secretary rolls his eyes and says, "Americans will understand that having modified, and I must stress this, modified B-1200 Stealth Velociraptor Unmanned Drone Bombers flying over our cities, is a necessary precaution to protect their lives and the lives of their loved ones. Yes?"

A different woman's face takes up the screen. "D. Noff-singer-Y37, Miami Herald. Are there plans for an invasion of Madagascar?"

"There are no plans to physically invade Madagascar at this time. An investigation is underway, and I am certain there will be reprisals for this attack on many levels. That is all. The Lord be with you." The screen goes black and retracts into the ceiling.

I relax and take a deep breath, the blood returning to my head. A babble of voices, male and female personal counselors, invade my thoughts before the television screens are out of sight.

Are you having a panic attack?

There is no reason to be frightened.

Would a mood stabilizer help lower your heart rate?

Mood stabilizer now being dispensed.

Your personal advisor will be with you momentarily. Please remain calm.

You have exceeded your maximum daily allowance of mood stabilizers. Paramedics have been notified, and a sedative is being dispensed.

A ripple effect ensues. Shoulders slump in a wave, past me,

and continue across the room. One man goes beyond slumped shoulders, banging his head on a table as he loses consciousness. His commemorative mug barely beats him to the floor. No one seems to notice, other than me.

My wrist glows green. Heart rate, blood pressure, breathing, sweating, muscle tension, all normal with no medication dispensed. I feel a wave of pride by dealing with the latest tragedy so well.

If I could just get a cup of coffee and find my car, I could go home, I thought. I realize I probably scared off the only employee.

I walk up to the counter. Ten seconds pass with my palms flat on the counter, glancing around for an Ishmael's barista. My eyes scan the toll-free, "How are we doing?" sign. Last week, I would have dialed the number after five seconds and had the entire staff fired before I finished my cup of coffee, but today, I am full of forgiveness. I am about to clear my throat and ask for help when a Terminal drops from the ceiling, hitting me squarely between the eyes. Eventually, I wake up on my back, with a screen wavering in and out of focus above me.

"Are you okay, sir?" says the boy's face.

I work my jaw side to side, wiggle a finger in each ear, and take a deep breath. The buzzing is gone. "I think that did the trick."

"I'm glad I could be of assistance," says the boy, unfazed by my non sequitur. "Can I assist you further?"

"Just a Mocha Monkey in the commemorative mug, and I'll be good to go," I say, still lying on the floor.

"I'm sorry, sir. The Mocha Monkey is not currently available in a commemorative mug. Would you like a Mocha Monkey in a regular cup, or would you prefer a Jumpin' Java Jive in the Never Forgotten commemorative mug?" A drink rotates next to the boy's face, showing the Hermod Winged

Spear, an illustration of an explosion, and, if my geography is correct, the outline of Tennessee.

"How long was I unconscious?" I ask, standing up.

"Only a few seconds, sir," he replies, as the Terminal moves out of my way.

"I'd really like one of the Forever Remembered mugs. I may have been involved in that incident, and..." I stop brushing the legs of my jumpsuit and try to give him a look, using whatever alleged celebrity status I had left.

"Which mug, sir?"

"You know, the one with blocks crushing cars on it."

"I'm sorry, sir?" he says, shrugging. The face on the screen is clean-shaven and devoid of adornments, but the actual person behind the counter is covered in facial tattoos and has a two-foot neon pink goatee.

"The Mocha Monkey was just in it when I came in."

"Oh, that mug. I'm sorry, sir. The old mugs are destroyed and recycled immediately to make way for the new mugs, you understand." I don't, but I nod anyway. "So, would you prefer the Mocha Monkey or Triple J in the commemorative mug, sir?"

"I don't know. Which one's better?"

He gives me a blank stare.

"Which do you prefer?" I ask him.

Silence.

"Which one has darker coffee in it?"

He hesitates, but then says, "The Mocha Monkey has Freedom Roasted Coffee in it."

"Fine. Grande Mocha Monkey."

"Are you sure, sir? I'm not allowed to put that in a commemorative mug."

"You know what? You're right, make it an Enormetron Mocha Monkey. It's a long drive home."

"Anything else, sir?" asks the boy, smiling at me.

"That's it. No, wait," I say, "lots of sprinkles and that should be it."

The boy's face falls. He gave me a moment to reconsider, then his eyes glaze as his heads-up display activates. His jaw moves side to side, as he works his mouth-mouse to operate the machine in front of him. The automated espresso machine whirs to life, steams, and praps, as I authorize the charge with my thumbprint on the Terminal.

A plain, white cup appears in front of me a moment later. "Thanks," I say to the boy. As I turn to leave, every customer has their wrist aimed at me again, as I take the first sip of my drink. I walk out of the coffee shop, trying to watch everyone in my periphery, their wrists tracking my progress.

Terrorist Tip Line, how can I help you help all of us?
Terrorist Tip Line, how can I help you help all of us?
Terrorist Tip Line, how can I help you help all of us?
Terrorist Tip Line, how can I help you help all of us?

The coffee cup is still to my lips, when the doors part and let me onto the street.

———

At Ishmael's, we know you're busy. We know the need for an Ishmael's can strike at any moment. We know you. With over forty-eight thousand locations in the greater metropolitan area, Ishmael's is always right around the corner.

Which corner?

Every corner.

Ishmael's.

The Patriot's Coffee Shop.

CHAPTER 3

The Mocha Monkey is devoid of aroma, flavor, and most notably, sprinkles. It did, however, have an acrid aftertaste that lasts a full ten seconds after each swallow. In other words, it is exactly as I expected. Once, while on vacation, I had an exceptional cup of coffee in Switzerland. I try to remember the subtle change in aroma as I brought the cup to my mouth and how each drop made my taste buds purr. Every cup of Ishmael's put me farther from the memory of what that tasted like. That was long ago, before the government advisory against travel to Switzerland due to terrorist activity. Come to think of it, the travel advisory was about the same time Switzerland refused to let Ishmael's into the country, though I could be mistaken.

The lip of stationary sidewalk on the front of each building is just large enough for me to walk and not bump into people whizzing by me. The liquid billboards had changed while I was in the coffee shop. Commemorative colognes, clothes, and, most importantly, shoes are the main topics now. Photos of the remnants of the Hermod factory are displayed and soft-spoken ad men tell me to take a stand, to be courageous in my everyday life, and to help the victims by buying their commemorative merchandise. Traffic cops are positioned along the sidewalk and street in front of the Hermod shoe outlet, keeping the weeping patrons in line down the street and around the corner. The first uniformed patrolman I come to stands with his back to the wall next to the Hermod entrance. The Terminal pivots back and forth on his helmet to watch the line. He locks onto me after a moment and when the screen turns red, I stop in my tracks, my coffee cup halfway to my lips.

"Where are you going, sir?" he asks.

"Just going to my car," I say, moving the Mocha Monkey to my side.

"End of the line is down the street, sir."

"I'm actually going to cross the street to get to my car."

"You'll have to wait in line like everyone else, sir. Move along." The screen turns from red to green and pivots away from me.

I follow the line for a while, debating whether I need anything from Hermod. My jumpsuit and boots look brand new, after all. Even if I do have twenty million credits, I really don't feel like paying the marked-up prices to help rebuild the factory. Instead, I decide to find my car and just send a donation when I get home. Two more uniformed patrolmen try to redirect me to the end of the line, but I explain, with all due respect, that I need to return home.

A block later, the streets are empty. They have diverted all slidewalks to Hermod, so I walk in the empty street toward my car. I find the silence comforting now that I am out of range of the billboards. Utterly alone, I traipse through the gutter. The bottom quarter of the now cold Mocha Monkey is even less luscious than the first three quarters, but I am determined to finish it.

We are Hermod.
We make you run.
Faster.

We help you jump.
Higher.
We keep you going.
Longer.
We are down now.
But we will always rise.
Together.
Never Forgotten.
All of us are,
Hermod.

A slight breeze ruffles my hair, and I stop. I look around, thinking I had heard whispers behind me, but there was no one in sight. Shrugging, I continue down the street for a few paces, then stop and look down.

Around my feet, red lasers paint a circle on the pavement. When I step forward, the circle moves, my feet remain centered. Realization dawns and I come to a halt. With my arms straight out to my sides, my head down, I wait. In my peripheral, I can just make out the silent hovercar perched ten feet above me. Ropes are deployed and four Homies in body armor rappel down from the car, landing in a rough square around me. A Sergeant steps into my line of sight, her rifle into her shoulder. The miniature Terminal at the end of the muzzle is two feet from my face. The Sergeant's identification badge appears on the screen as another Homie snatches the coffee out of my hand and throws it into a portable blast-proof box.

"Sergeant L. Demeritt, Homeland Security, don't move, citizen," the Sergeant says, as her actual face replaces the badge on the Terminal.

"It's clean, Sergeant, just coffee," says the Homie with the box.

"What kind of coffee?" Sergeant Demeritt asks.

"Ishmael's, Sergeant, Mocha Monkey, no sprinkles."

"The intel we received said our man ordered sprinkles," says Sergeant Demeritt to the man behind me, then focuses on me. "You're going to do exactly as I say, and we'll all be on our way in just a moment. First, follow the directions on the screen, and we'll get out of the street."

A video loops on the Terminal telling me to walk forward, keep my hands out to my sides, while a silhouette of a person demonstrates the moves for me. We cross the slidewalk and enter a narrow service alley between a toy store and a bar. Sergeant Demeritt back-pedals to keep in front of me. The screen turns red and I halt as an ache starts in my arms.

"Eyes closed while we scan you, citizen," the Sergeant tells me. I oblige and see a panorama of colors through my eyelids as I am electronically patted down. "Open your eyes and put your arms down." I comply and jerk back, the Terminal so close it almost touches my nose. "You're P. McGewan-X04?"

"That's correct," I say. I knew that whatever I say in the next few minutes, they will believe only half of it due to the 'four' at the end of my name. I am a decent citizen, but neither the best, a 'nine', nor terribly far from being a terrorist, a 'zero.'

"Where are you coming from?"

"I was discharged from the hospital, went to get an Ishmael's, and now I'm headed home, ma'am." I try to keep my voice calm and level.

"All true statements, Sergeant," says a voice behind me.

"And what did you order at Ishmael's?"

"Mocha Monkey, ma'am."

"In what kind of cup?"

"It came in a plain white cup, ma'am."

"Really? Why didn't it come in a commemorative mug?"

I take a deep breath. "Actually, I ordered it in a commemorative mug right before the President's Address, and by the end of the Address the Mocha Monkey wasn't available in a commemorative mug. So, they gave me a plain cup, ma'am."

"Untrue statement, Sergeant."

"Is that how it's going to be? You're going to lie to me? Why did it come in a plain, white cup?" Sergeant Demeritt shouts, moving the Terminal even closer to my face. "Were you talking directly to a woman on the street? Did you or did you not go into Hermod after leaving Ishmael's? Are you the leader of a terrorist cell? We have multiple reports of a man fitting your description acting suspiciously. What's your agenda? What organization do you belong to? Answer me!"

I take another deep breath and wonder, for a moment, why my L.I.F.E. hasn't asked to dispense a mood stabilizer yet. "I was attacked by terrorists four days ago," I say, picking my words with care. "They released me from the hospital less than an hour ago. When I went into Ishmael's, I found out I was the sole survivor of the terrorist attack. Before I could come to terms with that, I was bombarded with the news of the terrorist attack on the Hermod factory. My personal counselor recommended that I go directly home and meditate on everything that I just told you, ma'am."

"Checking, Sergeant," says the voice behind me. "We'll need a warrant to verify his conversation with his personal counselor, but everything else checks out. An employee even assaulted him while in Ishmael's. That could be our terrorist trying to misdirect us."

I keep an impassive look on my face, although I am relieved to hear that they need a warrant to find out if I had spoken to my personal counselor, which I hadn't.

"Call it in," Sergeant Demeritt says.

"Dispatch, this is one-Lincoln-niner, suspected four-oh-four employed at the Ishmael's on the corner of Eighth and Federal." There's a rapid reply from dispatch that I don't understand. "There's an Ishmael's on all four corners. Which were you in, citizen?"

I hesitate for a moment. "Southeast corner, I believe."

"That's the southeast corner of Eighth and Federal, dispatch." Another garbled reply. "Team is en route, Sergeant."

"Excellent. So, you're the sole survivor of the Highway Tragedy?"

"Yes, ma'am. Do you know how many other people were involved?"

"I'll ask the questions. You stated that you're headed home on the advice of your counselor?"

"Yes, ma'am."

"How about we escort you home?"

"Sure, if you'd like."

"It's not what I like, it's what I do. Don't move." She backs up a few paces and then everything went dark. A moment later, I realize the hovercar had dropped down and automatically restrained me in the prisoner compartment. Remote-controlled arms remove the black hood so I can see Sergeant Demeritt and her Homies watching from the other side of the blast-proof glass. My stomach rolls as the hovercar went airborne, the thick straps holding me motionless a foot off the floor.

The Sergeant removes the Terminal from the end of the rifle and holds it up to a slot in the glass. "Sorry about the restraints, standard procedure for everyone's protection."

"Not a problem, ma'am. I appreciate the ride. What about my car?"

"Your car will auto-drive itself home."

"Thanks. I know you guys, excuse me, officers don't hear this often enough, but I do appreciate all the hard work you do to keep us safe from terrorists."

"Stand by, citizen." She slides the slot closed and speaks into her wrist. I strain but can't hear what the Sergeant is saying. I can hear who she is talking to, though, which makes little sense.

He's just a concerned citizen grateful for the work we do, not a terrorist trying to misdirect you, Demeritt.

A pause while I watch the Sergeant's lips move.

The procedure would be to say 'you are welcome, sir' and leave it at that, Sergeant.

The Sergeant lowers her wrist and snaps open the slot in the glass again. She places the Terminal up to the opening and waits for a moment. "You are welcome, citizen," then slams the slot closed again.

A television screen turns on when the Sergeant closes the partition. The Department of Homeland Security logo appears.

This arrest is brought to you by Homies now in Super HD Plus. Tonight, at eleven, Big City, Little Terrorist. What happens when an enemy combatant slips up and orders an Ishmael's in a non-commemorative mug? The Homies are there. But what happens when the terrorist leads them to his home? Tune in tonight to find out. Homies, now in Super HD Plus. Click to subscribe to the Homies BluTube Channel.

The commercial ends. We ride in silence above the city, a faint trace of the skyline visible through the darkened windows. I don't recognize my building until the hovercar lands on the roof, and two of the Homies pull me from the back. They unbind my legs so I can walk on my own, but leave my upper body in restraints.

"Standard procedure," the Sergeant tells me as I walk towards the elevator with my hands strapped to my throat. The ride to my floor is uncomfortable with four Homies in bullet-resistant jumpsuits pressed around me. They aren't comfortable either, not having enough room for even one of them to point their rifle at me, but the ride was brief, thirty floors in a matter of seconds.

Sergeant Demeritt's palm moves up in front of my face as two of the Homies exit the elevator, and creep down opposite walls, rifles into their shoulders, barrels down at forty-five-degree angles. They stop thirty feet from the elevator, drop to one knee, and wait. The third Homie steps off the elevator to work on a keypad right outside the door. I hear a deadbolt on every door on the floor turn to lock and knew the message playing in each apartment by heart.

Homeland Security is conducting a routine exercise on this floor. We have sealed your doors for your protection. We will allow you to leave your domicile at the conclusion of this exercise. We greatly appreciate your patience and cooperation. May the Lord bless you and keep you.

In a tense whisper, the Sergeant's Terminal tells me to walk. The two Homies already down the hallway stay in front of me while the Sergeant and the Homie on the keypad fall in several paces behind me. I know who is home and who is still at work as I walk to my apartment. Voices of personal counselors come in snippets as I pass each door with a terrified tenant watching me through their plasma peepholes.

It is merely an exercise.

Terrorists do not live next door to you.

I recommend...

I recommend...

I recommend...

... you sit down, take a mood stabilizer, and watch television.

At my front door, I stop and wait. The two lead Homies go to the end of the hall, then return at a quick pace.

"Hallway's clear, Sergeant."

The Sergeant nods and unlocks my right arm from the restraint. "Is there anything you'd like to tell me before we go inside?"

"Like what?"

"Anyone waiting for us? Any booby-traps? Any contraband that you'd like to confess to? It will go easier for you if you tell us now vice after the door opens."

I try to think of everything in my apartment and for a moment thought that maybe terrorists were on the other side of my front door. I feel sweat forming on my left palm and running down my neck.

"His heart rate has increased, Sergeant."

"No comment?" the Sergeant says. "Fine, we can do it the hard way."

They take up positions on either side of the door. The two closest to the door on one knee, the other two standing close behind them. Each pull a grenade off their chest and thumb the actuator with their non-firing hand. I reach for the access panel on my front door, then stop just short.

"What are the grenades for?" I ask.

"If anything inside is going to kill us, we'll drop the grenades, and our deaths will not be in vain," the Sergeant says, not taking her eyes off the door. "Open it."

I press my palm flat against the access panel and wait.

Access Denied.

I check the number on the door, wipe the sweat off my hand onto my leg, and try again.

Access Denied.

Looking at the Sergeant, my heart rate is so high I couldn't find words. We all stand frozen in tableau for twenty seconds. Even the Sergeant's face began to collect sweat at the edges.

"Did you deactivate the lockdown?" the Sergeant whispers.

One of the Homies steps in front of me, punches a code into the keypad, and then resumes his position. "Lockdown deactivated, Sergeant," he whispers in reply.

"Open it," the Sergeant repeats.

Wiping my palm on my thigh, I position my hand on the

access panel. I can hear the four of them tense up in quadra-phonic sound as the door slides open to welcome me home.

———

Is the next terrorist plot being planned in the apartment next door? There is no way to know under current laws. But this November, you can help save the lives of Patriots everywhere. Vote Yes on Initiative 63, and Homeland Security can conduct random house searches in your neighborhood. We can never be safe from terrorists until we know where they live. Vote Yes on Initiative 63, and the life you save may be your own.

CHAPTER 4

The Homies sweep through my apartment, shouting, "Clear" as they go from room to room. I am uncertain whether they are disappointed or relieved that nothing, or no one attempts to kill them. Sergeant Demeritt keeps her rifle trained on me while I sit on the couch, my right hand on my knee, the other still strapped to my neck. The reconnoiter of my domicile for unfriendlies, as the Sergeant puts it, takes all of two minutes. After they deactivate the grenades and replace them on their bandoleers, my restraints are removed and I pump my left hand to regain feeling. One of the Homies goes to the hallway to deactivate the lockdown for the entire floor, then stands sentry outside while the other two search my apartment for contraband. The Sergeant slings the rifle over her shoulder and, with Terminal in hand, looks over my living room.

"These real?" she asks.

I had zoned out, staring at the sweat stain on each knee, worrying about what they might find in my spare bedroom. "I'm sorry?"

"Are these real?" she says, pointing to the fish in my aquarium.

"No, they're all mechs," I say, looking up at her. "The real ones don't last as long and they're expensive." She nods and continues around the room.

One of her men returns and shows the Sergeant something on his Terminal. The Sergeant nods and waves him off to continue his search.

"Is your second bedroom full of broken gear?" the Sergeant asks.

It was the thing I was most worried about, and they found it. I knew they were watching my heart rate, feeding my voice through machines to know if I was lying. I had to do the only thing I could think of.

"Yes, it is, Sergeant."

The Sergeant shakes her head. "What kind of freak are you? Taking up a whole room with broken gadgets and jump-suits and shoddy shoes? Everything comes a warranty these days. Send it all back to the manufacturer."

Oh, thank God, I think. They either hadn't examined the broken items closely enough, or Homies didn't care about the Refurbishment Statute.

Pausing at the window, she moves the Terminal around the darkened glass box sitting on the ledge, my spare bedroom forgotten. "Is this what I think it is?"

"I'm not sure," I say. "What do you think it is?"

"It's a—" She begins to say, but she stops when her Homies charge into the living room with my leather shaving kit.

"Sergeant, we found the mother lode," says the one holding the kit. He dumps the contents onto the kitchen counter. "We've got Mollie, heroin, Meow-Meow, cocaine, speed, GB-4, mushrooms, LSD, opium. You name it, he's got it in the bathroom." The Sergeant motions me to join them at the breakfast bar between the kitchen and the living room. I pull up a barstool and rest my elbows on the counter as the two junior Homies organize my drugs and paraphernalia in front of us.

The Sergeant nods at my stash, then aims her Terminal at me. "Now, what's in the box on the windowsill?"

"Hybrid bonsai marijuana plants, my own strain," I say.

"Go on."

"They only grow about a foot tall, but I can harvest one bud the size of my fist every six months." I take a deep breath. "If you open the box though, it will kill them. They're in the darkness phase of the flowering cycle."

"Do you want to tell me where all this came from," Sergeant Demeritt asks, "or shall I let the drugs do the talking?"

I shrug at her Terminal.

She turns to the Homies. "Scan it."

The apartment is silent except for the occasional beep of their instruments. After five minutes, they had scanned everything, including the barcode on the side of my marijuana grow house. Both Homies shake their heads at the Sergeant. She stops running her tongue over her teeth and aims the Terminal at me, again.

"Do you have receipts?"

I nod and bring up my bank statement on the Terminal laid into the counter.

"What about a permit for the plants?"

Five finger strokes later, she looks over my growing permits for the marijuana.

"What about this shaving kit, citizen?" the Sergeant asks.

I show her the Cruelty Free Leather tag.

"Well, looks like all the serial numbers match up. Everything came from an approved dealer. All your paperwork is in order. I guess I should apologize for wasting your time, sir. I will forward all my personal information to you so you can sue me and my department for harassment and/or profiling. Would you like us to put these back where we found them, sir?" she asks, waving her hand across the narcotics display in my kitchen.

"That won't be necessary, Sergeant. After everything today, I'll need help to unwind." I walk them to the door. The Sergeant lags behind the others.

She stops as the Homies enter the hallway, out of earshot. "I take full responsibility for this misunderstanding and for adding stress to an already stressful week for you, sir. I would appreciate it if you only went after me, Sergeant L. Demeritt, and not my Homies. They were just following my orders, which were obviously totally misguided."

"Okay," I say, unsure where this was headed.

"So, if someone has to go to the gallows, it should be me and me alone, not these young pups."

"I'm not planning on suing you, Sergeant."

"Right. Well, when you do, I hope you remember what I said. And send that junk in your bedroom back to the manufacturer. Have a good day, sir. God bless." The door slides closed as she steps into the hallway.

I slump against the wall, eyes unfocused, and attempt to process everything that had happened. I shake myself back to full awareness after a couple minutes and look around, trying to decide what to do next. My wrist shows everything as normal, though sweat output and heart rate are in the red, but no mood stabilizers recommended at this time. Pressing the house icon on my wrist causes the head-high lights to wink on throughout my apartment. A soft female voice in my head says:

At your service.

"Lockdown, shower, naked," I mumble. The door locks, the blinds close, and I hear the shower turn on in the master bathroom. Lifting my feet one at a time, my boots loosen, fall to the floor, and run into the nearest closet. The closures on my jumpsuit unfasten and fall away as I walk towards the bathroom.

Sklrda, my robotic butler, comes out of his cubbyhole and scoops up the jumpsuit. *Clean and press this for you, sir?*

"Sklrda, the jumpsuit is clean. Just fold it and put it on the bed."

I will take your lack of response as a desire to have your clothing cleaned and pressed. Sklrda opens the laundry panel and places my clothes in the cleaning receptacle.

"Sklrda, I don't want it cleaned or pressed." I poke the tentacled silver football of a butler with my toe. "Do you hear me, Sklrda? Just fold it."

The butler turns to look up at me. *I am not programmed for physical interactions. To assign me a task, simply state my name, followed by the requested task. For example, 'Sklrda, vacuum the living room.'*

"Sklrda, I do not want my jumpsuit cleaned. Sklrda, I do not want my jumpsuit pressed. Sklrda, I do want my jumpsuit folded."

When I press your jumpsuit, would you like starch, sir?

I growl. That is the one normal thing in a day full of abnormality. Sklrda still ignores me when I speak.

I go into the bathroom. The shower cabinet opens as I step up to it.

Shower is warmed and ready.

I lie down, the base of the shower conforms to the contours of my body before the lid closes.

Please select shower options.

By selecting 'Long and Relaxing' from the list, the soap-laden brushes and warm jets of water start a slow journey from my feet upwards. At least getting hit in the head at Ishmael's had stopped the screeching when I was confronted with a screen.

The hard plastic coffin was Mildew Resistant.

No Cleaning Necessary.

Ever.

Always the good things in bold, uppercase script.

About one out of five thousand people are allergic to the mildew-resistant treatment. Fatally allergic. If any abrasion on your body mixes with steam, the shower lasts the rest of your life. They state this in tiny script on the screen in the lid, with about a hundred other risks. Every drop of water in the recycling tank is purified, then "skeeched" out onto the body. Skeeched is not an official term; it is my own.

Skeech is the sound saliva makes when I force it through the gap in my front teeth. Years ago, my dentist squared off all of my teeth. They made each tooth rectangular, perfectly symmetrical with its neighbors. Each upper sat exactly on each lower, no gaps anywhere. About one out of one million people died after having this dental procedure. People go to sleep with a combination of blocked sinuses and clenched teeth, and suffocation results. The dental profession got so precise they gave people airtight mouths. I had the procedure before the "suffocation epidemic," so my dentist, by law, was forced to make a diamond-shaped gap where my four front teeth met. I could go back to my dentist now and have him fill in the gaps, but my bill would include a disclaimer that I would probably die in my sleep. When dentists realized the procedure was dangerous, they became liable, and had to undo every perfect set of teeth. Now, they will redo it with a disclaimer and make me responsible for my own death.

When the jets in the shower come on, they skeech. One-hundred-thousand skeeches hitting my body at once. About one out of five hundred people are allergic to the sanitizer in the water. Symptoms may include festering boils, eczema, psoriasis, endometriosis, and a low occurrence of death. Contact your healthcare professional or CleanSpa representative if any of these occur. CleanSpa offers a sensitive skin sanitizer that one person in three-quarters of a million is allergic to that costs twice as much as the more dangerous variety. All this on the screen over my face every time I get in the shower under the header Suspension of Liability.

One in five morbidly obese users have a chance of collecting enough water in the folds of their fat, that the jets will spray pressurized air powerful enough to flay the skin. One unit in eight hundred thousand has a faulty thermometer, steaming the occupant to a nice medium-well. One unit in two point two million has faulty wiring in the display screen in the lid, over the occupant's face. The next time someone calls, a jolt of electricity may run through my body, face contorted, my once perfect teeth clenching so hard, they snap in half. However, no one is to blame if any of this happens except me. I was warned by the manufacturer, the retailer, the installer, and by the shower itself every time it turns on. I wasn't in advanced placement math, but adding all these numbers on the screen means I should only be able to take seven showers before the shower kills me.

———

I fall asleep before the shower got to my ankles, and the jets of water pounding on my chest wakes me.

Continue?

Incoming phone call.

I select continue, sending the jets and brushes back down my body and check the caller I.D. It's my wife, who has an uncanny ability to always call when I'm in the shower. I accept the phone call, and her face pops up on the shower's display.

"Are you okay?" she asks without preamble.

"I'm fine, just a little car accident. I was in the hospital for a couple days."

"I know you were in the hospital. I was the nurse who discharged you. I meant the other thing," she says, her brow wrinkled with worry.

"What other thing?"

"It's all over the news. Homeland Security detained you for suspected terrorist activity."

"Oh, that was just a misunderstanding."

She turns away from her Terminal for a moment, then turns back. "I guess it was a misunderstanding. The news is saying now that it was harassment and profiling. Your lawyer is on the news now, talking about suing the Homies."

"What?" I shout, the sound of my voice echoing in the shower. "Please hold." My wife's face shrinks off to one side of the display as I dial my lawyer. He answers on the second ring. "What are you doing?" I ask.

"Holding a press conference on your behalf. Why?"

"I'm not suing the Homies. It was a misunderstanding and Sergeant Demeritt and her Homies were just doing their job."

"Need I remind you that you are either guilty of a crime or you are being harassed? End of story." My lawyer's face is smug as reporters on the monitor in his office shout questions at him.

There is a beep and a commercial for Ishmael's starts.

Wouldn't a Jumping Java Jive hit the spot right now?

I grit my teeth and try to hold on to my rage.

... and we'll waive the delivery charge if you order during this call. Ishmael's. What Patriots drink.

My lawyer's face reappears. "Do I need to remind you that there are a half-million lawyers in this town, most of whom would welcome the opportunity to have me as a client?"

His face drops. "You wouldn't."

"I would. So, tell the reporters it was a misunderstanding and I appreciate the Homies' diligence in keeping us safe from terrorists. And, most importantly, there will be no lawsuit filed against Sergeant Demeritt or any member of the Homeland Security Office on my behalf. Are we speaking the same language?"

"I don't agree with this decision."

"I think my retainer fee is large enough for you to get over any disagreements we may have. Do as I say or lose a client." I end the call before he can respond and get back to my wife. "Sorry about that."

"Hang on," she says, her face in profile to the camera, "I want to hear this." I could just make out the sound of the news over the shower as I try to relax again. "You need to call your lawyer right now," she says, turning to face the camera. "He just told the world that you appreciate the Homies' hard work and won't be filing a lawsuit."

"I just talked to him and told him to say that."

"What? Was your head separated from your body for too long? You need to sue those bastards for harassing you." Her face turns red as she speaks. "I'm sorry, hang on." Her jaw moves slightly as she selects the recommended mood-stabilizer. Her face returns to its normal color after a few moments, and she makes eye contact with me again. "Why aren't you suing the Homies?" she asks in a level voice.

There was a beep.

The brand new Vagues are rolling into Hagglin' Harry's and there's one waiting for you. All the features, all the price ranges. Schedule an appointment to talk to a dealer during this phone call and get ten thousand credits back or low, low thirty-five-point-two percent interest for sixty months. No one beats a Hagglin' Harry deal. No one.

My wife's face reappears, still waiting for an answer. "I was acting suspiciously. They picked me up on an anonymous tip, questioned me, searched my apartment, and then left. I wasn't mistreated or roughed up, everything was by the book. They were beyond polite and professional. There's no reason for me to sue them."

"Of course there is, you could win, that's reason enough. The news just said you had a ninety-nine-point-nine percent chance of winning. That's a couple hundred-million credits. From the government. Tax-free. Hello? Do you get what I'm saying?"

I shake my head at her and was glad that I don't have to be in the same room with her, ever. "Don't forget, they'd execute everyone involved at Homeland Security."

"So? It's not like those are the only four Homies left. They'll find someone to replace them."

Regardless of how hard the shower is trying, there is no way for me to stay relaxed while I am on the phone with my wife. "Listen to me. Are you listening?"

"Yes," she snaps.

"I am not suing the Homies. End of story. Segue to another topic."

"Fine." We stare at each other for a moment, while she works her jaw around, either as a nervous tic or an attempt to dispense more mood stabilizers. "How are you feeling?" she finally asks.

"Good, now that I'm home."

"Good. No problems?"

"No. How are you doing?"

"Well, I didn't want to bring this up but," she arranges her thoughts, "our son is freaking out."

"Oh?"

"Well," she rolls her eyes at me, "terrorists almost killed his father, then he's almost arrested for being a terrorist. Things are not going well at the Academy because of this."

"I'll call him."

"Good."

Continue?

I select continue to keep the shower running. "How long have you worked at the hospital?"

"Since I got out of the Academy, twelve years ago. Why?"

"Well, all those virtual dinners we had, and I never knew you lived in the same city. Just kind of amazing that I know someone here that I don't work with."

"Are you sure you're feeling okay?" she asks, as her brow furrows. "You're acting kind of strange."

"No, I'm fine, just thought it was odd."

"You realize that the computer matched us up for genetic compatibility, not for geographic proximity, right?"

"I know, I know. I am just trying to make small talk."

"Okay, if you're sure," she says, her eyes narrowing.

"I'm sure. So, what are you doing tonight?" I say, trying to change the subject.

"The usual, dinner, drugs, probably watch something on BluTube. You?"

"Same here," I say. "I will need a lot of opium to get to sleep tonight."

"I bet. Well, I'm going to let you go. Have a good night."

"Hey, wait, I have a question."

She nods.

"How many people were killed in the accident I was involved in?"

"The news said a couple hundred."

"I know," I say, deactivating the shower. "But how many were in the hospital?"

She shakes her head. "I don't know, I'm not allowed in the morgue. If the news said a couple hundred, it was a couple hundred. Why?"

"No reason. Have a good night."

"Don't forget to call our son."

"I won't," I say, as the shower dries me off with warm air.

"I love you."

"Love you, too," I say, as the screen fades.

When I am completely dry, the shower opens with a puff of steam. Slippers and bathrobe hang from the extended arms of my butler. Grabbing them, I shuffle into the living room and plop onto the couch. I debate for a moment whether to have dinner or call my kid. I would probably feel better talking to him on a full stomach, I decide.

"What's for dinner?" I ask.

CHAPTER 5

"I said, 'What's for dinner?'"

Normally, the space over the fireplace would change from an abstract painting to the kitchen's inventory, and I could scroll through every combination of food I had in the pantry, and it would be prepared with every technique I had paid for the kitchen to learn. For some reason, I have to walk into the kitchen and manually activate the program.

"Tossed salad, ranch dressing, grilled chicken pesto rigatoni, and a glass of Shiraz," I say to the room at large.

Sir, the virtual cook replied, Shiraz is a red wine. *You requested chicken.*

"I know, I prefer Shiraz."

Very well, sir. Dinner will be served in fifteen minutes.

My only bout of buyer's remorse in the last few years was the purchase of an 'Etiquette and Good Taste' upgrade for my kitchen. It was the big trend two years ago. Everyone had to have one. It was supposed to make me a connoisseur, open the world of cuisine to me, make me the envy of all my coworkers. All the upgrade does is second-guess every decision I make. It tries to force horrible combinations of food on me. Make me eat with tiny forks and other bizarre cutlery that the kitchen orders for itself, as I didn't own them already. I had disabled most of the more annoying defaults, but it still tries to make me drink white wine. I have never liked white wine, won't even order it from the grocery store, but the kitchen's computer keeps trying to sneak it onto my shopping list.

Sending the software back for a refund is out of the question, however. The hard-working, indigenous programmers of wherever would suffer if I return it. Upper-management would fire off memos to middle-management, middle-management would have meetings with lower-management, lower-management would have conference calls with supervisors, supervisors would scream over vid-links at workers, and workers would resign or be fired for creating substandard products.

My job was in jeopardy once, merely because customers got too many washers when they received their cubicles. The cubicles produced under my supervision are fully automated. Press a button, step back and in less than ten minutes, there are anywhere from two to two thousand sparkling new cubicles ready for work. After assembly is complete, three extra washers would appear in the upper right-hand drawer of each desk. Three washers, one a half-inch in diameter, the other two of the three-quarter inch variety. The three extra pieces of metal weigh six grams all together. Normally, not a big deal. Nobody even noticed until terrorists leveled all the Vague Automotive manufacturing centers, and Vague needed three-million cubicles for the rebuilding efforts.

Three million times six grams is nearly eighteen tons of metal.

The excess hardware initially confused customers, but the realization that around twenty tons of material had to be recycled following proper Environmental Protection Agency guidelines caused a little more than a strongly worded letter to the Chief Executive Officer of my company. I was nearly fired — robots had cleaned out my workstation — when a maintenance technician confessed to incorrectly calibrating one of the machines. After the obligatory press conference naming the technician as the perpetrator of the error and announcing his dismissal and execution, the factory returned to its usual level of productivity and boredom.

After that, I never complained about any product. Slow service maybe, but never a product. My spare bedroom is full of boots that don't conform to my feet, jumpsuits that won't close, and appliances that do nothing but smoke when turned on. I keep buying things, whether or not I need them.

Patriots are good consumers.

I grab a pair of boots out of my spare bedroom along with my toolbox and sit on the floor next to the coffee table in the living room. The boots are top of the line, Mark VI Auto-Form Technology. The most comfortable footwear ever created. Each step is predicted by fuzzy logic software, and the sole reshaped in accordance with the user's foot and surface microseconds before contact is made.

Concrete becomes like clouds.

That's what the ad campaign claims, anyway. Five minutes after I walked out of the store with them, they became the most painful pair of shoes I have ever owned. It wasn't a poor fit. The sole stabbed into my feet in unique and random patterns as I walked. Like my foot was stuck in a player piano made of nails.

At the Academy, I received some technical training and know how to fix most of the broken junk in the other bedroom. The training was useful for my profession, but the Refurbishment Statute technically made it illegal to use that knowledge outside of the office.

A thin-blade screwdriver releases the service panel in the heel, and I go to work, checking leads, re-soldering a bit of this and a bit of that. A couple days before the accident, I took a motherboard and some microprocessors out of an older pair of boots that had a habit of auto-lacing so tight, it felt like my toes would explode. They are slowly being integrated into the newer boots. Spending a few hours every night working on the boots or a malfunctioning toaster oven seemed ridiculous when in half a minute a new one could be delivered. And no matter how well I fix it, it won't bring that new electronics smell back. Nothing brings that smell back. But I know what will happen if I return it or throw it into the recycling bin. The manufacturer will get a report from the dumpster, if I discard it, and whoever was on shift the night my product was made will get fired. Or get sent to Patriot Rehab for disrupting the consumer goods flow. They're like me. They do nothing at work but watch robots build things. The robots are to blame. Why ruin the life of some human to improve my satisfaction as a customer?

The thought of buying something gives me a sudden pang of guilt. Using the keyboard sunk into the coffee table, I find the Hermod Website and send a donation for the rebuilding efforts. Brief clips of cheery people, walking in and out of the factory, smiling, waving at the camera. Now, all of them, dead. Unidentifiable piles of calcium around a scorched crater in Tennessee. Every one of them. No survivors. The terrorists are too good, too precise. Surgical, if surgeries were ever performed with sub-sonic incendiary devices.

The clip plays over and over. People walking out of the factory for a few seconds, then a slow pan up to the Hermod Winged Spear above the front door. It makes me think. I have worked at the cubicle plant for years, and I don't remember ever seeing someone smiling when they left work, let alone on the way in. That Hermod factory must have been one magical place for all those workers to be that excited to be there.

Pages upon pages of shoes are hard to resist. A cobalt blue pair with a projector around the ankle that puts out a hologram and makes it look like you have wings on your feet, like Hermod himself. They are the most magnificent things I have ever seen. I will die without them.

The boots from the hospital are brand new, I think. And I never wear anything blue, especially not that sexy, rich blue.

My hand freezes as I try to click away from the page. Sensing my indecision, arrows pulse and entreat me to put my thumb on the screen's pay-pad.

Just lay one right here, I could feel the screen begging me. Ooooh, you know what I want. Touch me right there, big daddy.

Electricity shoots through my skin, I clench my body, my knees lock together, elbows dig into my sides, one fist under my chin, the other in the grinder of my mouth. It feels dirty and wrong to not buy the shoes. In less than a minute, those shoes could be at my front door and seconds later, they could wiggle themselves onto my feet like animatronic puppies, set to scamper.

And I would be helping the rebuilding effort.

I would not only be helping the rebuilding by purchasing them, but by wearing them and advertising for the company every time I walk down the street in them. I am enticing other people to buy them. Then, the company would regain its strength sooner from one print of one thumb.

I shout as I lash out at the screen, unable to bear the tension anymore. Flailing, I click a link, any link to get me away from the shoe section.

The link that comes up is not exciting in a fashionable way.

It is not motivational in a tragic way.

It is boring in a chartered public accountancy way. The link shows the history of the company's stock in several ways: A series of numbers, bar graph, and line graph. Before the attack, Hermod stock was around a thousand credits a share. After the explosion, that number went up over a hundred-fold, which makes it one of the most valuable publicly traded stocks on the market according to the news crawl at the top of my screen.

Maybe the bombing wasn't such a destructive thing, I thought. Maybe this horrible event will make Hermod great again. I was disgusted with myself for even thinking such a thought.

Dinner is served, sir, the kitchen announces.

I make my way to the high counter and pull up a stool.

Will you be dining here or at the dining room table, sir?

"Here," I say, getting comfortable. At times, I believe the kitchen would turn its nose up at me, if it were capable. The two arms dangling from the ceiling in the kitchen finish plating my meal and bring everything to me on a hard plastic tray.

Will there be anything else, sir?

I look at the tray, take in the aromas. "No, that will be all."

Bon appétit, sir.

"Thank you."

You are most welcome, sir.

My mouth waters when I pick up a fork, not from the food, but at the sight of all the drugs sitting on the counter in front of me. Nearly five days with no drugs — not counting what they gave me in the hospital — is a long time for me. I work my way through dinner. My eyes never leave the display of syringes and pipes, balloons and vials, twisted spoons and all the pills in their Technicolor splendor. Every device has its own name, its own ritual.

If cocaine is on the chopping block, I am a submarine

captain. "Torpedo room, conn," I say as I chop it into a finer powder, "load tubes two and four."

"Tubes two and four loaded, cap'n," I reply to myself, as I finish smoothing out two perfect rails.

"Fire tubes two and four." The two lines would vanish, and I would sit back on the couch.

"Fish in the water, cap'n," I would grunt, as I wait for the cocaine to hit me.

I had a game for everything, every combination, except my new favorite — a hit of acid, two tabs of ecstasy, and a fat line of GB-4, with a bowl of opium for a chaser. The hallucinations were mellow and erotic, as long as I didn't watch the news. Spontaneous orgasms wrack my body for at least the first six hours of the high, then L.I.F.E. would intervene and dispense adrenaline. My heart had a habit of stopping at the beginning of the seventh hour because I didn't scrimp on the drugs. Nothing but the best went in my nose, down my throat, up my ass. But that was just the one time my dealer had nothing but heroin suppositories. It was cool losing consciousness, starting at my feet.

Last week, I wanted to build my tolerance so I could ride each drug out — the acid, the ecstasy, the GB-4, and the opium — until the end. I look forward to rising slowly from a dream state into full sober consciousness, instead of the usual jolt out of an overdose when the adrenaline restarts my heart. Now, as I eat dinner, the thought of even touching the hand carved wooden opium pipe frightens me.

I bottom out the wineglass and lean back. The kitchen arm brings the bottle to the counter before I set the glass back down. *More wine, sir?*

"Yes, to the top. You can clean up now, including this," I say, waving my hand over the drug layout.

Yes, sir.

I make my way to the living room with my full glass of wine and sit down on the couch. It takes all my effort not to run into the kitchen, snatch the opium pipe from the robotic arm and pack a bowl. The thought of opium makes me remember that my wife is somewhere on the other side of the city, probably on her couch, her head and eyes rolled back as dank smoke trickles from her nose and mouth. Half a glass of Shiraz did nothing to stem the tide of saliva on my tongue.

"Where's my son?" I say, suddenly remembering what I need to do. The word 'Searching' appears on the wall for a moment, then disappears, and is replaced with an exact location, his dorm room at the Academy. "Connect me."

After several seconds of silence, followed by his face appearing on the wall. "J. McGewan-YY2," he says from his end of the connection, "how may I assist you, citizen?"

"It's me, son. How are you?" There is a beep before he can respond and a commercial for Ishmael's starts.

I can't believe that he is YY2 already. It seems like only yesterday when I received a link to BluTube to watch the sonogram from the Procreation Licensing office. When I found out who the mother was, I called and introduced myself to my new wife, and drank a champagne toast with her over the phone. Once a week, I would go to the Procreation Website and stare at the gestation tank via vid-link, conversations with my son running through my head, trying to make them sound natural, so I would be ready when he needed them... and me. Now, he was in sight of citizenship.

... and if you order Ishmael's during this phone call, we'll waive the delivery charge. Ishmael's, the Patriot's Coffee.

"How may I assist you, citizen?" repeats my son.

"It's me, it's your dad. How are you doing?"

"I am very well, citizen. And may I inquire as to your overall health and well-being?"

"I'm... fine," I say. "What's with the tone?"

"Does my tone displease you, citizen? My apologies."

"Why do you keep calling me 'citizen?'"

"They executed a student this morning for undue familiarity with a citizen," he replies, his face blank. "Is there something I can assist you with, citizen?"

"I just wanted to tell you I'm fine. I'm out of the hospital. Taking a couple days off. Is there anything you need?"

"The Collective is my succor, I want for nothing. In three-and-a-half semesters I look forward to receiving my citizenship and repaying the Collective for raising me most properly." He speaks in a monotone, his eyes half closed. He no longer sounds like my son.

Granted, he is under a lot of pressure. He's in his last two years at the Academy, and the Crucible is not a place to make a mistake. Last year, he would have been sent to a remedial course. This year, he would be sent to the gallows. I remember all the sleepless nights I had, cramming for Advanced Consumerism oral exams, living on a constant diet of Ishmael's and terror.

"But everything is going well?" I ask.

"I have been in this building, training for my citizenship since birth. I have no experience to compare it with, but it is going as it usually goes, citizen."

The beep returns, this time for Vague Automotive.

Images of robotic nannies wheel through my head during the commercial. The first human I saw was the doctor that implanted L.I.F.E. in my arm at five years old. Then, nothing but classes, twelve hours a day, until I was eighteen. I wasn't even told who my parents were or how I was brought into the world until I was ten. Tears had poured down my face when I was told that Jane-49 — the nanny that had read me bedtime stories and changed my diapers — was a machine and not my mother. The Academy's methods were scientifically proven to create ideal citizens, and that's what the world needed, not troublemakers and shiftless lay-abouts.

... if you're an American, then you drive a Vague.

"I need to resume my studies, citizen," he says, as soon as the commercial ends. "It was a pleasure. God bless." He ends the transmission.

I stare at the blue screen for a moment before leaning back into the couch and sipping my wine. My tongue flips the screen to television mode. I scroll to my Favorites folder, tongue-click it, and find nothing. Just a line of text at the top.

There is no content in this folder.

A couple clicks more, and I am in my Viewing History.

There is no content in this folder.

"What happened to my Favorites and my Viewing History?"

The folders disappear, and a commercial plays.

Introducing the all-new, totally redesigned Wipeitall Gizmo. When unforeseen circumstances arise, you don't always have time to delete your Viewing History. Wipeitall has you covered. If you ever stop breathing or your heart stops beating, L.I.F.E. notifies Wipeitall, and the only thing friends and family will find is a clean slate. Wipeitall. Download it now in the Gizmo Store.

"Great. Why would that stupid Gizmo turn on? What am I supposed to watch now?"

The television flips to an ad.

Don't know what to watch? After a long day, the best way to unwind is to check out BPM. We have every form of entertainment for the Patriot on the go, with the largest selection of American-themed music in the world. Or, why not rent our newest release, Captain Patriot 15, Terror Begets Terror? Or if you're in a naughty mood, we've just expanded our adult section for those romantic nights alone. Visit us online or click the link to find the nearest self-serve kiosk. BPM. If you're not working, you're enjoying entertainment from BPM.

I wait for the advertising lockout to end, then say, "Activate slow crawl."

The television flips from channel to channel. I pause on one, and the doctor's voice from this morning pops into my head. He said I had been dead for a few minutes. I was alive, then I was dead, then I was alive again. A tremor shoots through my body. L.I.F.E. didn't ask if I wanted drugs or a chat with my personal counselor, so it couldn't have been anything serious.

"Riots in Europe today," the reporter says into the camera, a shot of the French flag over his shoulder, "as Americans are hunted down in the streets and executed for wearing sandals in the Louvre. The U.S. State Department has issued travel advisories and recalled all embassy staff—"

Click.

"—on its inaugural voyage," says the next talking head. "The federally funded light rail would have made the commute for citizens in the Denver-Colorado Springs-Pueblo Tri-City area more manageable and economical, but after today's tragedy, with the death toll exceeding five-thousand souls with more bodies still to be recovered, the project will most certainly be scrapped. In other news,—"

Click.

"This report is the sort of thing that boils my blood," a suit is yelling to his more casually dressed co-host. "Ninety-nine percent? Are you kidding me?"

"That's what the report says," casual responds, his voice matching his attire.

"The unmitigated gall of these, these rabble-rousing, neo-liberal, pseudo-fascist, dare I say it?"

"Say what?"

"You know what I'm going to say."

"Say it."

"Terrorists," the suit says. "These people are terrorists trying to destroy everything that you and I hold dear. Ninety-nine percent? Come on."

"These things happen," casual says with a shrug. "The government has had a hundred percent approval rating for three decades. Eventually, it is going to slip a little—"

Click.

As the next channel comes up, the Flanery Defense shield logo is just fading into the face of Jack Flanery. "Welcome back, citizens. If you're just joining us, Michael Stingle, Head of the Department of Transportation is my guest to talk about the train mishap in Colorado."

"It is a tragedy, Jack. No doubt about it. We conducted all the tests in the summer. Every car loaded with mannequins to simulate actual passengers. We took every precaution. We just didn't factor in the weather. It is horrible, simply horrible."

Flanery put his hands up, a mock plea for protection. "Tragedy, tragedy, tragedy. Stop it. I didn't ask you here for an operatic show of nursemaid hand-wringing. This is the Lord's will." Flanery slams his fist onto the desk. "This is the Lord's hand at work." Another slam for punctuation. "The only tragedy is that we had to scrap a ten-trillion credit light-rail project because a few entitled, welfare queens are too cheap, too stoned to save a couple paychecks and get themselves a used Vague to go back and forth from the local soup kitchen. I say, 'good riddance.' You make a couple of adjustments, you make sure the rivets don't fall out as soon as it snows, and you know what you've got?"

Stingle looks from Flanery to the camera, then back to

Flanery. "A free method of transportation for the less fortunate in Colorado?"

"A light rail that is five thousand dead terrorist-liberals lighter," Flanery says. The camera goes from the two-shot to a close-up of Flanery. "That's all the time we have tonight. Keep those shields up," he says, pointing at the camera, "and God bless every one of you." He makes the sign of the cross as the screen fades to black.

I tongue my way through the next dozen stations until I get to one of the XXXcitement channels. The news crawl at the bottom of the screen rehashes the Hermod bombing. Their political analysts are calling for war against Madagascar and all nearby countries of mainland Africa. The seven, leather-clad dwarves went on with their work, taking turns sodomizing the bound-and-gagged cheerleader, occasionally sipping their Ishmael's, heedless of war talk right below their diminutive feet.

Nothing about the Highway Tragedy.

Nothing about my run-in with Homeland Security.

Nothing about me.

"Television off, house lights dim, open the blinds."

The computer obliges, and I put my feet up on the coffee table and watch the dark skyline. Police and Homeland Security hovercars glide silently between apartment buildings. Lights turn on and off in the skyscrapers as people get home or go to bed. I wonder if anyone from the factory lives in that building, then dismiss the thought. Even if someone from the factory lived next door, I wouldn't recognize them, wouldn't speak to them if I passed them in the hallway. Sklrda appears and tops off my wineglass. As I watch the night sky, the dark Australian wine envelopes my brain in warm cotton.

I awake several hours later, sprawling naked on the bed. The wine buzz is still there, but fading. I can't remember if I had gone to bed under my own power or if the butler had done it. Sitting up causes my head to throb, and I stumble into the bathroom to splash some water on my face. The cold water clears the sleep from my eyes but does nothing for my head. My tongue is fat and dry, so I tap my wrist through several menus before I find 'Headache—Alcohol Induced.' I select, 'Yes.' The dispense prompt appears, but nothing happens other than the word 'Error' appearing on the display. I repeat the steps several times with the same results. After the fourth try, the display urges me to visit my authorized L.I.F.E. dealer and/or health-care professional for a system check.

Frustrated, I rummage through every drawer and cabinet in my bathroom searching for any form of pain reliever, as the headache gathers steam and ramps up into a migraine. When my right eye twitches from the pain building behind it, I call the computer for help. "Are there any headache relievers in the house?"

No, sir.

"None at all?"

None whatsoever, sir.

"Fuck!"

I'm sorry, sir, I did not understand your last request.

The shaving kit with all my drugs is the only thing in the medicine cabinet. They are good for a lot of things, but curing headaches isn't one of them.

"Never mind. Where's my car?"

In the garage, sir. Shall I warm it up for you?

"Yes, please."

I try to keep my right eye closed as I pull on a jumpsuit and step into my boots. The right boot is wearing out, I notice, as it takes three tries for it to seal around my foot. The clock on my heads-up display read two-fifteen in the morning. As a day worker, I wonder where I could get a headache reliever at this time of night.

When I get to the end of the hallway, I try to relax, try to will the pounding to slow, as I wait for the elevator to make it to my floor. That's when I heard it. Waiting for the elevator on the eighty-fifth floor of my apartment building, migraine trying to pummel my brain into submission. That's when I first hear the lullaby.

CHAPTER 6

It takes a moment, standing in front of the elevators, until I can make out the tune, distance muffling the words. I step back down the hallway, between the doors for 8501 and 8502, and the words are louder. It sounds like the lullabies Jane-49 sang to me at the Academy when I was very young. That is, the feminine singsong voice is the same, but the words are different than I remember. Much different.

The President / is your true friend / he'll fight the terror / until the end, the voice sang in a quiet soprano. *So, buy more things / and support the war / and remember what / we're fighting for... The elevator arrives behind me,* but I stand my ground and continue to listen.... *Consumerism / Consumerism.* I turn, but freeze when the second verse starts. *Hermod is / the choicest brand / for head and foot / legs and hand. / So, don't forget / the folks that died / to make the label / Made with Pride / in U.S.A. / in U.S.A.*

Eventually, I back into the elevator. A wave of nausea hits me as the migraine intensifies. I don't understand where the song could be coming from as I hit the button for the parking garage. All the apartments are soundproofed, so it can't be a television or radio. The pressurized elevator makes the pounding behind my eye increase as I plummet to below ground level and try to concentrate on headache relief.

Are you ready for some excitement?

A holographic automobile appears in front of me, taking up all the empty space in the elevator.

We are proud to introduce the all-new, totally redesigned 2234 Vague Automotive ID-Ten Turbo.

The hologram zooms in through the driver's door. Items on the dash explode toward me as the announcer speaks.

Fully integrated L.I.F.E. experience. Immersive surround sound. Onboard rocket fast Internet access. Top-of-the-line, upgraded auto-drive. And, of course, state-of-the-art Super HD Plus windshield, so all of your favorite programs and movies are brought to you in better-than-theater quality during your long commute.

All the parts zip back into the car, as the perspective pulls back. The driver's door seals itself as the vehicle rotates in front of me.

Are you ready for the excitement? Are you ready for the ID-Ten Turbo? Let's find out. If you're an American, you drive a Vague.

The hologram stops rotating when it is aimed at the elevator door. The rear tires smoke and deafening muffler noise comes from the speakers in the ceiling. The holographic car appears to shoot through the elevator doors at the same moment they open in the garage to reveal my identical car waiting at the curb.

The driver's door slides up as I approach, allowing me to get behind the wheel. A smile forms on my lips as I inhale the new-car smell. Lasers built into the roof flick on and off, each measurement raises or lowers the seat, slides it forward and back again. The manual controls on the dash in front of me shimmy this way and that until they are within reach, should I need them. The center console pivots. All of this takes less than a minute, and my new car is tailored to my body.

Destination?

"Out. I need a drugstore. Fast as possible." The car makes its way out of the parking garage with an electric moan as the electric engine screams onto the street at a breakneck ten miles per hour.

According to the console, most drugstores in my neighborhood are too specialized to carry headache relievers, so my search expands. The car drives further from my apartment as the search radius increases. The last two listings claim to have headache relievers, but only one is a 24-7. I select it on the console and the car turns to take the quickest route.

The store is larger than I expected, thirty square feet, half a dozen shoulder-high shelves run the length of the space. Each shelf is packed with merchandise out in the open, for anyone to touch or tamper with. I have only seen stores like this in old movies and am unsure how to behave for a moment. The computer does most of my shopping in my apartment or — when I do venture out — I use a little booth where I type in what I need, pay, and robots load my car.

A Terminal drops from the ceiling a few seconds after I arrive. A wiry black beard took up most of it. "Good morning, sir," the bearded face says in a thick accent, perhaps Indian or Pakistani. "And God's blessings be upon you. I am the franchise owner-operator of this American 24-7. Is there anything that I can assist you in locating on this fine American morning?"

"I have a headache," I grumble, not enthused by his chipper demeanor this early in the morning.

"Many fine American pain relievers can be found on the end of the last aisle, sir. Shall I show you?" He gives me a broad, eager smile.

"I think I can manage, thank you," I say, as I step around the Terminal.

"If there is anything I can do for you, as one American to another, do not hesitate to ask," the Terminal says to my back. The man doing the talking is visible out of the corner of my eye behind the counter.

I read the pain reliever packages for a few minutes before the décor grabs my attention. Every strip of metal, every window, even the floor and ceiling are covered with the stars and stripes–flags of all sizes, ranging from fingernail-sized taped to the front of each piece of merchandise to the giant flag that covering the ceiling. Even the owner is flag-festooned, his turban, his shirt, his trousers, probably even his footwear unseen behind the counter. I raise my hand in a wave toward the counter. "Excuse me," I say.

"My fellow American, I am at your service," he says, even before the Terminal stops in front of me.

"What's with all the flags?"

He gasps at the question and jerks back as if I had slapped him through the screen. "I am a naturalized citizen of the U.S. of A., not a terrorist, sir."

I run his response through my head a couple times, the headache making things difficult on me. "Terrorist? I didn't accuse you of being a terrorist, I was just asking about the flags. I've just never seen so many in one place before."

"As a citizen of this great country, and not a terrorist, I have every right that you do, which includes the right to display the stripes and stars in my business." His face darkens around the edges of his beard. "Have you found what you are looking for, sir?"

I wave the box in my hand at the Terminal. "I'm still reading labels," I say lamely. The Terminal shoots into the ceiling and I go back to reading the box in my hand. Just get something for the headache and get home, I think. You don't want another run-in with the Homies, do you?

It takes a couple of minutes for me to realize that the box in my hand is for menstrual cramps, not headaches. I nonchalantly put the box back and grab a different one, scolding myself for acting suspicious. "You are a terrorist and don't even know it," I mumble to myself.

The Terminal reappears so fast that it bounces on the end of its arm. "That is it," the man shouts, his exposed skin flushed, eyes narrowed. "I will not be accused of terrorism three times in my own store by the same person on the same night. You will conclude your shopping and vacate my store, or I will have you arrested for harassment, discrimination, slander, libel, profiling," spittle clouds my view of his face as he shouts into the camera, "prejudice, sodomy — "

"Sodomy? I haven't sodomized anyone!"

"Perhaps not yet, but I will have many a book thrown at you, my friend, my words will be marked." His image huffs and puffs at me for a moment, and then it dawns on both of us that another customer has entered the store and is watching us from just inside the door. "I will assist this gentleman, and then I will call the Homeland Security," he shouts. The Terminal disappears again.

The customer is a well-tanned older man with wispy white hair combed straight back, showing the widow peaks on either side of his temple. He walks up to the counter and gives me a sideways glance. I drop my head. In my periphery, once he thinks I am no longer watching, I see him speak to the owner face to face, a Terminal nowhere in sight. They whisper to one another before a stack of grayish papers and a metal jug comes from behind the counter. Both men glance at me as I try to increase the intensity of my search for pain relievers. The white-haired man puts a stack of golden discs on the counter, which the owner spirits away into a pocket. The customer takes the stack of paper and the jug and hustles out of the store with his head down. The owner's Terminal drops in front of me, blocking my view of the old man's route.

"A thousand apologies, my American brother," the owner says, his beard contorted up into a ridiculous smile. "Please accept my finest headache reliever free of charge as compensation for my rudeness." A box appears next to his face, with the words 'No charge' in the itemized total column.

I put the indicated box in my pocket and then follow the Terminal to the exit. "Have a wonderful day, my fellow American, and be assured that you are blessed by The Jesus," he says as I step outside. The doors close behind me.

A slight breeze comes up as I stare at my car. The migraine subsides, just for an instant, and I have a moment of clarity. I reenter the store and stomp to the counter.

"What did that customer say to you to change your attitude?" I ask the owner, staring into his eyes.

He hesitates for a moment, and then brings the Terminal down in front of his face, the image out of proportion to his body behind it. "We must use the Sanitary Terminals for all transactions, sir."

With both hands, I shove the Terminal back, catching the owner in the nose. His legs go limp. I catch him by his red, white, and blue collar before he can collapse and pull him halfway across the counter, bringing us chin to hairy chin. "What did that man say to you?" I ask, enunciating each syllable.

"I do not know who you are referring to," he says, as blood bubbles from both nostrils, pooling in his mustache.

"That customer said something to you, right into your face, that calmed you down. Who was he? What did he say?" My hands and arms feel electrified as I hold him there, headache forgotten.

"I took a mood stabilizer while I was talking to him. That is all. Please take the medicine with my compliments, sir." He tries to squirm out of my grip, but I pull him back.

"Bullshit," I shout, "your L.I.F.E. sensor isn't even functional."

He gasps and doubles his efforts to get out of my grasp. "I am a naturalized American citizen, not a terrorist. I am just a businessperson. I know nothing of the Librarian." He stops struggling as soon as he says it, his eyes go wide, then fill with tears. "I am undone. Death will surely come for me now," he wails. I release my grip, confused, and he slides off the counter onto the floor into a sobbing ball. Speechless, I leave him there and run to my car. The door opens, the engine starts as I approach.

Destination? The car asks, closing the door once I am inside.

"Define 'Librarian,'" I say.

Librarian, noun, antiquated. A specialist in the care or management of a library.

"Define 'Library.'"

Library, noun, antiquated. A place in which literary, musical, artistic, or reference materials, such as books, manuscripts, recordings, or films, are kept for use but not for sale.

"Define 'Books.'"

Book, noun, antiquated. A set of written, printed, or blank sheets bound together into a volume.

I was still unsure of what a Librarian was or why he elicited such a response from the store owner. "Is there a library nearby?"

Searching...

One result. National Public Library and Book Depository.

One-point-two-five miles north-northeast of present location. Destination?

"Same," I say. The car signals a left turn and whips around in a half-circle as the safety restraints pull me back in the seat.

"Why am I chasing this guy?" I mumble to myself as the car drives itself to the destination. "He's just a little, old man. Even if he is a terrorist, what am I going to do about it?"

The Terminal emerges from the dash and an anti-terrorism ad plays.

Terrorism knows no specific age, race, religion, gender, or sexual orientation. If you suspect someone of terrorism, contact Homeland Security immediately. Would you like to be connected to Homeland Security?

"No," I say, as I hit the cancel button on the ad.

I can't call the Homies. It had only been a few hours since I was at gunpoint because someone else had been overcautious. I couldn't do that to anyone, especially not some wispy-haired old man. But I have to know for sure. And if I do die while trying to find out, well, my son will graduate with honors and my wife will get a sizable reward for my heroism.

But is that even why I'm doing this? Is it really? Truth is, I'm plagued with questions. Questions I haven't formed into complete thoughts yet, that nag at the edge of my awareness. The accident... the terrorists... the lullaby... the accident... the terrorists... the lullaby....

Or maybe my migraine is the first warning sign of a brain tumor. Maybe my judgment is clouding as the tendrils of cancer spread across the sectors of my brain. If L.I.F.E. and the doctors and all the random scans I go through every day miss a brain tumor and I die, someone would have to invent a new word for the amount of money my wife and son receive. They would never have to work again. They could just buy and buy and buy anything they want. Anything and everything that I couldn't give them now. I smile as the car stops in front of the Book Depository.

I hope it is a brain tumor, I think.

The external cameras turn on, the building across the street illuminates the interior walls of the car. The building is dark and squat, four stories of brick with smudged and dusty windows every ten feet. No light escapes from any windows. A stone arch supported by two chipped columns stands over the entrance, with National Public Library and Book Depository chiseled into the arch. The solid-looking wood doors are locked tight, handles held together by a wrist-thick chain and a lock the size of my head. Seeing no signs of life, I sag back into the driver's seat, still staring at the building. The Librarian is heading home and not to work, and my questions remain unanswered.

A monster stares in at me from the passenger side of the car. I jerk back and slam into the door. No less than half a dozen cameras process the beast's visage and contort it into a curious nightmare. The white hair is vast, being nearest to a camera, making it an oversized hat resting above the ears. Each eye is out of proportion to the rest of the face and to its opposite, the right eye is pale blue circled by a starburst of scars, the left eye a rich brown, the surrounding skin smooth. The two separate halves of the nose don't line up. The tiny mouth is pressed into a frown. The entire image shifts, the proportions change as the creature moves its head from side to side, trying to see into the car. Surely, it had heard me gasp and slam against the door, saw the car rock. After a moment, the monster steps back, all of its features resolve into a single aspect ratio and form the face of the Librarian. Unable to see into the car that had pulled up next to him on the street, he steps around to the front end, crosses the otherwise deserted street, and ascends the twelve steps to the Book Depository.

My body relaxes as the Librarian works the lock. My chin drops to my chest and beads of sweat flow down my forehead. A solitary drop lands in my lap, beads on the fabric and rolls to the inside of my thigh on its way to the driver's seat.

The yellow bars on my L.I.F.E. display catch my attention. Each level — breathing, sweating, heart rate, muscle tension — is well above normal, but on a slow descent back into the green, with no medication dispensed or even recommended. I tap the display with my index finger, which, of course, has no effect. I stare at the display until every bar turns green.

When I look back at the Book Depository, the Librarian is nowhere in sight. The left-side door is open, just a crack, and the chain keeps it from closing all the way.

Leaving the 24-7, I was full of rage, ready to corner the Librarian and beat answers out of him, if necessary.

Now, after the drive cools me off, I have trouble getting the nerve to open the door of my car, unsure of what I would say to him, unsure of why I thought he would have answers, unsure of almost everything since I left my apartment.

It takes a few minutes, but I decide to go inside, tell him I was passing by and saw the door open.

That's what a good citizen would do.

That's what I will do.

Be a good citizen.

As I cross the street, I notice that I am not in a good part of the city. All the slidewalks are the stationary kind. There are no shops, no liquid billboards, no other cars on the street, and, I think as I walk, no hope of rescue if I am accosted by street thugs, rumored to roam streets like this, with no fear of the law. I quicken my pace and take the steps two at a time to the door of the Book Depository. It doesn't open on its own. I nudge it open with my foot, not wanting to touch the handle with bare flesh. The lock slips out of the way, allowing the door to close after I am inside.

A bare bulb shines just enough light for me to see a desk and three mismatched chairs against one wall. A bell rings somewhere in the distance, an alarm of some sort, but an honest man has nothing to fear. I'm being a good citizen. That's all.

As I enter the next room, the smell overpowers me. The rich, dusty odor assaults my nostrils and makes my eyes water. Shelves rise around me in the darkness, giving the impression that they go on forever, fading into invisibility five feet above my head. My L.I.F.E. gives off a bluish halo of light, just enough to define the darkness, not dispel it. The ringing continues and I try to follow it. Moving forward with careful steps, trying not to run into anything in the murky glow from my wrist, I realize what I must look like. If surveillance cameras are watching, and every building has surveillance cameras, they would bear witness to me sneaking through a huge warehouse that I shouldn't be in, trying to find someone that I don't know, to tell him something he doesn't care about. An honest man, a good citizen. It occurs to me that wouldn't do too well in a court of law, but I can't turn back. Looking over my shoulder, I can't see where I had started, the shelves swallowing up all the light from the lobby.

Then the ringing stops and I freeze, losing any navigational aide. There is a faint grumbling for a moment, but it seems to come from no specific location. I keep walking, hands out in front of me, hoping to find a light or door or maybe the Librarian. I walk a few paces when a loud rattle comes from somewhere far in front of me, and I stop again, trying to decipher the sound. The sound grows louder, seeming to come from everywhere at once. I consider running away, but to where? I don't know where I came from or where I am going. The floor vibrates, and it makes my heart jump into my throat, as if it were resolved to escape even if the rest of me isn't. Something is approaching, at speed, a faint flicker in the darkness now and then revealing that it, whatever it is, is headed straight for me. I swallow hard and realize it sounds like luggage rolling on concrete.

The thing slams into my face, throwing me back, my head hitting the floor. A buzzer sounds. A light flashes high in the rafters, then there's pounding of feet in the darkness. My arms and legs are too rubbery to push up off the floor — to defend myself against the next attack. A bright light comes around a corner and stands over me. Something cold and metallic presses into my throat. I lie still.

As quick as it had come, the piece of metal retracts. A voice behind the light says, "Oh, it's you. Well, come on, let's get you a cup of coffee."

CHAPTER 7

When the Librarian bends down, I can make out his face by the lamp attached to his forehead. He grabs my arm and pulls me to my feet with minor effort. "I expected you, but not so soon. Come on, grab the ladder." He guides me onto the thing that hit me, a long ladder attached to the front of a shelf. He steps onto the bottom rung with me and presses a button. "Hang on." A motor whirs to life and propels us down the aisle. The light on his head turns the two-minute journey into a drive through a darkened tunnel.

The ladder deposits us into an open area, the terminus of hundreds of shelves. He spends a moment pushing the buttons on the end of each shelf, recalling all the ladders he sent to ambush me. The open area contains several chairs, a ratty couch, a narrow bed, and a metal desk covered with kitchen equipment. Bulbs on long cords hang from the ceiling, illuminating an area thirty feet square. He hustles me into a cracked leather armchair before I can protest or even sanitize the seat. From there, I watch him hurry from one piece of furniture to another with no obvious purpose, moving clothing and other belongings from one chair to another, then to the couch, then the bed, then back to the original chair. His eyes dart around the room, then looks at me and snaps his fingers. "Coffee."

"Yes, please." I wasn't sure if he was asking me if I'd like some or announcing that he remembered something about coffee. He hands me a cracked ceramic mug and sat, sipping from a similar mug. "Thank you."

He nods to me and raises his mug in a toast.

"What is this exactly?" I ask, looking into the mug.

"Coffee. Do you need sugar? I have sugar, but no cream. Wait. Maybe some powder," he stares into the darkness to my left for a moment. "Nope, no cream, not even powdered. Sorry."

"Where's the steamed milk and the whipped cream and all the other..." I wave my free hand around in the air, "...the other stuff that goes with coffee?"

"Bah," he spat between sips of coffee, "that's not coffee. What's in your hand is pure, actual, good old-fashioned coffee. Trust me."

I stare at my reflection in the black liquid for a full ten seconds before the smell hits me. "Switzerland," I mumble.

He coughs, coffee splatters his chin. He lowers the cup. "What did you say?"

I take a sip that turns into a long pull, halving the contents of the cup. My shoulders drop and I sink into the chair. "It's just like Switzerland."

"What is?"

"The coffee tastes exactly like the last good cup of coffee I ever had. I was on vacation in Switzerland before the travel advisories." Don't waste this, I think, taking a small sip and holding it. When I allow myself to swallow, I look back at him. "Where did you get this?"

"You were in Switzerland?"

"Yeah."

"The one in Europe?"

"Yeah." I didn't realize there was more than one, I want to say, but don't.

"When?"

I chew my lip for a minute, trying to remember dates, then shrug. "It was a long time ago."

"You said before the travel advisories?"

I nod.

"Was it before the Collapse?"

I chuckle. "I wasn't alive before the Collapse. It was sometime between the Collapse and the travel advisories if that helps any." The plan is to finish this cup, maybe ask for one more, and get the hell away from the Librarian. No amount of plastic surgery or genome treatments could make a hundred-and-eighty-year-old citizen look my age. Slight disparity in appearance there, thirty-eight and one-eighty. Also, a huge disparity between reality and wherever the Librarian lives.

"What year do you think it is?" he asks me as he brings the silver jug over and refills my mug, then his.

"I know it's twenty-two-thirty-three, what year do you think it is?" My patience worn thin now, regardless of how good the coffee is, and I am not even aiming for polite.

He replaces the jug on the desk then resumes his position across from me, staring, not speaking, just examining me, waiting for something. Halfway down the cup again, I try to concentrate on the mug, my boots, the ratty area rug, anything but his two different colored eyes working me over. I move forward in the chair, ready to bottom out the cup, thank him for the coffee, and leave. He speaks before I have the chance.

"Where are my manners? I'm Herb," he extends his right hand across to me.

"P. McGewan-X04," I say, taking his hand, my arm lit with static when our palms meet. I can't remember the last time I had skin-to-skin contact with another person. "Pleasure to meet you," I lie as we break contact, the tingle gone.

"The pleasure is mine." He leans back, the mug in his lap. "Tell me, what does the 'P' stand for?"

"Excuse me?"

"The 'P' in 'P. McGewan-X04.'"

It takes me a moment to remember, not having been asked for years. The three-digit identifier at the end is the important part, the bit everyone needs to know for business matters, no one cares what the initial at the front means. It's window dressing. It's a frilly tassel in an otherwise utilitarian workspace. It's the appendix of my identity, the useless bit everyone is born with, but no one needs.

"It's Pat."

"Pat? Like a portion of butter?" he asks, with a smile, but without sarcasm.

"It was my grandfather's name. Patrick actually, but I just got Pat."

"Can I tell you something?"

I nod as I slide back into the chair.

"You don't look like a Pat. You look more like a Peter, no, a Paul."

"Thank you," I say, unsure of what he's talking about, but taking it as a compliment. "And you look exactly like a Herb." I am just echoing him now, trying to go compliment for compliment.

"Have you met many Herbs?"

"No, but the name conjures an image..." — I say, doing damage control, trying not to look like an idiot — "...and it is very close to what you look like."

"So, I resemble seasoning? Something you sprinkle on meats to add flavor? A clove of garlic, or perhaps a sprig of rosemary?"

"No, I didn't — "

He waves his free hand at me and shakes his head with a smile. "Save your breath for cooling your coffee, I'm just, as my people say, giving you a hard time."

I smile back and relax, reflexively looking at my wrist. Muscle tension is descending from yellow back to normal. The rest of the bars are higher than normal, but still in the green.

"Am I keeping you from an engagement?" he asks, over the lip of his mug.

"No, I was just checking my body's reaction to our conversation."

"You need a device for that? From five feet away, I could see your knuckles go white as I spoke. Your shoulders bunched up around your ears. Your jaw clenched. Your nostrils flared. Pat, why are we here?"

The jump from the physical to the metaphysical makes my head jerk back into the cushion. "To be good citizens. To defend and uphold the American way of life. To — "

A wave of his hand stops me, again. "I apologize. I was born in Germany, so English is not my first language. I think what I meant was, why did you come to the library? What brought you here? I don't mean your car, but what is your...?" His fingers swirl the air in front of his face.

"Quest?" I finish for him.

"Excellent word, 'quest,' a noble undertaking. Yes, what is your quest, Pat?" He sits his mug on the floor next to his foot and leans forward. Elbows on knees, palms cradling his chin, his different colored eyes nail me to the chair, sucking the words out of me.

"Terrorists. I want to find out about terrorists," I say with a calm I don't really feel, but keep eye contact, resisting the urge to look at my wrist.

He stands without a sound and grabs the silver jug, refilling both our cups. The last handful of drops crash into his mug, the sound exaggerated, amplified by the mausoleum of a room we are in and the rush of adrenaline flushing my face.

Once he sits again, he shakes a thick index finger at me and smiles. "Up until this point, I have considered myself a man of science. I have faith in what I can prove mathematically and through experimentation. There is no room for superstition, good luck charms, or prophecies in my life. But you...," his finger stops and points to the center of my chest, "... you are the one we have been waiting for all these years." He chuckles, clapping his hands together. "I will teach you about the terrorists. I will introduce you to the terrorists. Then, when the time is right, I will follow you as you lead the Revolution." He leans back in the chair and sips coffee with an enormous grin.

The Gizmo on my wrist flashes in the corner of my eye as every bar tops out, well into the red. My head vibrates side to side, my neck a bobble head's spring. "I'm not a leader. More importantly, I'm not a terrorist."

"But you are. You can hear the evil words spoken to your flock, in the privacy of their minds. You hear the songs the Evil One sings in the night. You have been sent to change those words, to make your people good once again."

I stand and place my mug on the desk. "This is ridiculous. How do I get out of here?" He rises and walks over to a ladder, gesturing with a wave of his hand for me to get on. "Thank you for the coffee, but I have to go. It was a pleasure meeting you and all, but, yeah, I need to leave."

"I will talk to you soon." It is a statement, not a question.

"No. No, you won't," I say, climbing onto the ladder. With a smile, he presses the button. The ladder jerks to life and hurtles down the aisle.

"You'll be back...," he shouts, as the light grows smaller over my shoulder. "... when you realize you have no choice but to help. I will be waiting for you."

Please standby, your consumer experience software is calibrating.

Based on your most recent interactions, the following commute is brought to you by the Department of Homeland Security.

Are you in over your head? Do you think you've uncovered a terrorist plot? The Terrorist Tip Line is available 24/7 and all calls are quick, discreet, and confidential. Would you like to be connected now?

CHAPTER 8

My heads-up display shows four in the morning when I return to my apartment. My boot comes up in anger, but I stop myself from kicking Sklrda when it greets me at the door. The electronic 'gentleman's gentleman' can't feel pain, but assaulting it would be considered Domestic (Machinery) Violence. Too many lawyers with too little to do would gladly take up Sklrda's cause. They would drag my name through the mud, find expert witnesses to decry the abuse of the poor, defenseless machine, have psychologists explain that my propensity for violence toward robots was a gateway to violence against humans. It would drag on and on, the day-long trial televised, the entire populace riveted by the proceedings, sitting on pins and needles during the commercial break for jury deliberation.

At the very least, I would get probation, and they would scrutinize all my actions in case of another violent outburst. If they could prove that I was a serial abuser of robots, I would get a sentence of five to seven years without robotic assistance of any sort. I would have to cook my own meals, launder my own clothes, and make my own bed. I shudder at the thought and put my foot back on the floor. After all, I want to inflict pain on

Herb or any terrorist, not learn how to make a sandwich or turn on the laundry unit.

The system lights wink on in the kitchen when I ease onto the couch. Now, it works properly when I want nothing from it. I shake my head and wait to be annoyed by another modern convenience.

Sir, would you care for a —

"No."

Then perhaps a —

"No."

Then may I recommend a —

"No."

Is there anything —

"No."

Very well. Do not hesitate to ask if you —

"Fine."

The standby light comes on and the kitchen leaves me alone. For a while. If I even glance in the stove's direction, it would go through its spiel again.

The blinds are still open, and I stare out into the partial darkness. Rain falls between my building and the next, each drop of moisture lights up the shielding with a brief lavender glow. The thought of how smart some people could be puts a smile on my lips.

The shielding is a prime example. People worry daily about being killed by terrorists, not only directly but also indirectly. The big fear, for a long time, was buildings being destroyed via terrorism, either with conventional bombs or aircraft, like the first 9/11 attack. If a person is in a building singled out for demolition by the Militant Independent Luxembourg Freedom Fighters, or whoever, they're pretty much dead, end of story.

What about the falling debris caused by the explosion?

What about the people that see the attack coming and dive from the windows?

What about the tons upon tons of broken glass shooting in all directions?

Some genius, his name lost to antiquity, invented the shielding five years ago for just that purpose. The shielding would solve all the problems caused by a terrorist attack on a high-rise building.

Falling debris?

Slowed to a pedestrian rate of descent, as it passes through subsequent layers.

Falling people?

They'll hit the ground no harder than if they stepped off the curb.

Shards of shattered glass shooting in every direction?

Stopped entirely, several feet from the window casing, then lowered gently to the ground.

All these benefits, but no one wants to pay to have the shielding installed. "I'll never have debris or people falling from my building." That was the general consensus. No one ever believes tragedy will befall them. Terrorist attacks happen to other people.

Then the break came. The Center for Disease Control released a report stating that "exposure to elemental precipitation could have long term, but as yet unknown effects on the health of humans." Shortly thereafter, a resourceful lawyer brought a class-action lawsuit against the owner of a skyscraper, because the building didn't offer enough protection from rain. The case went all the way to the Supreme Court, which unanimously ruled against the building owner.

Suddenly, the genius couldn't install the shielding fast enough because if you cranked the output all the way up, the shielding would slow down and dissipate rain before it got within ten feet of the sidewalk. For about a month, the genius was the richest man on the planet. Then, someone invented some device that everyone had to have, and the genius was forgotten. It's not the American way to remember the second-place finisher. First-place is all that matters.

A pleasant side effect of the shielding is the magnificent view during rainstorms. Lavender sheets of electricity pulse across the skyline in a shower, a frenetic light show during a downpour.

After a few minutes staring at the shielding, as it flashes on and off, I notice another flashing light. This one red and coming from my coffee table. I press the corresponding button on the keyboard, and an antique mailbox appears on the wall above the fireplace. A gentle female voice announces, "You have mail" as the flag goes up on the animated box. Pressing the receive button brings up the United States Post Service logo.

Thank you for your continued patronage of the United States Postal Service. For an additional charge of two hundred credits, would you like your mail scanned for dangerous substances and devices?

I select 'yes' without a second thought. When I left Herb, I kept saying to the instruments on the dashboard, "I'm not a terrorist. I'm not a terrorist." Everything I had been brought up to believe hinged on that fact. I'm a good citizen. I'm a Patriot.

Terrorists want me dead, so, as a Patriot, I want all terrorists dead. Then what happens if Herb is right? What if I am some sort of terrorist messiah? The patriotic thing would be suicide. Kill myself before I could hurt anyone. Engage the self-drive and swerve into a bridge abutment.

Now, back in my apartment, I am worried about letter bombs and chemical booby-traps. I barely beat Sklrda to the mail slot next to the front door. The robot tries to snatch the package from my hand so it can hand it back to me. I shoo the butler away and return to the couch. The box is as long as my forearm with a fresh green check mark and the legend "Scanned for your protection by the United States Postal Service" stamped across the mailing label.

Sir?

"What?" I shout at the butler who crept up on me, as I am about to open the package.

Your letter opener, sir.

"Thank you," I say levelly, taking the offered opener. "Now, Sklrda, leave me alone, please."

Will there be anything else, sir?

"Sklrda, go away."

I will take your silence as a 'No,' but do not hesitate to call upon me, sir.

It wheels out of the room.

The packing tape splits easily as I guide the laser letter opener around the top of the box. Inside an envelope of thick bond paper, a thumb-drive, and something heavy encased in a cocoon of shipping foam. I set both items on the coffee table and throw the box over my shoulder.

Allow me to get that, sir, Sklrda says. The little silver blur darts back into the room, then disappears with the box.

A small screen inside the envelope stands on its own on the coffee table and, after pressing 'Play,' my lawyer's face appears. "I apologize for questioning your decision yesterday. Hopefully, we can continue our professional relationship. I thought you might like to have this. They were sold out by the time they released you from the hospital. But I know a guy. Anyway, I hope this finds you well. Don't hesitate to contact me, if you need anything, anything at all. Sincerely, R. Willard-C73." The image freezes as the loop of data ends. My lawyer's mouth contorted into the shape for the number three.

I put the screen back in its envelope and push it aside. A

port opens on the side of my coffee table when I pick up the thumb-drive. When I insert the drive, the one-hour special about me, entitled 'Forever Remembered,' plays. The first half-hour only hints at the Highway Tragedy and instead concentrates on my past. Most of the information is slightly skewed to make for better television. My parents were good citizens, but not as heroic as the narrator claims. The narrator wavers between happy and tragic regarding my childhood. Which was neither. It was just like everyone else's. I stop the playback after a while, annoyed, and stare at the cocoon of packing foam.

Sticking my thumbnail into the foam lets enough oxygen in to make it sublimate completely, leaving behind my commemorative statuette, a miniature of the original in Remembrance Park, numbered three-hundred-seventy-five of three-hundred-thousand and signed by the artist. Because the statuette is signed and numbered, it is authentic and an exact duplicate of the larger version, down to the last detail. Being signed and numbered below one thousand makes it very valuable. The first thousand of any statuette never went on sale to the general public. They are sent directly to special collectors, and they auction a few off for ten times their original value. My lawyer spared no expense trying to keep me as a client. I am impressed.

The statuette is a Phoenix rising from rubble and flames, its wings spread, its eyes heavenward. The design of the statuette is confusing. Most of the statues in Remembrance Park are obelisks or simple slabs of stone with names and dates chiseled on the sides.

Why a Phoenix?

Turning the piece of stone in my hands, I notice my name hidden in the Phoenix's wings, P. McGewan on the right wing, X04 on the left.

I am the Phoenix.

Upon closer inspection, I see a name etched into each flame and piece of rubble at the Phoenix's feet. People's names. People that didn't rise from the ashes like me. People that were taken from their families by terrorists. Doctors and lawyers and scientists, people much more important than me, were destroyed so that I might live. These people could have brokered peace between the terrorists and the United States or found a better cure for cancer, but they died, and they allowed me to live. Out of two-hundred-thirteen people that could have survived, it was I, the Cubicle Production Technician, the least useful of all the victims, who got his name on the Phoenix. Everyone else, useful or not, became a grease stain on the highway. Personalized rubble in the artist's rendering of the last moment of their life. Tears start down my cheeks as I set the statuette on the coffee table.

I want to slam my car into the Phoenix erected in my honor. I want to breathe smoke as the engine shoots through the dash at a hundred miles an hour, charbroiling everything, starting with my boots and working up as I stare at the artist's homage to my pain from earlier in the week. I want to feel such excruciating pain that my convulsions of agony grow so intense that I snap my own neck. The coroner will list the cause of death as, 'self-inflicted statuary.'

No, that could be construed as humorous, not sterile enough, and then the coroner would be open to lawsuit, and someone else would suffer because of me. My teary-eyed survivors would take the coroner for every cent, then he — or she, I suppose — would be led to the gallows in front of City Hall. Citizens would pause for a moment in their busy day, turn to the nearest monitor and watch the coroner leave this world. Then, back to business as usual — production, consumption — without another thought about the coroner or the coroner's family or even a memory of why the coroner had to die.

This is just advanced hypothetical philosophy, not at all in the realm of the doable, I realize from the security of my couch. The car wouldn't allow me to slam into a bridge abutment or a granite bird any more than it would fly me to Pluto or drive me through the Marianas Trench. The car would automatically override the manual controls and, with the aid of the traffic collision and avoidance system, keep me on a safe and legal path. If I did go into the city's Remembrance Park, the car would slow to a sedate and reverential five miles an hour. Manual control would not be an option, as I tour through the monoliths, obelisks, and artist's renderings of past tragedies in chronological order, a deep and serious voice explaining the significance of each chunk of stone.

If I could, somehow, get to an unsafe speed under manual control and if, by some glitch, I could slam into a stationary object, the air-bag, impact foam, fire suppression system, Cocoon Enterprises Full-Body Impact Restraints, and emergency stasis field generator would all have to be disabled before so much as an eyebrow could be singed. Tampering with any of these systems would render the car useless, and a squad of armed Department of Transportation thugs would appear at my door. Whoever said, 'Where there's a will, there's a way,' never tried to end their own life in the twenty-third century.

The Feng Shui program turns on in my apartment while I ponder my demise. Lasers paint little red X's around the apartment to show me the most aesthetically pleasing spots to place the statuette. I center the statuette on the mantle, in front of the television. The Feng Shui program is satisfied and goes to standby. Lying on the couch, I turn the one-hour special back on, my eyes alternating between the statuette and the television. My tears stop after a few minutes, my breathing slows, my heart rate lessens. The status bars on my L.I.F.E. display sink to a low green. I am so calm that I doze off.

Sleep fully engulfs me when the narrator begins the roll call of non-survivors. I bring my eyelids to half-mast and watch the photos morph from one victim to the next. The narrator identifies each photo with their name, occupation, family status, and any awards they had won. At least six doctors scroll by, each with a family, each an award winner for ground-breaking research in their respective fields. Several dozen citizens, men and women, from different occupations had spent their free-time volunteering in the underprivileged parts of the city; tutoring, mentoring, helping at-risk children become good citizens, something I never had the courage to do. Every victim seemed to have something on me.

More kids.

More important job.

More awards.

More generosity.

More potential.

The program ends, and the main menu appears. I didn't realize I was crying again until the tears angle across my lips.

Why am I still alive?

Why didn't one of them live?

Why didn't the terrorists do a better job?

The apartment's computer interrupts me when I begin mumbling to myself.

I didn't understand your request, sir.

I sit up on the couch with no attempt to wipe away the tears streaking my face. "Start my car."

Yes, sir.

I grab the statuette off the mantle and head for the door.

CHAPTER 9

Rain pounds around me, and the wind whips it into the arch-
way. There is no shielding on this side of town, and with the
wind, no shelter. My jumpsuit wicks away some moisture, but
it can only do so much before the damp soaks through to my
skin. I don't care. If my plan works, I won't live long enough to
find out what long-term effects the precipitation might have
on me.

*Do you have commemorative paraphernalia at home or the
office that are worrying reminders of terrorist attacks? Perhaps
something willed to you? Perhaps bought in a zealous fit of
Patriotism, but now brings you panic and dread? Fear not. On
CraigsBay, you can sell it outright or setup an auction. It's three
easy steps. Our on-staff commemorative merchandise appraiser
gives you an honest starting price, and soon that statuette,
medallion, or commemorative mug will be out of your life for
good. Click below to set up or login to your account at Craigs-
Bay. CraigsBay — the simple, down to Earth, Patriotic trading
community.*

I dismiss the ad on my wrist display and stand for five
minutes in the downpour, toying with the idea of leaving, when
I hear a key working the lock from the inside. The door opens

and I shove the statuette into Herb's chest before he can say anything or bar my entrance.

"Give me answers or give me death," I say, through clenched teeth. The door closes behind me under its own weight.

"Did you think up that line on your own?"

"Yes," I sneer. "Yes, I did."

Herb snorts and stares at the Phoenix as he holds it with both hands. He turns and walks out of the lobby before he speaking again. "Lock the door and bring my keys," he shouts from the other room.

I want to protest, tell him to lock his own damn door.

"There are no answers in the lobby. They're all in here."

I lock the door and bring his keys into the other room. He stands on one of the ladders.

"Can we speed this up a little?" he scowls as he speaks. "I do need to sleep at some point."

The ladder moves down the aisle, almost before I can grab on. Herb doesn't speak, but hums a tune I don't recognize. His right hand holds the statuette, the Phoenix staring at me over his bicep. The wing emblazoned with X04 sticks out over his elbow.

Herb dismount before the ladder comes to a complete stop, and I follow him through the living area and across the width of the building. He stops in an open-sided freight elevator and presses the down arrow. The motor, visible five feet above our heads, groans to life.

The ride lasts ninety seconds, though we drop less than thirty feet. At first glance, the basement is a carbon copy of the main floor, nothing but floor to ceiling shelves as far as I can see. Our descent ends, and Herb sets out, still humming, and enters a small room next to the elevator.

My breath catches in my throat as I step into the room. He

is busy arranging the Phoenix on a shelf and takes no notice of my reaction. The room is full of statuettes, arranged by date. It is a miniature graveyard. At least a thousand miniature obelisks, monoliths, and abstracts stare at me. Each one equals how many dead?

Fifty?

A hundred?

A thousand?

How many people have died at the hands of this man?

Is this his trophy room?

"Now, I just need a Hermod statue and I'll be caught up again." He turns to face me. "Pat?" He steps closer. "Are you okay, Pat?"

My throat is too dry to respond, and my legs feel like rubber. Herb grows larger as I watch him. Then everything goes black.

I wake up on the floor outside the room. Herb propped me up against the doorframe and blots sweat from my face with a cool cloth. "I'm sorry I couldn't get you someplace more comfortable, but you're heavier than you look." He dips the cloth in a pan of water and wrings it out. "Can you walk?"

I nod. He helps me up and leads me, arm around my waist, to a small sitting area with a dozen mismatched wooden chairs. "Take slow, deep breaths and try to relax," he says. "I'll be back in a moment." He disappears and I stare at my wrist.

The deep breaths turn into hyperventilation when I see no data on my L.I.F.E. My vision narrows and unconsciousness comes for me again as Herb returns. He shakes me by the shoulder and shouts my name, but his voice comes from a great distance. The room is going dark and I can't keep my head up. Herb slaps me hard across the face, and I try to jump out of my seat. He keeps me in the chair with one hand and offers a glass of water with the other.

"Everything is going to be fine," he says, as I take a sip of water. "Your little computer won't work down here because of all the lead. You aren't dead. You just aren't getting a signal. Okay?"

"There's lead?" I ask, looking around, panic returning.

He takes a seat opposite me. "There's lead in the roof, in the pipes, in the support beams, in the shelves, even in the paint. Lead is dangerous to humans, but they inoculate newborns against lead poisoning, so we're in no danger." He leans back in the chair and points at my arm. "You won't get a signal at all while you're in the basement, too much lead between you and the satellite that tracks you. That's also why you hear the voices in other people's heads."

"What? You lost me there." I set the water on the low table between us.

"The box that landed on your car was full of lead paint. A construction company unearthed a cement bunker of it while they were building a new skyscraper. The paint was en route to Madagascar, where all lead goes to die. You have enough lead in your body now to turn your little computer from broadcast to receive. That's why you hear voices. That's also why drugs won't dispense."

I can't make sense of everything he says, so I first try to understand the terrorist angle. "Is that why the Madagascar Independent Liberation Force or Front or Whatever dropped the box on me? They didn't want any more lead in their country?"

"No one lives in Madagascar, regardless of what you hear on the news. It's just a big landfill now. Nothing but lead from coast to coast."

"Then why did you drop the box on my car?"

He squints at me and works me over with his eyes, then

shakes his head. "You really believe that a little, old man dropped a forty-ton box on your car?"

I can't hold his gaze any longer and look down at my boots. "You said you were a terrorist. I thought you were trying to rub my face in the fact that you let me live."

He chuckles. "'Give me answers or give me death,' that's what you said when you showed up here, right?"

I nod, still looking down, his face barely visible in the corner of my eye.

He sighs and leans toward me. "So, you think I need to explain why I let you live," he holds up a finger, "or I need to finish the job. Is that right?"

I nod again.

"Look at me, Pat. Look me in the eyes."

I lift my head.

"I had nothing to do with the box landing on your car, okay? It wasn't a terrorist attack. It wasn't even user error on the part of the person piloting the container ship. It was just old-fashioned mechanical failure. That's it. All right?"

"What about the one-hour special? What about the other names on the statue? I saw the news clips of those bodies being dragged from the wreckage. I heard the names and saw the faces of the two-hundred-and-twelve people who died that day," I say, as tears streak my cheeks. I bury my face in my hands before I can continue. "Why did they have to die? Why did I get to live?"

He moves around the table and sits next to me, his arm on mine. He pulls my head onto his shoulder as I sob. "Pat, I know this will be hard on you, but what I'm about to say, I can prove beyond a shadow of a doubt. You need to believe me, okay?"

I sniffle and raise my head. "Okay."

"Those two-hundred-and-twelve people don't exist. They were made up by a computer."

"What are you talking about?" My face flushes with anger.

"Let me show you."

I follow him further into the room, away from the elevator and the graveyard to an area full of electronic equipment.

"What is this?" I ask, as he pulls up chairs for both of us.

"This is what computers looked like before they started putting them into people. Everything is hard-wired, so it works despite the lead." I take a seat next to him, as he types on the keyboard. A sheet of paper comes out of a bulky printer that's the size of a shoebox. He hands me the printed page. "That's a list of everyone that supposedly died in the accident you were involved in, agreed?"

I scan the list. A few names are familiar. "Agreed."

"This is a Website that shows us the public records of anyone on the planet. We'll start with you, get all the survivors out of the way first." He types my name in, and the computer displays my entire life. My parents' names, my birthday, transcripts from the Academy, my employment record, marriage license, my procreation license for my son, everything in black and white for both of us to read. "I also can find out the toothpaste you prefer, the drugs you buy, and the last five movies you watched, if I wanted to. We agree that this is you, this is accurate?"

I nod.

"Give me another name."

"A. Spriggs-G48," I say, reading the first name on the list.

Herb types the name and a similar page of records comes up along with a photo that I recognize.

"What does this prove? He's a pediatrician who was on the one-hour special. He's dead and I'm not."

"You're right, he is dead. Look at the date on his Death Certificate. Hell, just look at the cause of death," Herb says with smug assurance.

"Fifth of May..." I pause to make sure I read it correctly, "... twenty-two-twenty-five. That's not right."

"It is right. He died eight years ago in the Amazon rain forest," Herb says, leaning back in his chair. "Death by piranha, not terrorists. Here, you try." He slides out of the way and pulls my chair over so I'm centered on the keyboard.

The next five names produce similar results. Every page comes up with a picture I recognize and a Death Certificate dated at least five years ago. Except for the piranha incident, every person had died of natural causes. I jump around the list after the first five names, thinking it is a trick. I think if I can find at least one person that died the day of my car accident, from any cause, I can prove Herb wrong. I can go back to believing. I can go back to business as usual. I can relax and think everything is running according to plan and no one is trying to deceive me.

I can't. Herb's argument is bulletproof. I pivot the chair to face him. "I don't know what to say. What about the one-hour special? All those bodies?"

"Some of it was archival footage, some of it was filmed on a set. What do you think happens to winners on reality shows that have no acting talent?"

I mull this over for a moment before he interrupts me.

"What's your father's name, Pat?"

"J. McGewan-Q44."

"Construction worker?"

I nod. "He was a plumber."

"Was? He passed away?"

"Twelve years ago."

"Look him up. Find out if anyone else has the same name. I need to grab something."

I turn back to the computer and do what I am told. No other entries come up besides my father. I feel a tug in my chest when his photo loads. I don't have any photographs of any of my relatives, least of all him. The last time I saw him was at my graduation from the Academy. I remember feeling embarrassed when I got my diploma. Everyone else in the audience just sat and applauded as each name was read. My father jumped up when my name came over the public address system. He whistled and shouted, "Way to go, Pat."

I wipe my eyes before Herb returns, a statuette in one hand, a sheaf of papers in the other. He sits the gray block of granite next to the keyboard and flips through the pages.

"Four years ago, in March of twenty-two twenty-nine," he reads, "the Mutually Incendiary Liberators of France dropped a fuel-air-explosive onto a BPM Entertainment Super Store in Hayes Center, Nebraska. Do you remember that?"

I nod. "It sounds familiar, yes."

"Now, a fuel-air-explosive is a huge canister with a parachute attached to it which is pushed out of a cargo plane. About fifty feet from the ground, it explodes with enough heat to turn people into piles of calcium. They say it's instantaneous death for everyone inside of a square mile, but you can't really prove that sort of thing."

"Okay. Why are you telling me this?"

"This is the statuette from that attack. Read the names on the side facing you."

I move my finger down the face of the stone and halfway through the list, I see: "J. McGewan-Q44."

"Your father was a tough man. Died twelve years ago of natural causes, then came back just long enough to be killed by French terrorists in Nebraska four years ago."

"I don't understand why they would blame the French for killing my already dead father."

"That was Phase One" he says with a sigh and wipes his forehead. "Phase Two was the United States carpet-bombing

Paris for one-hundred-and-fifty-five consecutive hours, the number of alleged victims in Nebraska. Roughly, a half-million Parisians were killed — men, women, children. They never found most of the bodies, just pieces. Did they teach you about the fire-bombing of Dresden in school?"

"I've heard of it."

"This was worse. Some people fled, some hid in old bomb shelters, some just went to the museums."

"The museums? Why?"

"During World War II, Hitler ordered his bombers to stay away from the museums. He was an artist, after all. Parisians thought the Americans would save the museums, too." He shakes his head. "Didn't matter, they bombed everything this time. They say the heat was so intense that the Champs-Élysées flowed like a river of magma." His eyes focus on a spot above my head, his voice low and even. "The Arc de Triomphe sank. The Eiffel Tower melted. Rodin, Monet, Picasso, all their museums destroyed. Nothing was left but ash and pieces of rubble smaller than your thumbnail." He sits silent for a moment, still focused on the wall above my head.

"But the French didn't really attack the United States?"

He shakes his head.

"Why did we bomb the French then?"

"They refused to trade with the United States. They were crying about how we treated the rest of the world and our own citizens," he says, looking down at me. "So, we gave them something to cry about."

We stare at each other for a minute.

"Wait," I say, "didn't anyone notice that the BPM store was still there?"

"Oh, they bombed it. It's a crater. I've seen it. There's a pleasant garden on the perimeter of the site now. It's actually beautiful."

"I thought you said the French didn't bomb that store."

"They didn't, it was the United States." He waves his hand to calm me down. "No one was hurt. It was the safest, most well supervised, faux-terrorist attack in the history of the world. They would have stopped the entire thing to relocate a family of rabid sewer rats." He chuckles with a grim look on his face. "Actually, they dug up all the trees surrounding the store a week before the bombing, then replanted them in the exact same spots a week after the bombing in memory of your father and the other victims."

I massage slow circles into my temple for a moment before I feel ready to continue. "Let me get this straight. The French said they didn't like what we were doing, so we bombed ourselves and blamed it on the French so we could bomb the shit out of the French?"

He nods.

"That's crazy." I say, pacing in front of him. "Why did we bomb ourselves? Why didn't we just cut out the middleman and bomb the French?"

"Insurance pays off triple in the event of a terrorist attack. Everyone knows that. The building was insured, as were all the people who allegedly died. And BPM needed something to boost their stock, so — "

"Stop," I say, still pacing. "A half million people died in my father's name to boost stock prices and commit insurance fraud?"

He nods. "Happens all the time."

I stop pacing. "The Hermod factory? That wasn't real, either?"

He shakes his head. "Who is the President of the United States right now?"

"It's, wait, I know this—"

"Matthias Jackson," Herb says. "What was his job before the presidency?"

"He was the Chief Executive Officer of Vague Automotive," I say.

"And who was his opponent? Where did he work?"

"He was a Chief Executive Officer, too. Right?"

"Logan, Chief Executive Officer of Hermod," Herb says. "During the campaign last fall, they tried to destroy each other by any means necessary, on television, billboards, in commercials during every phone call. But the commercials paid for by Vague were a bit more convincing. Mud thrown at Logan and Hermod stuck a little better than the mud thrown at President Jackson and Vague Auto. The President is re-elected, and the ads stop. But we all have a lingering memory of the campaign ads, and that made everyone buy less from Hermod.

"Understand that the five richest men in the country run the five biggest companies in the country. They're all friends. They play Zero-G racquetball together. The President was roommates with Logan at Harvard and best man at Logan's wedding. And they both had weddings. They can get married and live with their wives and have as many kids as they want, unlike you and I."

"What does this have to do with the bombing in Tennessee?" I ask.

"Logan's stock is in the toilet because of the campaign ads. He's laid off as many people as he can to keep his paycheck where he likes it. Shut down a couple plants, notably the one in Knoxville. Gets to the point where he's not comfortable with his bank statement. Granted, if no one in his family made another credit, just spent the money they already had, it would take four generations to fritter all his credits away. So, he asks his old roommate, his buddy from Harvard, President Jackson for a little help. Those drone bombers they have floating overhead all the time, that's their purpose. There was no one in that factory; there was no one near that factory. They bombed a deserted building to get the Hermod stock back up. Then, all you Academy grads, as you've been taught, buy as much of their merchandise as you can. The song you heard is reprogrammed to tell you what to do in your sleep. There's a lot of data saying that narco-hypnosis doesn't work, but it doesn't need to. You're all guilted into consuming on every television station, radio broadcast, and billboard until the stock price climbs back up."

I groan and rub my eyes. "When President Jackson first got elected, who was his opponent? I mean, what did he do?"

"Very good," Herb says with a smile, "you're thinking now. He was the Chief Executive Officer of BPM. The campaign ads from that election brought their stock down, so they had to kill your father again."

I stand and pace the room again. Too many thoughts are running through my head. The words want to form. My mouth opens. I want to say it's madness. That it's impossible. Or that I am still in sensory deprivation, dreaming. But I look at Herb and all I can say is:

"I need some air."

Herb nods and leads me outside in silence. We walk for a block and come to a disused square. Benches are sprinkled around an old fountain, stunted shrubs line the paved pavilion, water gurgles quietly. Herb sits down and I pace around the fountain in the pre-dawn morning. Lamps light the streets on all sides of the square, but the illumination runs out just before it reaches me.

Herb could be crazy, but everything tells me that he is telling the truth. Where did I get my truth before? Flanery? I replay his show in my mind. All I can conjure is angry accusations and him pounding on his desk. Had I ever heard him actually make an argument, or was he blaming everything on so-called terrorists? Had he ever debated anyone? Everything I'd ever heard him say sounds like such nonsense now, and not even well-written lies. Maybe it is the accident, or the headache, or my sudden sobriety, but I know, despite how ridiculous and world altering Herb's story is, he is telling me the absolute truth for the first time in my life.

A voice breaks through these thoughts and I freeze in the darkness. A night-shift worker, young, on his way home from his pointless job, shouts into his phone, an Ishmael's in his hand. He can't see me or the fountain or the aged Librarian just a few paces from him. He strolls through the light, talking to someone unseen, both unaware of the thoughts in my head. From this distance, the boy looks like my son. Roughly the same age, roughly the same build. Youthful and concerned only with being a good citizen, a Patriot, a consumer. But what would that get him? Worked to death for the sake of a grand lie?

He throws the Ishmael's at a trashcan, never slowing his pace, never losing the thread of his conversation, never looking back to see if the cup made it into the trash. The cup teeters on the edge for a moment, then a gust of wind pushes it just enough. It hits the pavement, lid spinning off in one direction, cup rolling the other way.

Another breeze, this one more pointed and full of menace, ruffles my hair. The street lights up, the young worker freezes on the sidewalk, ends his call. He looks up at the lights on the bottom of the hovercar, then over his shoulder at his discarded Ishmael's laying in the street. Then he sees me, staring at him, our eyes lock. Naked terror pours out of him, reaching for me.

"Citizen, you are charged with littering," the voice booms down from the hovercar's speakers. "Patriots do not litter. How do you plead?"

"Guilty," he says, still looking at me.

"You are sentenced to ninety days of Patriot Rehabilitation. Do not move. God bless."

The hovercar drops from the sky and swallows the citizen, the boy, before another word escapes his lips. The vehicle leaps back into the air, its lights extinguished, and disappears as quick as it arrived. The boy's discarded Ishmael's still in the street.

Herb appears next to me, still silent.

"Do you have any coffee?" I ask.

He smiles. "I could get some. Why?"

"You need to explain what the Chosen One does."

"Welcome aboard, Pat."

CHAPTER 10

Who funds terrorism? If you drink black-market coffee, you fund terrorism. Drink Ishmael's or nothing at all.

———

Herb and I stand in the library's foyer, waiting for the coffee to arrive via courier. The courier's nose is swollen to twice its size from where I hit him with the Terminal.

"Pat, this is Sameer. I believe the two of you have already met," Herb says, taking the jug from the 24-7 owner. Sameer gives me a nod as we walk to the library's elevator.

"Is this black-market coffee?"

"Did you just hear the commercial about black-market coffee funding terrorism?" Sameer asks. His red, white and blue outfit is gone, along with his accent. He now wears an unadorned black jumpsuit instead and speaks flawless American.

I nod.

"If you stick around long enough, we have a tech guy that can disable some of those functions. Not all of them, but the more annoying ones."

The three of us board the elevator.

"I'm sorry I attacked you," I say to Sameer, as we descend.

He shrugs. "It's just the drugs, don't worry about it."

I take a cup of coffee from Herb once we are in the basement and stare into the cup for a moment. "No, it wasn't the drugs. I've been stone sober for at least four days now. What I did was," I try to find an appropriate word and settle on, "barbaric. Totally uncalled for and I'm sorry."

Sameer sips his coffee before replying. "I know, it's a lack of drugs I was referring to. You're having THAW withdrawals, sudden bursts of rage and bouts of depression, disorientation. Modern conveniences stop being convenient. Maybe you don't understand why your boots are automated or your butler is suddenly a nuisance, instead of helpful. You probably think reporters are lying to you or your dead-end job seems stupid. All that and most people OD or drink themselves to death because their L.I.F.E. usually malfunctions when the THAW stops. That's why I run the convenience store. I'm the recruiting office for would-be terrorists. Didn't Herb explain this to you?"

"The night and I are both very old, and there is much I need to explain," Herb says.

"The sun's up," says Sameer.

"When you get to be my age, you find that what you used to do all night takes longer than one night to accomplish." Both laugh, then look at me and stop.

"Call if you need anything," Sameer says. He puts his coffee cup down, shakes Herb's hand, and heads for the elevator.

"What did you mean by the 'all night' comment?" I ask, after the empty elevator returns to the basement.

Herb motions to a chair. "That's the least of our worries at this point. There're a lot of things that I need to explain."

"You're going to tell me everything?"

"I probably won't live long enough to tell you everything, and I suppose you won't just believe me when I say that everything you know is wrong and go from there?"

I shake my head.

"Well, I'll tell you the important parts of everything."

He starts his account right before the Collapse. Every Academy student knows that a terrorist army descended on the United States, intent on destroying the American way of life. The surface of North America became unlivable from the chemical and biological agents and the lone nuclear suitcase bomb. Citizens not attached to the military were sent underground until the armed forces won the war, or at least cleared the surface of enemy combatants.

The truth is, Herb explains, that when the Middle East ran out of oil, we took away trillions of dollars of funding. Middle Eastern economies crumbled. The United Middle Eastern Coalition was formed to replace the Organization of the Petroleum Exporting Countries. People that had fought each other for centuries united against a common enemy — the United States.

"There was no 'army of terrorists.' There was just an army. Or, more precisely, armies made up of Saudis, Kuwaitis, Iraqis, Iranians, the whole lot. The terrorist angle was overplayed because they were predominantly Muslim. Terrorists don't have fleets of aircraft carriers and destroyers or squadron upon squadron of fighter jets or thirty armored divisions. That's an army, navy, and an air force. Before the Collapse, terrorists were suicide bombers, and then they developed overnight into a unified and uniformed sea, air, and land forces. That's a rather obvious deception."

They detonated the lone nuclear suitcase bomb inside an underground bunker in Wyoming, killing more than a million innocent civilians, which I knew. What I didn't know was that most of the civilians were middle-class, working men and women, funneled to the Wyoming shelter because of their income, blue-collar workers one and all, leaving doctors, lawyers, and bankers with no one to take out the trash or fix the toilets. It was a tragedy, not because they were Americans, but because someone with a doctorate got the short straw and wound up a garbage man.

"That's why you have X04 at the end of your name. They want to make sure there are enough peasants left to do the dirty work for the lords, if another attack happens."

"Lords and peasants?" I ask. "You act like we're living in the fifteenth century."

"The other reason you have X04 at the end of your name," he continues, ignoring my comment, "is in case they don't have enough room in the next set of bunkers. They'll just leave everybody with, let's say M through X out in the cold. Nuclear winters, I hear, can get quite chilly."

The peasants that survived rebuilt the cities, made the surface habitable again. Most died or had horrible enough diseases from a lack of chemical suits to warrant euthanasia. They used the ones that were not contagious or dying horrible deaths for medical experimentation.

"People don't enjoy being underground, especially without sunlight. When they think everyone on the surface is trying to kill them, especially when paranoia makes them believe terrorists are lurking around every corner. They needed a new kind of drug. Something to keep people docile. Something to keep people from killing themselves, or everyone around them. Something to make people think yesterday, when the attacks happened, was a long time ago."

Something called THAW.

"There really isn't a chemical called THAW. It started out

as a joke that only humorless scientists could enjoy. People were frozen with terror and this made them relax, ha-ha, let's call it THAW. Test subjects did more than relax. They melted into a big pile of I-don't-care and if-you-say-so. Bad things seemed farther away to them, and they were highly prone to suggestion, simply accepting that those terrible things they lived through were just stories from the time of their grandparents. They believed they had been born underground, had never seen the surface except in pictures. Then a genius for acronyms, probably a General, came up with a definition for THAW — Time Heals All Wounds.

"Every citizen had a L.I.F.E. computer installed before the Collapse. When the surface was inhabitable again, they modified it to administer THAW, a constant drip into the bloodstream. After a few months, no one remembered what living underground was like. After a year, everyone thought the Collapse happened a decade ago."

"I was alive before the Collapse?"

"You said yourself you were in Switzerland before the travel advisories to not travel outside the country."

"Yes."

"The travel advisories happened first, before the Collapse. There were negotiations when the oil ran out, but the Middle East no longer had anything we needed. So, the United States walked away from the table. That's when the travel advisories were put in place."

"But that means I was underground. I don't remember that," I say. "I've only seen it in movies."

Herb smiles. "You're making my points for me. Think about the last five movies you've seen. All of them are super hero movies, yes?"

I nod.

"Is there a flashback in every movie where Captain Patriot

or whoever is in an underground bunker during the Collapse? Or a group of citizens coming out of the bunkers and rebuilding the surface?"

I am reluctant to answer, because of what he is implying. "Yes," I say at last.

"All of it brought to you in Super HD Plus, more real than real life. What is Captain Patriot's origin story?"

"He took an experimental drug underground before the nuclear suitcase bomb exploded. The drug and radiation combined to make him into a super soldier."

"Correct," Herb says. "Everyone knows how the aged B. Kaufman became invigorated by the drugs and radiation, and was transformed into Captain Patriot, the perfect example of an upstanding citizen. Why do we have to watch the origin story, from a different angle each time, the bunker slightly different, the actors around him a little bit shorter or taller, more women, fewer men and vice versa in a dozen different movies?"

"Fifteen," I say. "They just released the fifteenth Captain Patriot movie."

"Twelve, fifteen, doesn't matter," he says. "What matters is that you have a memory of Captain Patriot, over and over in the bunker. Add the drugs that are constantly fed to you and your memory of life in the bunker is replaced by Captain Patriot's memories of life in the bunker. Think hard. The drugs are leaving your system. Were you underground when the Collapse happened?"

Thoughts flood through me. Cement walls. People strapped to gurneys around me, screaming, crying...doctors and nurses injecting them with drugs... a doctor standing over me, discussing my dosage with a nurse. It was a flash of a memory, but it wasn't Captain Patriot, it was me. My memory.

"There's something there," I say. "I don't remember a lot."

"It will come with time. There will be other memories, genuine memories that will surface. Anyway, the government conducted surveys, and the drug worked so well, they had to change the date, jump forward a hundred-fifty years in time. No one believed that it was 2070, anyway. So, on New Year's Eve, thirteen years ago, it went from 2070 to 2221."

"No one noticed this?" I ask, refilling our coffee cups.

"You were alive, and you didn't notice it."

He has a point. "This seems too big an operation. How did they pull it off without a coast-to-coast riot?"

Herb sips his coffee. "Easy. They cranked the THAW dosage up nationwide after Christmas, so no one was sober enough to notice anything. Then, to make sure there wasn't any conflicting paperwork, they decided to go paperless across the board. They instructed everyone to bring in any documents they had in their home or office to designated locations. If they were over three years old, they were destroyed. If they were newer than that, they were scanned and put into a central computing system with the dates moved forward a hundred-and-fifty years and the originals destroyed. Birth certificates and any form of identification or licenses were done away with and put on universal ID cards. Does that set off any buzzers?"

"It sounds vaguely familiar." I try to digest all the information as I sip my coffee. "Computers alone couldn't have done this. There had to be programmers and clerks. Certainly, one of them would come out and say something, expose this whole scheme."

"They were all handpicked and in on the scheme. They don't take THAW, they aren't taxed, and they don't worry about retirement like you and me. They also know that even a whiff of disloyalty and they're nothing but a name etched on a statue in Remembrance Park."

"How do you know all this? Why do you remember and no one else does?"

He points to his wrist. "No L.I.F.E. I'm part of the one percent of the population that is allergic to biomechanical implants."

"Then why does the government let you live? You could be..." I wave my hand around the room. "You could be doing exactly what you're doing."

Herb stands to stretch. "There was a raid a long time ago. Lost my right eye, whole thing was gone, blood streaming down my face. I dragged a friend, an ally that wasn't a terrorist, out of the building with a bullet in his stomach, but he drowned in his own blood before I could get him to a doctor. He donated his body to the cause, and I got his eye. The authorities found my eye along with a lot of parts of friends and comrades, declared me dead." His finger traced the starburst of scars around his right eye. "My left eye is Herb, the Dead Terrorist. My right eye is Herb, the Upstanding Citizen. That's why I'm still alive." He bottoms out his coffee cup.

"Besides, who would listen to a crazy old man with a job that no one needs? I'm technically Z-class. The Y-class is the mentally and physically handicapped and rookie reporters. I'm below them, useless. I'm a Librarian in a country that can't pay attention long enough to read anything longer than a ten-character text message. I remember when ROFLMAO was cutting edge technology. Now kids can get a doctoral thesis into a six-emoji combination."

I don't know how to respond. I can't conceive not having a purpose. Instead, I sort and file everything, match it with information I already have and replace it with new truth. Then, a big flaw rears its head. "What year does the rest of the world think it is?"

"Twenty-eighty-three."

"And they know that we think it's twenty-two-thirty-three?"

He nods.

"Then, why don't I see them every night laughing at me via the news? All I see are riots, mobs, looting. An entire continent believing it's a hundred-and-fifty years in the future should be a unifying laugh-fest. They could stop shooting each other with rubber bullets for a couple minutes and chuckle at the stupid Americans."

"You have a point, and I'm sure you think it's a deal breaker. If old Herb can't disprove your suspicions, you'll scrap everything and go back to life as you knew it. Am I right?"

"That's a bit extreme, but it is a big discrepancy."

"You need to understand two things." He holds up a finger. "Except for isolated pockets, the rest of the world is at peace with itself. All the riots and mobs and teenagers throwing rocks at tanks and platoons in riot gear, firing rubber bullets and tear gas into unarmed civilians, doesn't happen anymore. It's all archival footage. Some of those clips are older than me. We shut out the rest of the world and live in our little delusion, and they really don't miss us. The whole world is pretty much the first world now. Free medicine, cheap transportation, excellent working conditions, central air conditioning. Large countries help build the infrastructure of smaller countries, which fosters a feeling of brotherhood between all nations. If some country is struggling, every other country fights to be the first one in line to help.

"America is the third world now. Perhaps not sweatshop conditions, but workers are treated like cattle, disposed of if there is a dip in the stock prices of the five guys that exchange the Presidency every four years. Human rights violations at every turn: can't procreate, can't marry in the traditional sense, a caste system that oppresses everyone, healthcare that is unfeasibly expensive. And, if a single person protests or says they have a better idea, they are dubbed terrorists and executed in the Town Square. If they lose their boss's money, or if they demand lower food or healthcare costs, it's the gallows on every station, tried by a jury of pundits, with no hope to defend yourself or see the inside of a courtroom."

"But the guy that dropped the box on my car got a trial. Right?"

Herb shakes his head. "Actors made a show of what we perceive his trial would look like, but the actual pilot was dead five minutes after they took him into custody.

"There is now an uneasy détente between America and the rest of the world. No one can match us militarily, and our borders are too well defended. But the rest of the world does not allow us to step outside our borders and bomb, say France, over a dip in someone's stock. We still trade with the rest of the world, and they allow citizens to leave, if they wish. The world has made it very clear that the American government can do whatever it wants to us, they won't try to intervene. But if the U.S. Military steps across the border, there will be repercussions. The government would have you believe that the walls along the east and west coast and on our borders with Canada and Mexico are to keep terrorists out," he says, shaking his head. "It is to keep us in."

"That's why we blame random terrorist organizations now," I say.

"Exactly. The terrorism angle serves multiple purposes. There is no winning against terrorism, there is no home country for the terrorists, and there is no end to fear and war profiteering from the ceaseless war."

I take a moment to mull that over in my mind. "So, the richest people in the country have created an endless loop of misery to gain control of more wealth? It doesn't make any sense."

"There's an old saying in my country, 'Tragedy is when I get a hangnail, comedy is when you fall down a well and die.' It may not translate properly. They trade your misery for their wealth, which apparently makes sense to them."

He holds up a second finger. "The second thing you have to understand, reality television is everywhere, except on the news. All those news programs, updates, scrolling marquees on every channel, every bit of it is contrived. Scriptwriters were out on the streets when reality programming took over. Now, they have jobs making up the news. There's a monopoly everywhere. Ishmael's controls all the food and coffee in the country. Vague Motors makes every car. BPM controls every form of entertainment. Hermod makes all the clothing and shoes. Hasp-Hearken-Lewis makes every piece of military equipment. And, if something isn't in one of those five categories, it's owned by a subsidiary of one of those five.

"The only industry that has any competition is the news. The news program that gets the scoop on a story and makes up the most watchable lie, gets the bulk of the advertising money. Then, other programs have to follow suit, play catch up, and hope they can come up with the next big lie. They manufacture our beliefs, and none more so than Jack Flanery."

"What's so special about The Flanery Defense? He's certainly the loudest on television, but I still have the right to a mute button."

"So, you know who Jack Flanery is, but you don't know the name of the President?" Herb asks.

"I see Flanery every night—"

"And the President isn't on television every day?" he asks.

"Well—"

"Name another reporter."

"There's the guy in the suit that yells at the guy in the polo shirt. Then the white-haired guy with the whiny voice." I run fingers through my hair. "Oh, there's the two guys in suits that sit on either side of the blonde woman with the giant teeth, and they smile like they're on laughing gas regardless of the story, but I don't watch that show much because they seem mentally defective. And the other one I watch is the fat, sweaty guy who yells at everyone."

"No names?" he asks. "Not even the names of their shows?"

I shrug.

"All the money put into Flanery's show is well spent then," Herb says. "You know his name out of an ocean of channels. Forty-eight half-hour shows a day on three-thousand channels. That's in the hundreds of thousands of programs, but you only know Jack's name."

"What's the problem with Flanery? I don't see the connection to all this."

"Ishmael's owns him."

"So? He gets his money from a coffee shop, big deal."

Herb shakes his head. "After we ran out of oil, coffee became the most traded resource on the planet. Unless you meet someone that has a greenhouse of coffee trees, you can't get a cup of coffee anywhere in America that doesn't have an Ishmael's stamp on it. Flanery has the biggest budget, the best writers, and more lies per hour than any other two shows combined. The Flanery Defense is reality. If he says it's raining tomato soup in Bosnia, by God, it's raining tomato soup. Or, a few years ago, when we could still take our craziness global, he might say that terrorists were hiding in the mountains of South America, suspiciously close to a coffee plantation that Ishmael's doesn't own yet. Probes by the intelligence community, whose field agents get to stay in nearby luxurious coffee plantations owned by Ishmael's, declared that the terrorists funded their operations by selling black market coffee. Public service announcements rile up the public. Where do terrorists get their money? If you buy black market coffee, they get it from you. Then everything happens quickly. Obligatory public outcry. Patriots text their Congressperson. Congress passes a bill. The President signs a bill. The U.S. military precision bombs a villa. The clip of the bombing plays every five minutes on every channel. The President gives a speech turning the newly liberated plantation over to an American company, which is either Ishmael's or a company owned by Ishmael's. All that for a figment of Flanery's imagination."

"I just watched him last night," I say. "He was talking about a train derailment in Colorado."

"Flanery's second job," Herb says. "The government knows who gets watched the most, who gets the most airtime, replays, advertising credits. When they screw something up, Flanery spins it for them."

"Isn't his big thing that there is no spin? Doesn't he say, 'Spin is dead,' at the start of every show?"

Herb put his hand on my shoulder. "I'm going to enunciate, so you do not misunderstand me. If. It's. On. Television. It's. A. Lie."

"So, there was or wasn't a train derailment?"

"There was," Herb says, nodding, his hand back around his coffee mug. "Several thousand people died because the President's brother-in-law has no idea how to do anything, except beat up hookers and rape chambermaids."

"Stingler, Flanery's guest last night, is the President's brother-in-law? And he doesn't know how to do the job? That's bullshit."

"Really? I told you that we've bombed people over made up

news stories and that a government official rapes maids and only the nepotism gets you angry?"

"It's a lot to process," I say. "I'm working on the perspective."

"Keep working," Herb says. "What did Flanery say about the accident in Colorado?"

"That it was just a bunch of moochers that died, and now the train would run faster without all the hippie socialists on it or something," I say, running my tongue across my teeth. "That's awful coming out of my mouth, and I thought he was making a good point last night."

"Flanery's shtick doesn't really work without the THAW dripping into your cerebral cortex," he says. "Do you know about the rapid transit projects in the Midwest?"

I shake my head.

"Companies had to build factories on cheap land after they got thrown out of every other country because they wouldn't treat the workers right. After the Collapse, the Midwest was sparsely populated at best, so there was plenty of room to build factories. The workers weren't centrally located, but they could commute. Screws to them, as you say in America."

I raise a finger.

"Don't interrupt. The workers at all the factories were getting enough money to feed themselves and pay to recharge their cars to get to and from work. That was it. A few of them organize back a state representative who promises to get them a light rail that will be cheap and fast. Then, the hope is they can save up and make their lives better somehow. That's the closest this country has come to a worker's union for decades. The government doesn't make a big deal about it. They agree to build the light rail, but they build it cheap, cheap as the dirt. The first passengers are the union organizers and the state representative, and they happen to die on the maiden voyage."

"They were murdered?"

"No, the lowest bidder built the train. You don't ever go with the lowest bidder. You get the second or third guy from the bottom, if you don't care, and the most expensive guy, if you really care. Eight-year-olds with plastic mallets could have built a better passenger train."

"Then, Flanery comes in. He takes the government's mistake and spins it in such a way that the passengers take the blame and all the would-be complainers are now terrified of riding on trains."

"That's not very Christian," I say.

"Don't even get me started on that." Herb pours us both some more coffee.

"What do you mean? Is Jesus in on the conspiracy, as well?"

"Actually, he is," Herb says. "After the Collapse, the government could have picked anything as the State religion. They could have made up a religion. They had most of the citizenry so doped up, they could have told us that Americans have always worshipped a used popsicle stick. Instead, they went with Christianity."

I put my hands up. "I may have to draw the line here, Herb. I can't believe that Jesus is bad for us."

"What is the major tenet of Christianity?"

"The major tenet?"

"The big one."

"That if we believe in Jesus, we will get eternal life," I say.

"Right," Herb says, nodding. "No matter how shitty your world is here, no matter how poorly you are treated by the rich bastard that runs your factory, if you believe in Jesus, you will have a kingdom when you die."

"Okay? What's wrong with faith in an afterlife?"

"When you die," Herb repeats. "You don't get doodly-squat

in this life. Your religion tells you about all of your predecessors that were killed and tortured and lived in poverty. That's fine, because when you are dead, you will be rich beyond measure in the presence of Almighty God."

I nod. "Yeah, that's what I remember from church."

"And that doesn't sicken you?"

"Why would it sicken me?"

"There are a lot of things the Bible talks about, but that's the only thing the media and churches talk about, to keep you from rising up and killing the rich."

"No, that's just silly. The Bible tells us that if we happen to have a rough life, we needn't worry because the afterlife will be glorious."

Herb sighs. "The Bible is giving the people that are oppressing you permission to oppress you, and telling you to turn the other cheek. They are working you to death in horrible conditions sometimes and if you lose an arm, hey, God will give it back to you in Heaven. The rich are using your forgiving nature against you, so they can torture and kill you at work and protect themselves against a popular uprising. 'It's easier for a camel to pass through the eye of a needle than for a rich man to enter the gates of Heaven.'"

"The Bible is against rich people," I sip my coffee. "So what?"

"No. The Bible is telling poor people that they don't want to be rich. They need to live in poverty if they want to get into Heaven, which also gives protection to the rich people who purport to be Christian from poor Christians robbing them. 'Thou shalt not steal.' If you are poor, you have nothing worth stealing, so that commandment is only protecting rich people who have something worth stealing. 'Thou shalt not covet.' Again, if you're poor and have nothing worth coveting, you have nothing to worry about. But the commandments are saying 'Hey, poor guy, don't steal and don't think about stealing that rich guy's stuff because God is against that.'"

"I'm Christian, Herb, and I stand by that. Maybe you're right about the government playing with my brain, and maybe my bosses use me like a rag and throw me in the garbage when they're done, but there's no way you're turning me against my religious beliefs."

"What if there's no Heaven?"

"But there is."

"What if there isn't?"

"But there is."

"Humor an old man," Herb says. "Picture in your mind that this life is all you have and when you die it stops. No reincarnation, no life everlasting at the right hand of God, just a stopping of vital functions and loss of awareness. Close your eyes and think about it for a moment."

I close my eyes, but it is ridiculous, and I can't take it seriously.

"If this were all we had," Herb says, "people might treat each other better. With any religion, there is an afterlife and people on this plane are promised all sorts of things on the next. If there were no next, we wouldn't let five rich assholes get away with treating us like shit because they can't hide behind the promise of Heaven. The Good Times Tomorrow sign hanging over their desk. There is no tomorrow, there is only today. What about Flanery's or the President's behavior is Christian? They belittle people that die in accidents and the poor and they bomb their own people and innocent people abroad. How is that Christ-like? How is cruelty on any level equal to being Christian? The only thing they do is end every sentence with a hollow 'God bless you' and all of America says, 'Oh, I need to listen to him because he's Christian, just like me.'

It's a scam to keep you down. That's all it is and that's all it ever was."

I look at the old Librarian and don't know what to believe. "So, the government and Flanery are using our fear of not getting into Heaven to keep us docile?"

"Yes," Herb says. "They want you to be weak and obedient, so they can do anything they want to you."

The whole, 'religion as mind control' bit is a bit much for me. But there is a lot going on. I put a pin in that and consider everything else I've learned. If everything Herb told me is true, and it seems, at the very least, to be possible, what does that mean? I mull it over, consider it from a dozen angles. Herb sits silently, watching me think, waiting patiently for me to come to my own conclusion.

Religion aside, I focus on one thing. "Flanery is basically concentrated evil. That's what you're telling me?"

"Not really. He's just good at his job. He also hates the French, so, not to rub salt on your raw nerves, but the BPM bombing, that your father supposedly died in, that was his idea."

"If I were the Chosen One, and I am, I would start by dealing with Flanery and spiraling outwards."

"We're working on that, Pat." He stands and claps me on the shoulder. "First, we have to find out how."

"Is there a terrorist simulation program running through scenarios, eliminating the unfeasible, as we speak?"

"Nope."

"Is there a camp where you hold mock invasions, preparing for your attack?"

"Nope."

"Then, what do you do?"

"I ask a question until someone can answer it. It's low tech, but it works, eventually."

"Stick with what you know, I guess." I rub my palms on my thighs. "What should I do?"

"We find ourselves in unique circumstances. To do the right thing, we must do the wrong thing. But to know which is the right wrong thing, we must first determine how wrong the right things are. So, to do the wrong thing, we must begin by doing the right thing. It's quite simple, really."

"I didn't understand a word of that."

"Just show up to work," he says, smiling, "like a good citizen."

CHAPTER 11

The electric eye over the main entrance scans my ID card and directs me to Door Six. Door Six verifies my thumbprint before allowing me into the pre-foyer, where I am instructed to utilize Gate Charlie. In the foyer proper, Gate Charlie checks my Eye-D, the laser licks across my retina for the barest moment, before I am allowed through to the body scanner. When no metal or incendiary devices are found, the blast doors unseal and I enter the lobby of the cubicle factory. The routine varies daily, sending me through random Doors and Gates, but even with the latest terrorism prevention technology, it still takes more than thirteen seconds.

Welcome to the cutting edge of cubicle manufacturing. We are United States Cubicles. Our ready-to-deploy designs are self-cleaning, ergonomic, hypoallergenic, and fit any space, any budget. If a worker "punches out" while still on the clock, our cubicles won't just sanitize themselves, they self-sterilize to be new-hire ready just five minutes after the corpse is removed. All colors of the corporate color spectrum available in all models: Tan, Beige, Taupe, Light Grey, Medium Grey and Matte Gunmetal. And we are proud to announce our newest approved color, a sexy mash up of our two best sellers — Light Grey and Beige — Greige is available on all sizes and all model cubicles. We can't stop the productive Patriot. We only hope to contain them. We are United States Cubicles.

Two paces in, the slidewalk activates and puts me in line with the rest of the day-shift workers waiting to punch-in with the "receptionist." Every employee knows she isn't a real receptionist. It is as plain as her nametape, M. Paulson-F37. F-class is law enforcement. If she were an administrative technician of any sort, she would be O-class. The obvious deception amused me at one point. What criminal would be stupid enough to slide right up to an officer of the law? And, if said criminal got past her, three more armed guards stand behind her, waiting to give everybody one last body scan, as well as a urinalysis, DNA test, and full-body cavity search before entering the factory.

Staring at my boots, I realize I am that criminal. Last night's conversation with Herb made me question if I could still call myself a citizen. Was there still a four at the end of my name, or had I been downgraded to a terrorist? Herb wants to see how screwed up my life is by seeing my employer's reaction when I show up to work. Have my duties changed? Is my supervisor acting differently? Is my desk now in the furnace room? Instead, I am sliding my way to a containment cube for twenty-five to life, if I'm lucky. I am about to get out of line and walk back to my car, when I hear the voice of doom.

The Inquisitor Branch of Homeland Security is in the building, the stern voice says directly into everyone's ear. There is no need to be alarmed. A routine investigation having nothing to do with you is under way. Please go about your business. Thank you, and God bless.

Even if I couldn't hear it myself, I know everyone in line requests a mood stabilizer before the end of the announcement.

I envy my medicated coworkers for the first time since my L.I.F.E. went haywire. They are as calm as can be expected, doped to the gills, with a Black Coat standing in line behind them.

I know a handful of things without turning around. There's a single Inquisitor with two Homies shadowing him. The Inquisitor is bald and wearing mirrored sunglasses. He — it is always a 'he', as Inquisitors are not equal opportunity employers — is wearing black, knee-high boots, a black suit, and a black leather trench coat, the genesis of their nickname. The Black Coat is also thin and pale, in direct contrast to his robust subordinates.

If the investigation was routine, a squad of Homies would have crowded to the front of the line, arrested everyone within earshot, and questioned them in a frightening, if not monotonous fashion. Black Coats wait with patience. Waiting not just to negotiate a line but trying to coax someone into snapping and running for the door by just staring at the back of their head.

Every few months, a Homeland Security Regular is arrested, tried, and executed on charges of detainee abuse. If there is one instant where a Homie's actions are not recorded by a surveillance camera, any lawyer worth the weight of their press conference podium will have that Homie's badge, followed by his life. All accused must prove their innocence, even Homies. No Black Coat has ever been accused of anything, let alone stood trial for a crime. Black Coats enforce the law, they do not abide by it.

The last thing I know, without turning around, was that the Black Coat was here for me. In eleven years at the cubicle factory, a Black Coat had never entered the building. Now, hours after I decide to become a terrorist, they show up for someone else? I'd have better odds of sneaking money past the military wing of the Internal Revenue Service, the Re-appropriation Enforcement Council of Taxation, Usury, and Monetary Systems.

Sweat pools in the small of my back. To break from the line would prove my guilt. My only hope is to get through the security checkpoint, into the factory, across the production floor and out the opposite entrance. If they haven't detected my presence from ten feet away, they probably can't detect me from ten blocks away and accelerating. Not even a Black Coat would wait patiently behind an Enemy Combatant they were tracking, only behind innocent people they wanted to frighten. The trio is searching. They aren't stalking someone they have already found.

Or they wanted encirclement. Three security guards and a faux receptionist on one side plus a Black Coat and two Homies on the other side equals the rest of my natural life, all eighty-plus years, in a containment cube or the rest of my natural life, all eight hours of it, strapped to a gurney with a Black Coat standing over me. It all depends on who grabbed me first.

A terrorist for less than a day, and I already thought like a criminal.

The police officer posing as a receptionist says, "Next," with the edge that meant she had just said the word twice and wouldn't say it again. I step up to the counter and notice for the first time the brunette sitting there, not the Super HD Plus, disproportionate image on the monitor over her desk. Given a less severe hairstyle, a more form-fitting coverall, a brief exposure to unfiltered sun, and a dimming of the lights, she would have been quite utilitarian in appearance, with the minimum amount of response to her looks for the maximum amount of people. As it is, she is just extremely unremarkable. This raises my spirits, ever so slightly, to be dealing with a person who has not spent all her hard-earned credits to tattoo and pierce every inch of exposed skin.

I feed my ID card into the slot, place both thumbs on the electronic fingerprint pad, and look in the retinal scanner. "Clocking in," I mumble, trying to sound groggy. A green light indicates that all my data has been recorded. I straighten and retrieve my ID card.

The woman does not speak, but at the press of a button, a loop of frequent responses play on the screen. "I'm sorry, but that employee is deceased. Next."

"Wait," I whisper, trying not to draw more attention to myself, "how is that possible? I'm that employee."

The woman scowls, but her recorded face says, "How can I let you speak with an employee that is no longer with us? Next."

"One question. Who do I speak to if Accounting believes I'm deceased?" I try a different tack, wanting to put as much distance as possible between me and the Black Coat.

Her scowl softens, and she shakes her head. The next loop says, "The information booth is directly behind you. They can answer any further questions you may have. Next."

I nod my thanks and exit the line. The Black Coat pays me no heed as I pass within arm's reach of him. My mug shot must not do me justice, I think, as I bear down on the Information Booth. The actual O-class receptionist attending to the Information Booth has a smile on his video screen as I approach. His actual mouth stays shut and impassive, but a cheerful loop of tape asks, "How may I be of assistance?"

"I can't clock in because the computer says I'm deceased. Who should I talk to about this?"

He presses a string of keys on his knowledge base Terminal. A pause, an apparent decision, and a frequent answer button fingered. The face on the screen disappears and is replaced by static. The attendant flips a switch above his head. From the bottom of the screen, a metal sign descends. "We are experiencing technical difficulties, please stand by, and may the Lord smile down upon you as you are being inconvenienced."

I tap my foot as a release for the kinetic energy that my body wants to expend fleeing from the building. Soft music plays from a hidden speaker as long seconds stretch past. The attendant tries countless combinations of keystrokes, to no avail. The music stops and my foot freezes. A faint voice comes through the speaker, instead.

"I'm here to see P. McGewan-Xo4." The low accented monotone could only be the Black Coat.

"He hasn't clocked in yet," the fake receptionist's voice says through the speaker.

"Then I shall wait in his supervisor's office."

"On what authority?"

"Is the black trench coat too subtle?" There is a smack of leather on metal. "Here are my credentials and my authority. I wouldn't waste any more of my time."

"Proceed to the checkpoint and have a pleasant day. God bless."

My head stays locked on the screen of static throughout the conversation, so I have no trouble noticing when the fake receptionist's face appears on it. She mouths something, but I don't understand. I shake my head and look over my shoulder. The Black Coat places his hands on the exam table and bends over. One robotic arm lifts his coat over his head as another descends with the disposable probe tip. The privacy glass turns opaque and I turn back to the screen. No one, not even Black Coats, can escape law enforcers determined to search a cavity. The face on the screen scowls, then fades to static. A letter appears, three inches high in one corner, then another a few seconds later, followed by a third.

R–U–N

I understand, and I do.

CHAPTER 12

Herb's question has an answer. The next challenge is living long enough to tell him about my screwed-up life. In the parking lot, I press my thumb on my car's door handle, once, twice, five times, before I realize I am off the grid. No bank account, no apartment, no vehicle. Soup kitchens won't serve me without an ID. The Black Coat has disabled all of my identity software, but the fire code saved me from being trapped inside the building with him. I leave the grounds on foot. Buses won't let me board. Robotic cabs drive by me like minorities in Racism Awareness training videos. My only choices for movement are slidewalks and the old heel-toe express.

Law enforcement could also give me a ride. With no idea how to get around the city — let alone back to Herb's — without my conveyance's Global Positioning System, this seems probable. The Gizmo store on my wrist is inaccessible as well. So, I can play one of the already downloaded game Gizmos, like Hangman, while I wait to be captured, but I can't download a map Gizmo to keep from becoming a hanged man.

The slidewalk moves me toward the shopping district, people shout over the liquid billboards and into their wrists as I try to think of a way to contact Herb.

Herb and the Library might as well be at the South Pole. Without ID, there's no way to contact him or purchase a map. My head drops and I decide to ride the slidewalk until the Black Coat finds me, or until terrorists drop a building on my head. If only my thoughts didn't have to contend with all the people shouting inside and out of my head.

A grim thought comes to mind. If the Black Coat takes me in, would it be quiet there, or would he pause in his ministrations for commercials?

And now, a message from our sponsor.

Are you tired? Weak? Low on blood? Running out of skin? Maybe you should have tried Patriotism. Side effects are generally mild and may include martyrdom and/or death at the hands of a foreigner you have no personal quarrel with. We now return you to your torture already in progress.

A conversation behind me catches my attention. "I'm about to get stopped by Auditors, so I may be late." My head snaps up. Vehicle traffic is being diverted and people are pulled off the slidewalk by Auditors to line up in the street. All the Auditors are very muscular, very tan women in black-sequined short-shorts, bulletproof sports bras, and knee-high wrestling shoes. The chemical enhancements they take make them a little too masculine for my taste.

Thirty people are lined up in the street, double arm's length away from each other. If it had been a Patriotism audit or a Morality audit, I would have been found out with alacrity. This audit will be a breeze.

The leader of the Auditors puts on a headset that feeds her voice into our ears. "How's everybody today?" Her voice is high and chipper.

"Outstanding," everyone drones.

She puts her hands on her hips. "I heard 'outstanding,' but

it didn't feel like an 'outstanding.' How's everybody doing today?"

"OUTSTANDING!" We all shout, knowing that it will go badly for us if we don't.

"Super." She claps her hands together and smiles. This makes her face look like an alligator purse made from an alligator face. And someone forgot to yank the teeth. "I'm Jeannie, and this is Brit," she points to her right, "and this is Amber," and then to her left, "and we're from FEA, the Fitness Enforcement Agency." FEA agents and celebrities are the only citizens allowed to use their first names. "And we're conducting a routine audit. Everybody follow along, and we'll be on our way in no time. Okay?"

"OKAY!"

"Outstanding. Let's start with two steps forward with a right knee raise, then two steps back with a left knee raise. Ready? Exercise." The crowd mirrors the cheery federal aerobics instructors through the ten-minute audit routine. A man several rows in front of me collapses on the last eight-count bodybuilder. He's handcuffed and loaded into an FEA ambulance. Poor bastard, I think as they made the rest of us get down for Hello Dollies. He probably has a medical condition. Now, he'll get at least six months in physical conditioning prison.

The Department of Homeland Fitness has cracked down in the last few months, ever since the Donut Deadlock. A half-dozen morbidly obese citizens had hijacked a transport full of pastries and locked themselves in a warehouse. The Fat Czar, in his striped shorts and tank top of office, had cried into a megaphone for hours. No variation of "Food is not Love" had worked. All six ate themselves to death before the FEA could break through the barricades.

This is the third fitness audit for me this month. All I have to do is make it to the end, get a hermetically sealed slice of orange, and be on my way. They would only check IDs if a citizen couldn't finish the routine.

We do the last of the Jumping Jacks and Jeannie starts the obligatory round of applause. "I'm so proud of all of you," she says. "Fit citizens are good citizens. Let me hear you say it."

"Fit citizens are good citizens." Our collective annoyance and breathlessness isn't heard over the FEA agent's bubbly personality and pride in a job well done.

"That's right. Come grab an orange slice and have a blessed day," Jeannie says, as she waves, puts on a giant smile and trots off with the other agents. Loud, peppy music blasts from their armored personnel carrier, while the rest of us take our citrus slice and go about our business. All the buildings around us go white, and a beautiful, toned woman appears on every building.

At the Fitness Enforcement Agency, we want you to be happy. Healthy people are happier. We want you to be productive. Healthy people are more productive. We want you to live longer, and that's exactly what healthy people do. We want you to get rid of that spare tire, but we also want to get rid of depression and sick days and poor productivity. Run, jump, swim, lift, or climb. We want to move you, so you can move the country forward.

The commercial over, I mount the slidewalk, the orange halfway to my mouth. Something Herb had said came to me. "Ask a question until someone can answer it."

Who can answer all your questions discreetly? the commercial announcer would ask. Children shout the reply, *Public Information Services.*

There is a PIS box at the end of the street. A tearful woman steps out as I approach. A moment passes while it sanitizes the interior, then the door opens for me. A recorded voice plays the disclaimer. *All questions and answers are completely private and will be shared with no outside party or agency unless criminal acts are admitted to or described.*

This stops me short. Roaming free with a disabled ID is punishable by death. My words come out carefully. "Are there books in the city?"

Yes, citizen. There is a large depository of books in the city, the last remaining one in the country.

"Where is the depository located in relation to my present position?"

Six point three miles east-southeast of your present location.

"Can I have a map?"

Certainly citizen, I will upload it to your L.I.F.E.

Damn. "Can I have a hard copy of the map?"

A digital copy will be much more detailed, citizen. I will upload it now.

"No, wait. I'm a... I collect maps and would like a hard copy for that purpose." I hope that works. Getting a piece of paper out of a government machine is nigh impossible.

An hourglass appears.

Very well, the voice says after a moment. Remember, a good citizen recycles.

"A good citizen recycles," I repeat to get it to dispense the scrap of paper no larger than both my thumbnails.

"Thank you." The box's door opens and urges me to make way for the next citizen. I squint down at the map, then zip it into a pocket. Six miles is a lot of law enforcement infested city. I try to pep myself up as I bite into my orange slice. "Are you an Ameri-can or an Ameri-can't, Pat?"

Well, at least the orange is fresh.

CHAPTER 13

"I'm getting really tired of hearing that I'm to blame for every-thing wrong in this country," I say, as I flop onto the couch in Herb's living quarters. Herb and Sameer stare at me in shocked silence, coffee cups halted in midair, as if they are giving a toast but can't remember the end. "Every billboard and newsfeed on the way here said that I am solely responsible for the Hermod bombing and the Highway Tragedy. How could I have bombed a factory in Tennessee while I was in a hospital sedated? They even blame me for some attack I've never heard of, that happened when I was seven. Seven, can you believe that? World's Youngest Terrorist is what they called me. That's three strikes, so I don't even get a trial when they catch me, now. Some citizen called in and said he wanted to buy thumb drives of me being executed in the street, so he could send them out with his Christmas cards." I stop talking for a moment. Herb and Sameer haven't said a word since my arrival. "What? Say something."

"You were captured fifteen minutes ago," Sameer says, then remembers the coffee cup and takes a sip.

"Says who?" I ask, as I take off my boots.

"Flanery just showed Homeland Security dragging away a

hooded figure that they identified as you," Herb says, nodding to the muted television.

"Homeland Security never came close." I say, peeling each sock off and stuffing them into my boots. "However, the Black Coat that's chasing me got within arm's reach." Sameer sprays coffee out of his nose. "He didn't see me, though. And what are these sacks of skin on my heels?"

"Blisters," Herb replies. "Sameer, get that ointment out of my medicine cabinet and rinse the coffee out of your beard." Sameer leaves the room. "So, they brought in an Inquisitor just for you?"

I nod.

"Are you sure he was looking for you?" Sameer says, as he tosses me a tube of foul-smelling ointment.

I nod and recount my morning's adventure while working the ointment into my blisters.

"So much for Plan A," Herb says.

"Refresh my memory, what was Plan A?"

"Well, I was hoping that you could work for us on the inside, give us information, give us access to certain restricted areas if needed. Then, when the time came, tens of terrorists would rise as one and disable important necessary services throughout the city, allowing the revolution to proceed as planned."

I nod and picture my version of the planned revolution, starting with the destruction of Flanery's office building. "Wait. Tens of terrorists? You mean tens of thousands, right?"

"Nope, tens. There's about thirty of us," Herb says.

"Thirty-six counting the three of us," Sameer says.

"Three dozen terrorists? That's all? What can you do with an army that size, except maybe start a Zero-G baseball team?"

"You're thinking about it the wrong way," Herb says.

"We're highly mobile. Elusive. Camouflaged. They'll never see us coming."

I scoff. "If we all attack at once, they still won't see us. Thirty thousand, that's a realistic number. People would notice that, the government would sit up and take heed. But thirty?" I shake my head. "What's Plan B? I mean, what am I supposed to do now that I can't join this all-powerful silent opposition?"

"That's tricky," Herb says, my sarcasm ignored. "Usually, if Plan A works, you go about your business like a good citizen. If it doesn't work, you're picked up by the Homies and executed. So, we've never really had the opportunity for a Plan B."

Something catches my attention. With Herb's hand-held remote, I unmute the television, as the new Hermod commercial starts. The camera cuts back and forth between an army of athletes in the full spectrum of Hermod merchandise. The gravel-voiced announcer speaks after a few seconds.

Run...

A man sprints toward the camera.

... because you want to.

Climb...

An aerial shot of a mountain climber.

... because you need to.

Sweat...

A tight shot of a woman's face, perspiration pours from her brow.

... because you have to.

Remember...

A black-and-white shot of a bomb crater.

... because McGewan-X04 doesn't want you to.

A terrible photo of me appears.

McGewan-X04 Manhunt Memorabilia now available at all Hermod superstores and wherever Patriotic citizens shop.

An American flag billows in the wind.

Hermod. What good Americans wear.

"Your mug shot looks nothing like you," Sameer says.

Speed-metal guitars cut off my response, as red and white stripes slam into a blue field of white stars. An announcer's voice, "Now, back to The Flanery Defense, the Patriot's shield against terrorist media bias. Here's your host, Jack Flanery." The graphic dissolves into Jack Flanery's face.

"Welcome back," Flanery says into the camera.

The news crawl at the bottom of the screen restarts. They have upgraded the terror level since this morning from the orange-red of High-Severe-High to the tangerine of Severe-High, and it was all my fault. Only the red-orange of Severe-Severe-High stands between America and the beginning of an all-out terrorist war, the red of Severe.

"First, a correction. We reported a few minutes ago that Homeland Security had captured McGewan. In fact, it was this man." A black-and-white photo of a man complete with beady eyes, buzz cut, and facial scars hovers over Flanery's shoulder. "Known as Grievous, he is one of McGewan's chief lieutenants."

"Who is that?" I ask.

Sameer and Herb shrug in unison.

"Grievous is being questioned by the Office of Homeland Security and the whereabouts of McGewan should be forthcoming." A profile shot of Flanery appears on the screen, and he pivots to face camera two. "And now, as part of our continuing coverage of the manhunt for the most dangerous domestic terrorist in U.S. history, a look into McGewan's terrorist upbringing."

"This should be good," I say with a snort. "Is he going to blame a preschool nanny-bot for teaching me how to make dynamite out of building blocks and old diapers?"

Herb chuckles. "No one uses dynamite anymore, Pat."

"All the cool terrorists are into Semtex," Sameer adds.

Soft orchestral music accompanies an aerial view of the suburb where my parents lived. "This quiet community was the home of Mr. and Mrs. J. McGewan-Q44, parents of P. McGewan-X04. Mr. McGewan-Q44 had a lucrative plumbing business, but secretly, something darker loomed." The music is discordant for a moment, before Flanery's voice-over continues. "McGewan-Q44 headed a domestic terrorist cell and terrorist training facility right under his neighbors' noses." A slide-show of still photos shows a group of hooded figures in various terrorist poses — firing weapons at unseen targets in the first, then the group working with chemicals, their black hoods in sharp contrast to their white lab coats, and finally, hand-to-hand combat training. The camera zooms in on the last photo. In the crowd of onlookers, behind the combatants, is a child, without hood or mask. From the quality of the photo, that child could be the President, Jack Flanery, me, Herb, or anyone. "This is where P. McGewan-X04 got his first taste of terrorism. His father groomed him to one day take over the family business..." says Flanery, pausing for three beats, "... of terror!" The music kicks in with deep horns, "Done, Done, DONE!"

"Pat," Herb says.

"What?"

"Pat," he repeats.

"WHAT?" I shout.

"You're grinding your teeth."

"Sorry." I take a deep breath and work my jaw side to side to relieve the tension.

Flanery continues. "The elder McGewan taught his son something new every day, from weapons handling and lethal martial arts skills to manufacturing Semtex, a powerful explosive, from easily obtained ingredients."

Sameer smirks at me at the mention of Semtex.

"Then, McGewan-X04's tutelage ended abruptly when his father was killed in one of the elder's own terrorist plots." Photos of the crater where the BPM store used to be fade in and out of one another. "McGewan-X04, distraught, traveled nomadically after losing his mentor." A picture of a desert fort fades into a mountain chalet that fades into a shack surrounded by swamp. No people, only landscape photography. "Throughout the world, he was taken in by terrorists, trading knowledge from his father for new knowledge and techniques, honing himself into the ultimate terrorist," an over-dramatic pause, "the first Super Terrorist."

I mute the television. "This is such bullshit. I can disprove all of this."

Herb and Sameer shake their heads. "No, you can't," Sameer says.

"Flanery's staff doesn't just find facts," Herb says, cutting in, "they erase all the facts that conflict with his stories."

"I went to the Academy. I wasn't a nomad."

"Do you have a hard copy of your Academy transcripts?" Herb asks.

I stop short.

"Every bit of data now says that you were never in the Academy. What they're doing now is proving you have the terrorist gene, not just a repeat offender."

Sameer says, "Your father was a terrorist, you're a terrorist — "

I cut him off. "My son's a terrorist. Shit."

"They're trying to flush you out," Sameer says. "If your son disappeared from under their noses, you're a brilliant terrorist, not to be underestimated."

"But if you sit here and do nothing to save him, you're a cold, calculating terrorist, not to be underestimated," Herb says.

"What should I do?" I ask, standing and pacing in front of

the television. "My parents are dead, so they can't do anything to them now — other than ruin their reputations. I'm fine with that. My life is in the toilet. I'm strangely comfortable with that, too. But my son? He doesn't deserve this. He's the definition of an innocent bystander."

"And your wife," Herb says.

"Yeah, don't forget your wife," Sameer says.

"My son and my wife, great. I don't mind being martyred, but my wife and kid did nothing wrong. What should I do, Herb? How do I save them?"

Herb regards me first with his blue donated eye, then fixes the brown one he was born with on me. "You don't." His voice is grim and flat. "Sit down and act like a clever terrorist."

I lunge at him, but Sameer grabs me to hold me back. "Fuck you," I shout over Sameer's shoulder. "I'll chew through you like a meat grinder and anyone else that stands between me and my family. I won't let this happen."

Sameer whispers in my ear. "It's okay, Pat. Everything will be fine." He pinches my shoulders hard. My already tired knees buckle and I slump back onto the couch. He stands between Herb and me, waiting for me to lunge again.

"For a guy that was shat out of the Consumer Factory, you are witty at times," Herb says. "Meat grinder. That's good." He takes a deep breath and leans forward in his chair. "Your wife and son are strangers, Pat, but you'd risk your life to save them?"

"They're not strangers."

"You've never been in the same room as them, that's the definition of strangers."

"That's not true. My wife was at the hospital with me."

Sameer does a double take. "She visited you?"

"She was my nurse."

"Did you recognize her?" Herb asks.

145

"No, she told me it was her on the phone later."

"Still strangers in my book," Herb says with a wave of his hand. "My point is that you want to save them regardless of the risk. That's good. If you had disregarded them, well, this would have been a different conversation."

"How so?"

"I would have sent you out on a suicide run. I have no time for people willing to sacrifice the innocent."

"Really?" I brighten up. "How can I save them?"

"You can't," Herb says.

"What? But you just said—"

Sameer cuts me off. "They're already saved."

"Wait," I say, "what do you mean they're already saved?"

"We knew this would happen," Sameer says.

"But how?"

"The news claims to be a lot of things, ground-breaking, award-winning, thought-provoking, but really it's a fill-in-the-blank form. Get a questionable citizen, put his name in Blank A. Put his parents' names in the blanks marked with B. Put a little twist near the end, Super Terrorist in your case, to keep it from sounding like last month's story. Throw in some graphics and photos from the archives and read it to the public repeatedly until they believe it. The public sends text messages to their government representatives. The government releases statements, enacts laws, mobilizes troops. Then the ratings start to wane, and they find someone new to target.

"If there isn't a threat, terrorist or otherwise, the government thinks everything will grind to a halt. People will stop selling back their vacation days, and they'll think it's safe enough to step out of the country to visit the rest of the world. Who knows, maybe people would think Europe or Asia are better than here, and they don't come back. Then, who would make cubicles and coffee for people?"

"That's ridiculous," I say.

"Who knows what would happen if a thousand people in Nebraska went to France. They would enjoy the rebuilt museums and the coffee and the food. Strolling musicians in night-time cafes. People laughing and smiling together, not in the same room, but together, looking into another person's eyes and talking to them directly. Maybe they would think what we are doing here is ridiculous, and they would tell their friends and family. More people would go, they would tell their friends. Someone would complain to a congressperson or write something nasty on the Internet."

"Nasty how?" I ask.

"Anything," Herb says.

"Ishmael's coffee sucks," Sameer says. "You should try the coffee in Paris. By the way, I wasn't martyred by terrorists a single time on my two-week vacation."

"Exactly," Herb says. "Americans believe that we are behind the walls of a castle, and the President is the king defending us against an everlasting siege by nations that would slaughter us wholesale. But that's the trick. We're behind the walls of a prison, and the President is the warden. The media, the Homies, the Inquisitors are the guards forever quelling the riot, feeding us nonsense to make us afraid to live any other way."

"But what about my family?"

Herb sighs as if he has a lot more to say but answers my question first. "As soon as the news hinted that you might be a terrorist, your wife and son went with some of our craftier cohorts and were taken to Mexico. There, they boarded an ocean liner bound for Europe. Our overseas sympathizers already have an apartment for them. Your wife has a job lined up, and your son will get the finest education that France has to offer."

"They just went with strangers that claimed to be taking them to Europe?"

"God, no! They were kidnapped. We don't have the luxury of time," Herb says. "They were drugged and woke up on a ship in the middle of the Atlantic where a marvellous woman explained what was happening. Your wife is no longer speaking to you, but your son seems relieved he doesn't have to take the Consumerism final exam at the Academy."

I blink. All that, already? I was just declared a terrorist this morning. How long had it taken me to walk back to the Library?

"Thanks for saving them." I say, sinking into the couch next to Sameer. "Thank you."

"You're welcome. I'll try to think of a way for you to repay me."

Your family is already safe, echoes through my head, but this time it isn't an advertisement. They are no longer in danger. Herb was correct. They are strangers in so many ways, but they are the only family I have. They might have been imprisoned, tortured, killed simply because a computer had matched me with my wife, and we had made a son. The thought sickens me. Now, they are safe and where that pain and fear had been is a jagged hole in my stomach. The hole needs to be filled, but with what?

If I believe what's on the news, I'm not just a terrorist: I'm a Super Terrorist. Truth is, I hadn't been doing anything other than trying to survive. The government will not stop until they catch or kill me. I need to start acting, not reacting.

Think.

Think like a terrorist.

I close my eyes and take a deep breath.

No. Think like a Super Terrorist.

"What did you say?" I ask.

"I'll find a way for you to repay me," Herb says.

I smile. "No need. I know exactly what to do next."

"Really?" Sameer asks.

"Am I the Chosen One or not?"

Sameer laughs. "Yes, the Chosen One. You've been the Chosen One for almost a full day now."

"Quiet, Sameer," Herb says. "What's your plan?"

"My father was Q-class, so I should have at least been P-class, a manager at Hermod or Ishmael's. I left the Academy as X-class, though. One step above being classified as mentally deficient, or worse, a reporter. That doesn't happen unless you do something really shady, right?"

They both nod.

"What did you do?" Sameer asks. A grin lifts his beard.

"I need some supplies first," I say.

CHAPTER 14

It takes Herb and Sameer an hour to find everything I asked for, giving me time alone with the books. Herb shouts my name when they return.

I walk back to the couch, book still in hand. "Did you know you can learn to make food without the use of a robot? None of these pages update or define a word when I put my finger on it, but these book things are interesting."

Sameer rolls his eyes. Herb nods. "You can learn how to do many things in here if you just take the time," Herb says. "Will this stuff work?"

I sit on the couch and put the book on the floor, next to my feet. Sameer picks it up and places it on a table.

"We don't put books on the floor," he says.

"Sorry." I root through the boxes of supplies. The equipment is dated, but I nod to Herb that it will do what I need it to do. "I need some tools, screwdrivers, small wrenches, you got some?"

Sameer hands me a small black box, but I'm unable to identify most of the contents. "What else do you need?"

"Sit down, and I'll tell you a story," I say. Herb and Sameer sit, and I spread half the supplies out on the low table in front of the couch, the rest on the floor. "I haven't done this for years. I've always been too scared. But I'm a Super Terrorist now, so I might as well go all in. Anyway, I was dead-on average at the Academy. Good at some things, mediocre at others." I work as I talk, taking components apart, wiring pieces together. "Neither of you went to the Academy, right?"

Both shake their heads.

"Okay, once a week we had a seminar. A different instructor taught something outside the core curriculum. If you showed interest or promise or something, they would take a few students out for private classes in that area. They would try to train you for a job that was semi-skilled, not just button-pushing. Some students were gone for a day or a week, then returned. Others left and never came back. I was pulled twice. Once for electronics repair and once for, well, a government job, I assume. I only say that because they refused to tell me what the job was, so it had to be a classified position, to be explained if I passed all the tests."

"What kind of tests?" Sameer asks.

"First, there were word games. There were four of us at the beginning. The instructor would upload a string of words to our L.I.F.E. and we would have to substitute letters until the words made sense. I created a program to run through all the variables and that impressed them. One student was sent out after that. Then, the three of us listened to a conversation in a made-up language, and we had an hour to decipher it. It was utter gibberish. I ran it through the voice-recognition software in my L.I.F.E. and created a similar program to decrypt it. The other two were sent away. The third thing they did was —" I rub my temples, another headache.

"Are you okay?" Herb asks.

"Just a headache," I say. "I don't remember the third thing. Every time I try to, I get a migraine. What I recall is the instructor entered the room, and I was the only one there. He told me we were going to try something new, and then I woke up in my dorm room with this horrible headache. There was a notice on my heads-up display that they quarantined me for three days because of suspected exposure to a virus."

"You really can't remember what he showed you or leaving the classroom?" Sameer says.

I shake my head. "He said, 'We're going to try something new today,' then there was this flash of searing white light, and I was back in the dorm."

"Did they put you back in the regular classes after that?" Herb asks.

I nod. "But here's the weird thing. I understood everything about computers, how to build them, how to program them. It just all made sense. I would look at my L.I.F.E., see an icon, and know exactly what the line of code looked like to put that particular icon in that particular spot."

"I don't understand," says Sameer. "What's the use of knowing how to put an icon on the screen?"

"That's just the first thing I noticed. After some experimentation, I could sit in my dorm room and read everyone else's homework. I could see the lesson plans on the instructor's L.I.F.E. I could go anywhere, and no one was the wiser." Satisfied with my hardware setup, I boot up the modified laptop and began typing. "I could have coasted through the Academy after that. Download every scrap of homework, pick the best of the best, and ace all my classes, but I got greedy. I wanted to alter my old grades so I could graduate as H-class, not P-class."

"You wanted to be a banker?" Sameer says.

"That's where the money is," I say with a smile. "Well, the part of the Academy's mainframe that houses transcripts was encrypted differently. The first layer is the same, but I didn't even see the second layer until it was too late."

"They caught you?" Herb asks.

"In a sense. As an experiment, I changed five students' grades, mine included. They pulled us from class the next day, and they inspected everyone's L.I.F.E. I had wiped all the evidence from the hard drive, and they couldn't prove anything, but I was the prime suspect. No, now that I think of it, there were two of us. The other guy had tried to modify his L.I.F.E., but didn't do a good job of hiding it."

"What did they do to you two?"

"His parents were rich, and they took him out of school. I never saw him again."

"What about your folks?"

"My dad said I didn't murder anyone, so he didn't under-stand all the fuss. As punishment, I graduated as X-class. Done," I say as I finish my work on the laptop and spin it for them to see.

"It's a tic-tac-toe Gizmo," Sameer says.

"Exactly," I say. "I can upload it to my L.I.F.E., or anyone's L.I.F.E. really, and they can walk around with tic-tac-toe on their wrist. It also has a laptop version."

Herb and Sameer exchange a look.

"I don't understand," Herb says.

"Try it out," I say.

Herb clicks a box and an 'X' appears. The computer places an 'O' in another box. "So, I'm playing tic-tac-toe against the computer?'

"If you give me a few minutes, I can program it so you can play against Sameer if you would prefer. Does the thing on your wrist do anything, Sameer?"

Sameer looks at the device he wore that looked like a L.I.F.E. He unclips it from the hidden magnets embedded in his forearm bone and hands it to me. "It does everything yours does, but no drugs. No voices in my head or lasers in my eyeballs."

"Do you mind?" I ask.

"Go ahead."

After a few minutes of tinkering while his mock-L.I.F.E. is hooked up to the laptop, I hand it back to him.

"What does it do?" Sameer asks.

"You can play tic-tac-toe against Herb now," I say.

"And that's all it does?"

"No," I say, "that's all you can do with it. And, more importantly, that's all a Homie will be able to do with it when you get stopped with that Gizmo on your wrist."

"But what does it really do?" Herb asks.

"Can we get on the roof?"

Herb nods.

We could have gone out the front door, but I wanted to be dramatic and stand on the roof. I didn't realize the elevator didn't go to the roof. I didn't realize there were no stairs to the roof. I didn't realize it was even legal to have rusty ladders attached to the masonry that squeaked and shook with every step.

I got my composure in line, had the sweating situation under control. "Open the Gizmo, Sameer."

Sameer clicks the tic-tac-toe Gizmo on his wrist and plays a game against the computer. I open the version on the laptop and watch his game progress while Herb looks over my shoulder. "Then I do this," I say as I drag Sameer's game to one side. Underneath the game board, millions of lines of computer code scroll by.

"What is all that?" Herb asks.

"Right now, that's every broadcast signal in the city. Not phones, not radio, just the frequencies used by television.

Coming from Sameer's wrist to this laptop. It's not saving anything, just observing."

"How does that help us?" Sameer says. "It's all encrypted."

"I can get around that," I say.

"Okay," Herb says, "there are thousands of channels, hundreds of thousands of programs. Not all of them originate from here, and they're just rebroadcast through the local affiliates. I don't understand what you're going to do. Are you planning on hacking into every single station and messing with every single broadcast?"

I shake my head. "There's only one that concerns me, and it's broadcast from here, not a rebroadcast. We do what the government does and go with the guy that gets the most viewers and the most advertising."

"Flanery," Sameer says.

"I need you to play some tic-tac-toe downtown at around seven o'clock tonight," I say.

Sameer nods. "How dangerous is this?"

"Not even a little. It won't broadcast any traceable signal. It will just absorb signals from television stations. I need about an hour of data for it to be usable."

"Then what?" Sameer asks, closing the Gizmo on his wrist.

"Then I'm going to kick Jack Flanery's ass."

———

Waiting is the difficult part. The three of us check Sameer's car before he leaves to make sure there is no reason to pull him over. All the lights work. License, registration, and insurance are current. There are nine pieces of magnetic memorabilia on the bumper. I remove three of them.

"We need all the help that we can get," Sameer says, as I toss the three magnets in the trash.

"Trust me, six is the exact right number."

The headlights get polished twice out of nervous energy. We check and re-check everything, but I can't stop the worst-case scenarios running through my head. Sameer wears his red, white, and blue work uniform and mumbles to himself in his phony accent for practice. My biggest fear is that he's so nervous he will cause an accident.

When Sameer leaves, Herb reads a book in his chair, feet propped up on the table. After a few minutes, I hear him snoring. Up to this point, I've always thought snoring was a gimmick in movies, not something that real people do. I wonder for a while if I snore, then go back to worrying about Sameer.

"He's back," Herb says, eyes still closed.

"How can you tell?"

"I've been in this building for a long time. I know what every creaky board sounds like. Another one will creak right about," Herb says, pausing for a heartbeat, "now."

I hear a floorboard moan on cue and am impressed that Herb is so in tune with his surroundings.

"Only Sameer is heavy enough to make that particular board creak. He also walks down the same aisle every time. Pick up a book and pretend you weren't nervous."

I do as he says and read more about fried chicken when Sameer walks in, turban in hand.

"Back already?" Herb says, peering over his book.

Sameer puts the turban on the table, then collapses into a chair. His bronze complexion is faded to a dull gray, sweat hangs from the end of his beard.

"Any problems?" I ask, as I scroll through the recorded data on the laptop.

"The law is out in force today," Sameer says.

"Were you stopped?" Herb asks.

"Three times, but they were looking for him," Sameer says,

nodding at me. "It was interesting to get waved through a road-block, while a bunch of white guys stood around in holding pens."

"You hear that, Pat?" says Herb. "You're breaking down the ethnic barriers of terrorism."

"That's what white people do. We take another culture's idea and make it our own." They both scowl at me. "What? When was the last time you saw a black rapper?" They nod and I go back to the data. I compare the encrypted data from the broadcast to a recording of Flanery's last show. Lines of code are isolated into groups until I find what I'm looking for. Hours go by as I write a new program. Sameer leaves at some point and returns with two jugs of hot coffee. Herb makes me a sandwich which I chew on while I type.

When I finish, my thighs and lower back are stiff. I stand and pace around for a few minutes while the program compresses itself.

"Well?" Sameer asks, his color and excitement back to healthy levels.

"The hard part's done," I say. Herb and Sameer nod with a smile. "Now, the program needs to be uploaded." Their nodding continues. "And, it needs to be done from inside Flanery's building." They both freeze, their expressions gone blank. "I don't suppose you have a terrorist working in that building?"

"No," Herb says.

"What about Mikey?" Sameer says.

"Yeah, Herb, what about Mikey?" I ask, the name unfamiliar to me.

"Well, Mikey is the only human working maintenance for most of the buildings downtown," Herb says, "but if we use him, he'll be the main suspect."

"Good point," Sameer says. "They'll execute him when they find him."

It is happening again. Putting some stranger's life in danger because of me. Mikey, whoever he is, doesn't deserve to die any more than my wife and son. But for this to work, we need access, and Mikey is the only one that has it.

You're thinking like a citizen. Think like a terrorist.

"What if we kill him first?" I ask.

"What?" Sameer shouts.

Herb nods to himself. "That's an excellent idea, Pat."

"Herb, we can't kill Mikey."

I pat Sameer on the back. "Of course we can. Good job, Sammy."

———

Herb and I go to Mikey's apartment without the furious Sameer. After our introduction, I learn that Mikey is a maintenance human for one reason, his size. He is just over five-feet tall and wiry. The only non-robotic member of maintenance must be able to enter the pipe and wiring chases—circular ducts crisscrossing the buildings—and retrieve stuck or broken maintenance robots. Most of Mikey's predecessors had died in the chases, unable to move because of their size, or their claustrophobia induced panic attacks. Mikey loves being in the chases he tells us as he runs around his apartment, unable to remain motionless for even an instant. He visibly vibrates with energy, offering us drinks, food, asking if we're comfortable. He is in awe of Herb and beside himself that his hero has come to his home. He only acknowledges me as an obstacle blocking his view of Herb. Sameer didn't think we should kill Mikey, but his behavior suggests that he would dive out the window if Herb asked him.

After ten minutes of watching the wound-up Mikey, Herb

asks him to sit down. "There's something important that we need to talk about."

Mikey sits across from us, slowed, but not stopped by Herb's tone. "Anything, anything at all, sir."

"Go ahead, Pat."

"I need to get into one of your buildings," I say.

"Sure, sure, easy," he says, his feet tapping non-stop. "Will you be carrying anything?"

"A laptop about this big," I say, holding my hands apart, "and some tools and wiring that will fit into my pockets."

"Not a problem. Not a problem at all. What else?"

"I need to hard wire the computer to a data feed."

"Yeah, yeah," Mikey says, his head bobbing to the beat of his feet. "One of the hot spots won't work?"

I shake my head. "A hot spot would get me to the mainframe, but that would be monitored before broadcast. I need to wire in between the mainframe and the broadcast array."

"Hey, hey, I've got the perfect spot. None of the robots can get anywhere near it, and it's right before the array. One problem, though. Only I can get that far. A guy your size wouldn't make it within a hundred yards of the spot."

Herb and I exchange a look.

"I can do it, sir. I can wire it," he says to Herb.

"Are you sure?" Herb asks.

"If Pat has a diagram, I can wire it, I can wire anything. What else?"

"A little bit of chaos, maybe?" I ask. "Nothing lethal, just some panic and confusion."

"Chaos, I can do chaos. The way they designed the building, chaos is easy. Order would be a difficult request. What else? I feel like you're holding out on me."

Herb clears his throat. "You're the only one that has access to this area, right?"

159

"Right, right."

"So, you'll be the main suspect."

"Right, right."

"So, you're dead if you're caught," Herb says.

Mikey freezes for five seconds before his feet start to tap again. "Okay," he says, a nervous edge to his voice.

"So, we're going to kill you before anyone else gets a chance. Show him," Herb says to me.

I drop two documents on the table, between Mikey and us. Mikey skims through both, his head bobbing, a smile on his face. "Hell yeah, hell yeah. Let's do it. I'm ready to die."

CHAPTER 15

Mikey is a juggernaut all the time, never half speed, always full-bore. Except when he reads. His fingers move across the page like he's dragging it through honey. The first script isn't that long, but I could have etched the entire thing into the floor of Herb's living quarters with a spoon in the time it took him to read it. I pace as he reads, then sit for a minute, and then back to wearing the floorboards down. Sounds of hammers and furniture being dragged around comes up through the elevator shaft, as Herb and Sameer work in the library's basement.

"I'm glad Herb finally realized that I can help the cause," Mikey says at one point, then goes back to reading, tapping his feet as he mouths the words.

Not for the first time, I look at him in awe. We're about to kill you and you're excited about it.

The hours hunched over the computer have taken their toll. The muscles in my lower back are tight with a dull, constant throb of pain when I sit. As I stand, the dull throb turns to a sharp, shooting pain, every step feels like bone grinding on bone. My neck is locked into one position, straight-ahead, shoulders up around my ears. When I look to the side, a hot dagger inches up under my skull, telling me that further movement will bring the real pain. What stretches I can think to do only pinpoint each pain point and did nothing in the way of relief.

"Why don't you take something for your back?" Mikey asks.

I point to my L.I.F.E. "Doesn't work. A couple days ago it showed my stress levels and nothing else. Now, I can't get it to do anything, but pull up the more useless Gizmos."

"Aren't you some sort of computer savant? Why haven't you fixed that?"

"It freaks me out. What if I touch a bone?" I shudder.

"Let me see."

I sit and Mikey takes a small multi-tool from his belt. He selects a tiny screwdriver and fits into a slot where the biometric implant meets the skin of my wrist. The blank display screen rises and levers itself open so we can both see the inner workings of my L.I.F.E. I expect to see blood vessels, muscles, bone, something. Instead, there is a wafer-thin motherboard. That's it.

"Where are all the drugs?" I ask.

"There's a dozen vials under the board. I don't have the equipment to open that." He takes another screwdriver out of his pocket, one for each hand. He touches one to the back of the display screen. "You may feel a little prickle." He touches the other screwdriver to the board. There's a screech in my ears and my right leg shoots out, my foot connects hard with the table leg. "You've still got power. That's good," he says. A wisp of blue-black smoke curls out of my wrist. The room filled with the smell of singed hair and the tinny aroma of burnt electrical wire.

"Is that normal?"

"A little smoke, no big deal." He gulps and wipes a single drop of sweat off his forehead. "You need to hold still, or I might do some serious damage."

I am about to tell him to stop, when a tone sounds in my head, followed by the L.I.F.E. voice.

Life-force Input and Feedback Equipment System. Diagnostic Mode.

"It's in diagnostic mode," I say, shocked. "How did you do that?"

"I just messed around with mine one day and found this manual override for paramedics. Tell me when you get visual." He twists a screw clockwise until it stops. "Nothing?" He twists it the other way.

The laser projectors in my eyelids wink on and paint a picture across my eyes. "I've got the grid."

"Try the mouse."

My tongue moves the trackball in the roof of my mouth and takes me through all the menus, most of which I've never seen before. "I think it's working."

"Do you have a Manual RX option?"

I nod and scroll down.

"There should be a back-pain menu, then several dosage levels, after you click that. Pick the lowest dose."

I obey and my wrist vibrates as it mixes chemicals.

Now dispensing back pain medication.

No side effect warnings, no message from the manufacturer about this or any other fine product, just drugs, glorious drugs.

The knotted muscles in my back and neck unwrap, like fists unclenching. "That's nice," I say. Everything slows and my words make the remaining smoke ripple in front of me. "Thanks."

"No problem. I'd have to completely remove it to fix it

more, which would probably kill you, so, it won't do anything but give you meds. Everything else is still shut down." He closes the display, and it sinks back into place. "There's some safety measures still, but in this mode, you can overdose easily, so be careful."

Sameer walks in and puts his hand on Mikey's shoulder. "Someone cooking hot dogs?"

I shake my head.

Sameer shrugs. "You ready, Mikey?"

Mikey nods, takes the scripts, and we follow Sameer downstairs.

Herb talks to a woman on the edge of the stage that they have constructed. When she sees Mikey, she gives him a hug, then sits him in front of the camera and stands to one side of him. The corner of the basement is cleared out, so only the bare brick walls show. Mikey sits in a metal chair, forearms perpendicular to his body, palms flat on the metal table. Two bright lights sit out of the shot and illuminate his face. There's no doubt about his identity. The woman is barely in the shot. On the monitor off to one side, her hip and part of her torso are all that can be made out. She's wearing an official looking uniform, not Homeland Security, but law enforcement of some sort. Herb and I watch as Sameer moves the two of them around.

"Mikey, chin up, roll your shoulders back. Good. Sit up a little straighter, hold it. Right there. Mary, draw your gun and —"

"Pistol. It's a pistol," says the woman, Mary.

"Draw your pistol and press it against Mikey's head." Sameer grunts. "No, wait a second." He zooms the camera out. "Now, move to your right a little, Mary. Keep the gun, uh, pistol, to his head. Good." Sameer looks at the monitor, then through the small screen stuck on the side of the camera. "Don't move, I'm just going to adjust." He picks up the camera on its tripod and takes two steps back. He centers Mikey in the shot, Mary's arm is straight, pistol in hand, but no other part of her visible. "How's that look, Herb?"

Herb nods. "I'm happy if you're happy. Pat?"

"Can I move that light back a little?" I point at a spotlight that is now in the frame. Sameer nods. I step forward and pull the light back two feet. "You ready, Mikey?" He smiles and gives me a thumbs up. I turn to the woman. "How are you doing?" She scowls in response.

"All right, everybody happy?" Sameer says, looking at each of us for a nod or sign of affirmation. "Good. Mary, holster the pistol, hands clasped in front of you. Good. Nobody move. I'm recording. Mikey, whenever you're ready."

Mikey recites the first script with confidence, eyes into the camera, just stating the truth in a smooth, and above all, slow voice. That is the difficult part, getting Mikey to go against his nature and speak with a normal rhythm for everyone to under-stand him. He speaks the last line, and the red light fades on the video camera. Sameer plays it back, turning a monitor for Mary and Mikey to watch.

"What do you think, Herb?" Mikey asks.

"Son, if there was something other than reality program-ming and news on television, you would be a natural. Done in one, get the star into make-up," Herb says, giving Mikey a playful punch on the shoulder. Mary turns Mikey in his chair and pulls out a make-up kit. She proceeds to make him bloody and beat-up without all the time-consuming pain.

Mary says, "Stop smiling, Mikey. The make-up won't look right if you're smiling."

Sameer helps me hang a wood sign behind Mikey's chair. Bright-white streaks of paint worm across the front. "What does this say?" I ask Sameer.

"Think of dead puppies, Mikey. Dead puppies and kitties. That's good," Mary says.

"It says 'Kill one infidel, get one free.' I'm Nepalese, I don't read Arabic. How should I know? Herb found it in a book."

When the sign is in place, I step to the front of the stage, curious about this woman's presence. "I'm Pat."

"I know," she says, not looking at me. "I'm Mary."

"Have we met?"

"We work together."

It takes me a moment to recognize her out of context. "You're the receptionist at the factory. Hey, I want to thank you for getting me away from that Black Coat."

She stops in the middle of creating a black eye for Mikey and looks at me. "If you had asked one more stupid question, I was going to arrest you myself." Her tone makes my face want to crawl to the back of my head. She scowls. "Do you mind? I have a lot to do."

I go over to stand next to Herb and Sameer. "What's her problem?" I whisper.

"Mary? She has a lot of stress in her life right now," Herb says.

"And it doesn't help that you're about to kill her brother," Sameer adds.

"Mikey is her brother? Do you think I should apologize? I mean, I'm new to this whole Chosen One thing."

Sameer coughs and turns away from me.

"Why do you do that every time I say, 'Chosen One?'"

"Sameer is not as strong a believer as I am, Pat."

"Really? Doesn't every major religion have some sort of messiah?"

Sameer turns to me. "By every major religion, you mean Christianity and Islam, right?"

I nod.

"There's more than two religions on the planet, and just because I have a darker complexion than you it doesn't automatically make me a Muslim."

"I'm sorry. What religion are you?"

"He's a Greek Pantheic Revivalist," Herb says. "They have no messiahs."

"Really? I'd like to hear more about that."

They both stare at me for a moment. Sameer bites his lower lip as his face turns red. Then they laugh at me. "Herb's kidding. I am Hindu," Sameer says, "but I was forced to convert to Christianity to get my U.S. citizenship."

"So, being Hindu and being Muslim isn't the same thing?" I ask.

Sameer shakes his head, his smile gone. "My people have dealt with Muslim extremists for longer than Americans even knew they existed. A Mughal king came to Nepal centuries ago and destroyed all the Hindu temples, going as far as Lumbini, the birthplace of the Buddha, and he desecrated those temples as well. My forefathers fought the extremists for generations. When the Middle East attacked America, that's when I became a U.S. citizen."

"To keep fighting the Muslims?"

"To fight the extremists in the United States that make war on the rest of the world. They are the terrorists."

Mary comes over, lasers me with a scowl, and then turns to Herb. "We're ready."

Herb, Sameer, and I stand behind the camera again and watch the screen as Mary and Mikey take their places. Mikey sits at the table, facing the camera, one eye blackened, his lip and forehead caked with dried blood. Mary stands next to him, only her arm and gloved hand, pressing a pistol to Mikey's temple visible on the screen. Sameer jostles them around a bit until their positions line up with the first recording.

"Looks good," Sameer says, after a nod from Herb. "When you're ready, Mikey." Sameer presses 'Record,' and Mikey recites the second script, his voice choked and unsure. He reads pages this time, a forced confession. Arabic mission statement in the background, generic interrogation room setting, beaten prisoner, gun to his temple, everything the nightly news dreams of.

When Mikey finishes the last line, Mary pulls the trigger. The gun's report is deafening. Blood shoots out the opposite side of Mikey's head and his corpse drops off camera. Sameer stops the recording and plays it back on the television.

"That's excellent," I say, after the playback stops. Sameer and Herb nod. "What do you think?"

Mikey pulls out his earplugs and wipes the fake blood off his neck. "Looks like I need to find a new job."

"Edit both and start making copies," Herb says to Sameer. "Mary and I will work on the memorabilia, and you two know what to do, right?" Mikey and I nod. "Good. We have four hours until the broadcast. Let's make it happen."

———

Half an hour later, the freshly showered Mikey opens a crate of replacement parts and lets me out into fresh air. "Sorry, we didn't have a bigger box."

He takes the backpack with the laptop as I stand. My back pops in several places as I stretch. I want to stay sharp and pass on dosing myself, again. "I'll be fine. Where to?"

He leads me through the giant sub-basement that connects the four buildings on the block. Different colored arrows line the cement floor, all pointing in different directions. Mikey explains briefly where each color leads, but red is the color I need to remember. If I have to run, all the red arrows lead to an emergency exit.

The only sound is our heels squeaking on the cement and the distant hum of hidden machinery. Few employees in the buildings above even know about the service tunnels. Mikey had told us that usually only he and his robots were ever in these giant hallways, below street level, that house the chases that access every part of the building. Every space needs climate control, water, electricity, data, and it all starts here, three levels below the street. Only Mikey knows the way.

We stop under a manhole-sized grate in the ceiling, no different from any of the other hundreds we have passed under. He presses a button on the wall to open the grate and a ladder descends, which Mikey climbs before it stops. He retracts the ladder, closes the grate, and I see his outline above me in the chase's darkness. "Give me about ten minutes," he says. "And, even though there aren't any cameras, you might want to stay out of sight." Then he is gone.

I step out of the main hallway, into one that dead-ends after about thirty feet. I alternate between watching the seconds tick by on the heads-up clock and worrying about what could go wrong. Amidst every negative theory I think up, I smile, thinking we might pull this off. Once Mikey does his part, hooking my laptop into the data feed right before it's broadcast, I will be on the run. Officially. Not just one reporter screaming and one Black Coat searching, but an entire army, the full weight of the government set for "seek and destroy," as Herb had stated.

An icon flashes green in my heads-up display, Mikey's signal that he's finished his part. The Gizmo program I had written and installed on my L.I.F.E. accessed the laptop, now in some inaccessible part of the building. I open several other new Gizmos, one of which let me watch the data stream out of the building's studios, through the laptop, and out into the world in the huge broadcast array on the roof. There is only the slightest lag due to our tampering, less than a millisecond if my math is right, and not enough for anyone to notice. If an engineer detects anything, they will isolate the problem to one of the chases and submit a request for Mikey to investigate. By that time, Mikey will be deceased. They will have to find a replacement for him before they make any repairs. I open the laptop's word processor remotely and type a message for Mikey that everything's working. He types back that he is on his way out.

I step back into the main hallway to see a guard under the grate Mikey will come out. He turns at the sound of my boots and raises his sidearm, the big scope and barrel pointed at my chest. "Identify yourself," his disembodied face shouts from the Terminal mounted on the scope.

"Maintenance," I say. I wave my L.I.F.E. around, as if scanning the area with it. "I've got a power drain that I'm trying to locate." I don't know what Mikey does exactly, and I hope this guy doesn't either.

"Where's the other guy?" he asks.

"Called in sick. I'm a temp, borrowed from down the road. They wanted this fixed hours ago, I guess."

"Why doesn't your ID register on my scope?"

"They rushed me over here, man. Payroll probably hasn't uploaded my info to your net, yet."

"How'd you get in, then?"

"Some supervisor met me at the door and rushed me down here. I didn't catch his name, big guy, dark hair." I'm running out of lies to tell him, and I want him to go away before Mikey reappears.

"Johansen," he says with a nod, "that figures." The pistol moves from my chest to threatening my left knee. "How does a guy your size get around in those chases, anyway?"

"The ones down the road are a lot bigger. I'll have to use the robots for most of this job."

"Well, I've probably slowed you up enough already. Sorry to have bothered you." He turns and holsters his pistol as he walks off.

Mikey chooses that moment to open the grate and deploy the ladder. The guard looks back over his shoulder. I expect him to keep walking. Instead, he turns and runs towards us, pistol back out of the holster, as soon as he sees the two of us. Mikey shouts, "Security," for the guard's benefit, out of cunning or a sense of self-preservation. I run. I have a slight lead, but not far enough ahead of the pistol for my taste. Any moment I expect a bullet to rip through my spine. My shoulders bunch together protectively. Or will he aim for my knee?

"Intruder in the sub-basement," the guard shouts. "I repeat, intruder in the sub-basement."

The reply comes into my head as clearly as it does the guard's. *Lethal force approved*, says an unseen supervisor.

I try to speed up, but my legs won't go any faster. The shot never comes.

"My weapon is malfunctioning. I can't take a shot."

The red arrows take me through the corridors and outside, up a ramp, around a corner, and I freeze on the slidewalk. The people already riding ignore me, just continue shouting into their wrists, leveling up on their game Gizmos as they go about their day. I wait for a hand to yank me off the slidewalk, into a waiting police van, but my jumpsuit looks like everyone else's from the back.

My feet aren't healed yet, but I have another walk ahead of me. I step off the slidewalk a few minutes and ten blocks later, and head for Herb's. I don't know if Mikey got away. No one will believe he is dead if Homeland Security has him in custody.

Worrying won't change anything, but I do it anyway, just to pass the time.

CHAPTER 16

Broadcast Corporation now hiring IT professional with computer maintenance experience to oversee daily computer performance, provide technical support, and install new software for computer users. Daily duties may include fielding inquiries, running diagnostic tests to resolve issues, and installing updates to existing software. Additionally, technicians may be responsible for setting up new equipment, performing minor repair work, and keeping records of service. Technicians may also create manuals and train others on hardware and software. Click the link below to apply.

————

The library is silent when I return, everyone still running errands. I flop onto the couch and take my boots off. A brief sense of ritual passes over me, as I stuff my socks into my boots and take up the tube of ointment, still on the table where I left it yesterday. The day-old blisters are simply loose skin now, but fresh ones are cropping up from today's walk. All of them, new and old, get a coat of ointment for good measure.

A board creaks behind me, but I don't flinch, don't whirl

around to see who is approaching. One boot at a time, I thought, that way it isn't so difficult to run away some more. As it is, bootless and unable to successfully flee, I apply ointment and wait for the person to identify themselves.

"Where's Mikey?" asks Herb. Not a muscle in my body twitches, but I am relieved that Herb returned first, not Mary.

"We got separated," I say, remaining solely focused on my left heel. "Everything's ready."

Herb moves around the couch to sit across from me. "Broadcast is in thirty minutes. How long ago did you see him?"

"Hour and a half," I say, trying to judge the walk, half on slidewalks, half off.

"Two hours, a diligent Black Coat, a bag of tools, and a gurney." He sighs. "They could find out enough to stop us."

"I know." I look up at him for the first time. "What do you think I've thought about for the past ninety minutes? We're this close to being truly fucked," I say, holding my thumb and forefinger so close together they're one ointment-covered blob. "What do you want me to do? Maybe if I worry some more, I'll develop a tumor big enough to be confused for Mikey." We stare at each other for a moment, then I turn my attention to my other heel.

His voice is conciliatory when he speaks again. "It isn't all that bad. We have contingency plans."

"Really? What's the contingency for Mary? What am I supposed to tell her? That her brother was captured, and I walked away? That sounds like I sold Mikey out. If Homeland Security walks in here, it's because I sold everyone out to save my own ass, regardless of what Mikey may have told them. What's my Plan B, Herb? Oh, that's right, you never got to Plan B."

"You have a point." Boards moan in the distance and Herb's head snaps up. "Sameer and Mary are back."

I cap the tube of ointment and put my socks and boots back on. Sameer sits on the couch with a nod to Herb and me. Mary stands off to the side.

"Where's Mikey?" Sameer asks.

"Detained," Herb says.

"Is that the polite way to say he's in the bathroom having a movement?" Sameer asks. "Or is that the direct way to say he won't be joining us again?"

Herb shrugs.

"He sure as hell isn't in the can," I say.

"What's that supposed to mean?" Mary asks.

"Of all the places Mikey might be right now, Mary, Herb's bathroom is not one of them," I reply, my eyes locked on hers.

"What happened? Where's Mikey?" Her face turns red, as she steps toward me.

"They got separated, Mary," Herb says. "Mikey's probably on his way here now."

"Thanks, Herb," she says, "but I want him to tell me."

I stare at her accusing finger for a moment. "A guard saw us when he came out of the chase. Mikey yelled for security and I ran, that's it. I don't know if they took him."

"That's great, just great," she says.

"We planned for this, Mary," Sameer whispers. "It will work out."

Herb heads for a book-strewn table and returns with a bottle and four glasses in his thick fingers. The germaphobe in me cringes when he blows the glasses out before filling each a quarter full of amber liquid. "Who wants a drink?" he asks with a glass touching his lips. "I'm having one."

We each grab a glass before Herb allows himself a sip. Mary throws hers back, her eyes boring a hole in my head.

Sameer rolls his glass between his palms, staring at the tide of whiskey lapping the sides. The nanny-bots at the Academy and their human counterparts had drilled me with Christian rituals, but I never had much use for them. All the same, I say a generalized, all-encompassing prayer for Mikey, in the hopes that the patron saint of inept terrorists is on the clock and alert, then down the drink in two pulls.

Herb sloshes the last sip around the glass and squints at it with his brown eye. He's going to say the right thing, not the popular thing, as I had learned from watching him take things in with his two different eyes. "We proceed as planned. If Mikey was taken," he glances at Mary with his blue eye, "God forbid, we don't want it to be in vain. Right?"

Sameer and I nod. Mary pours herself another drink.

A board sings out in the distance. Sameer and I jump up in unison. Herb empties his glass.

"Mikey?" Mary whispers.

Three more creaky boards sound off, each down a different aisle.

"It's not Mikey, it's the law," Herb says, his voice low. "Sameer, the basement, get them out of here."

Sameer slams his drink and grips Herb's shoulder.

"Go," Herb says, "I'll be fine."

Sameer nods, and Mary and I follow him to the stairs. I look back to see Herb pour himself another drink and hide our glasses. Calm and composed, he sits in his chair and picks up a book.

Sameer leads us across the basement, to the corner closest to the street.

"Help me with these," Sameer says. He moves boxes from a tall stack against the basement wall. "There's a tunnel out of here somewhere in this corner." I grab a box and pause, look at Sameer. "Anywhere, put it anywhere, just get it away from the wall. Mary, there should be a crowbar on Herb's workbench."

Mary is gone for a moment, returning with a lengthy piece of bent steel. "Sameer?"

"That's it, just hold on to it for a minute." His voice is smooth, but sweat covers his face, and the dust being kicked up sticks in places. "That's good." We uncover a section of brick wall with a dozen boards running across it. "Pat, get those boards off." He is hunched slightly, trying to catch his breath. I step onto a box and grab a board. "Use the crowbar."

I nod, take the crowbar from Mary and study it for a second. The whole bar is half as wide as my palm, bent at a ninety-degree angle at one end with a V-shaped notch at the tip of the bent end. It feels solid, heavy for as thin as it appears. Bar, boards, nails. It's a lever. I smile, having figured out a new tool on my own.

"You planning to pry a board off the wall?" Mary asks. "Or you just going to smile them off?"

It takes a couple of tries, but I wedge the bar at the top of the boards and push up. The nails moan as they come out of the wall, an eighth of an inch at a time.

"Do you know what that thing's called?" Sameer asks.

"What thing?" I say, with a grunt as I work the boards further from the wall.

"The crowbar."

"It's not just a crowbar?"

"The brand name."

"No idea. What's it called?"

"Wonder Bar," he says with a smile. "Wonder Bar, get it?"

"All the emails from Sanity are getting returned undeliverable, aren't they?" Mary asks.

"Herb bought it because it was funny. He's German. Wonder Bar?"

I pull the crowbar, the Wonder Bar, out and look at it, trying to understand why it is funny.

"It's a play on words," Sameer says.

I step toward him just as the boards come off the wall of their own accord. Dust billows up from the floor, obscuring the opening in the wall. A tiny light turns on in the dust, bright red, almost like a —

"Laser sight," Mary says. "Don't move."

I look down to see three marks, the points of a triangle, over Sameer's heart. A second later, it jumps to Mary's chest, then back to Sameer, again and again, skipping me every time.

"That's my line," a voice says, through the dust. "Hands up. Nobody moves and nobody dies." Our hands go up, my fingers still wrapped around the Wonder Bar.

A figure emerges from the hole, dressed entirely in black, night-vision goggles and a mask obscure his face, a small pack on his back, and a very large rifle with target lock on Mary and Sameer in his hands.

"Apparently, this tunnel isn't that much of a secret," Mary says.

"No kidding," Sameer replies.

"How is it a play on words?" I ask.

Mary and Sameer look at me, confused.

"What are you talking about?" the officer asks, his voice cool, knowing that no one would dare assault him. He steps off the box and strolls towards me.

"How is Wonder Bar a play on words?" I ask Sameer. Our arrest is imminent, but I'm not afraid. Without all the recreational drugs or the secret drip of THAW, everything seems crystalline. I know, or think I know, exactly what needs to be done to get Sameer and Mary to safety.

Sameer looks from the assault Homie to me. "In German,

wunderbar means wonderful. That's why he thought it was funny."

I nod. The Wonder Bar falls on the crown of the officer's head and he drops to the floor, unconscious. His rifle skitters away. "It's all right, I guess. Let's go. If there's one Homie, there's bound to be more." I step up into the hole and turn to give them a hand. Mary goes to get the rifle. "Leave it," I snap.

"Why?" she snaps back.

"People with rifles get shot by other people with rifles, that's why."

"We need weapons."

I shake the Wonder Bar at her. "Just call me Mr. Wonderful. Now get in the fucking hole."

CHAPTER 17

Backs bent, and chins on our chests, Mary and I follow Sameer into the low tunnel. After twenty steps he stops. With just a faint light coming through grates in the ceiling, Mary walks into him and I plow into her.

She spins and shoves me. "Don't touch me."

"Sorry."

"This way," Sameer says. The tunnel branches to the left and right, both appear identical to me, but he leads us to the right.

"Do you know where you're going?" Mary hisses.

"Herb said this goes to an abandoned building." Even in a whisper, Sameer's voice seems too loud.

"That doesn't answer my question."

"I think if we keep right we'll be fine."

"You think?"

He stops and turns. "I'm sorry, Mary. Herb told me about this tunnel a long time ago, and he never actually brought me into it. What else can I tell you?" He walks on.

"Great. We're either going to walk into a nest of Homies, or we're going to get lost and starve to death. Fabulous."

Sameer mumbles something.

"What did you say?" She turns to me. "What did he say?"

I heard him say, 'Then, you lead,' but I would eat broken glass before I admitted it. I just shrug and try to change the subject at the next intersection. "Do you know what these tunnels are for?"

"Oh, sure," Sameer says.

"Well, what are they?"

"Are you deaf?" Mary chimes in. "He said, old sewer."

"Oh, that's what I thought he said."

Silence for a few paces.

"What's a sewer?" Mary and I ask in unison.

"Before toilets and showers recycled everything, all the waste came down here on its way to the purification plant."

Mary puts it together before I do and freezes. "So, when people talk about being 'up shit creek—'"

Sameer stops and looks at her. "This is the place." Even in the dark, I can see his grin.

"I'm going to be sick," Mary says.

"It was probably more of a river, though."

"Oh, god."

"It's been sanitized, I'm sure," he says.

"Really?" I say. "Do you think they sanitized that rat crawling up your leg?"

Sameer yelps and presses against the wall. "Get it off. Get it off me." He shakes his leg until the rat loses interest and runs away. "I hate rats." He slumps to the ground, his breathing fast.

I move around Mary and kneel beside him. "You're fine. Let's keep moving. We'll keep the rats away, and you get us to that abandoned building. Right, Mary?"

Mary stares past us down the tunnel.

"Mary?" I ask again and notice the laser sight painted on her chest.

Lethal force approved.

I jump in front of her before I know what I am doing.

The round picks me up and slams me backward, taking Mary down with me as I fall.

The Homie materializes out of the shadows, steps up to Sameer and presses the rifle to his head. The Homie cocks his head to the side as he listens to the computer chip on his eardrum.

Firing at unauthorized targets is a criminal offense. Weapon disabled. Report to your commander.

The Homie shakes the rifle and tries to fire, but it just beeps and the voice in both our heads repeats, *Weapon disabled.*

"The gun doesn't work," I say. "Hit him. Sameer, hit him!"

There isn't much skill in the punch, but Sameer's a big guy coming from his knees. His fist connects with the Homie's chin and drives his helmet into the ceiling. The Homie wobbles for a second, then his pack drags him down backwards.

Sameer rolls me to the side, and Mary wiggles out from under me.

"How did you do that?" Sameer asks.

"I can't believe you saved me." Mary's voice is soft for a moment until she says, "Hero." It came out the same way as, "Idiot."

"How did you stop him from shooting me?" Sameer repeats.

It's hard to breathe, and I feel the walls closing in. "I heard a voice say something about unauthorized targets and that the weapon was disabled."

"What?" Mary says.

"I'll send you a link to the Gizmos," I say, scrolling through my L.I.F.E display. "You two can still make it. Don't worry about me."

Mary smacks the side of my head. "You aren't dying. What hit you was the concussion from the round self-destructing. It thought you were an innocent bystander." She stomps down the tunnel and darkness envelopes her.

I pull open my jumpsuit. No spray of blood. No chewed-up organs hanging out of my torso. Just smooth skin starting to bruise.

Sameer pats me on the shoulder. "Well, at least one of us can't get killed by smart bullets. That's good news, right?" He helps me up, as my suit seals itself. I step over the Homie with Sameer behind me. "Pat?"

"Yeah."

"Pat?"

I turn and Sameer is stock-still, one foot in mid-air. His arms shake as he tries to force them to move. The Homie is trying to stand. A day-glow orange anklet is around Sameer's leg. "Run, Pat." The Homie gets to one knee and mumbles into the microphone in his wrist. "Run," Sameer repeats.

———

Mary is fifty yards down the tunnel already. I run to catch up with her, my head pressed into my shoulders to avoid the ceiling. She plants her feet when I grab her arm, and my head rebounds off the tunnel's curved roof. For a second, I hear a Mariachi band, then back to static and Homies mumbling to one another.

"Let go of me. Where's Sameer?"

"Homie..." I say, trying to get it out between gasps "... inhibitor cuff... backup coming."

"Let's go," she heads right at the fork. "What are you waiting for?"

"They're coming from there. This way." I go left at a jog, a welt forming on the back of my head.

"Sameer said to stay right. You're going to get us lost."

I pass through a doorway and stop. "That won't be a problem."

The room is a dead end. A bare light bulb hangs from the ceiling and I see a dozen rusted wheels on the wall opposite the door. A metal grate is sunk into the floor. The ceiling is high enough for me to stand erect. I stretch and rub the back of my head.

"We have to go back," she says.

Flashlights and laser sights bob down the corridor toward us. Without a word, we grab the door and muscle it shut on rusted hinges. I slide the Wonder Bar into a bracket and lock us in just as the Homies reach the other side. "Now what?" I ask, as various Homie body parts pound on the door.

"Homies don't carry cutting torches, that's good. The tunnel is concrete, and this room seems to be entirely metal," Mary says, "so, if they try to blow the door, the tunnel will cave in on them and we'll be fine."

"Trapped in a room with no food or water, and one door that has a caved in tunnel on the other side?"

She scowls at me.

"No, that's fine with me if it's fine with you," I say.

The pounding stops. She pushes me against the door and waves me to silence. A black plastic snake with a glowing red eye works its way under the door and pivots its head. Mary kneels and slowly wraps her hand around the body of the snake and yanks hard. The sound of a helmet banging against metal, a muffled curse, and the control box for the Snooper all come under the door at once.

"This is nice. I didn't think the new model was out yet."

She fits a piece of plastic in her ear and goes through the options on the display screen. "Damn."

"What? What's wrong?" I ask, as I feel my way around the room trying to find another door.

"Stupid talking badge wants me to register." She pounds keys as she speaks. "Yes, I'm a new user. Yes, I'm law enforcement. No, I don't have a password from my supervisor. Yes, I would like a ten-day trial. Yes, you can have my firstborn."

"Is that really a question?"

She snorts at me and shakes her head. "There we go. Very nice. This thing has thermal, night-vision, sound, ooh, X-ray, it can smell explosives, and the resolution is amazing. I want one of these."

I try to turn each rusted wheel on the wall. "Well, if we don't get arrested in the next couple of minutes, I'll let you keep it."

"Thanks." She aims the eye at the door and fiddles with the controls. "The X-ray won't go through the door." She kneels and feeds a bit of the snake through the gap, being careful not to give the Homies enough to grab ahold of. "There's four pairs of boots. Two are leaving to get another Snooper and a cutting torch." She stands and faces me. "The odds are even now, two of them, two of us. I say you rush them with the Wonder Bar, and I'll stay in here and try not to get shot. Okay?"

"Help me with this wheel," I say.

She rolls her eyes, and we both grab the wheel, the only one that seems to have any play in it. With a screech, a small piece of metal slides open by our feet.

"Good," she says. "If we were six inches tall, we could walk right out of here. Good work, Pat." She slaps me on the back. "Now, can we get back to you attacking those Homies, Mr. Wonderful?"

"What about this grate? Can you see what's down there?"

She aims the Snooper's probe through the grate in the floor. "There's a ladder, but it looks like the last thirty feet or so have rusted off, then it drops into a small room with some water running through it."

I grab the grate with both hands and pull it out of the floor. "Let's go." I step onto the metal rung sticking out of the wall of the shaft and start down.

"Wait," she says, as my head reaches floor level. "What if there isn't a door down there either? If we drop off the ladder, there's no way we could get back up to it. The Homies could just drop a grenade down there and we're done for."

The hole we opened in the wall is directly in front of me and something is moving in it. After a moment, a slow-moving rat emerges and stares at me, then rears back and sniffs the air.

"What else is in this room?" I ask, as the rat and I conduct a staring contest.

"There's an old bucket, some trash," Mary replies, as she sweeps the room with the Snooper's night vision, "a couple bricks. That's all."

"What are you carrying?"

"What?"

"Do you have anything in your pockets?"

"I've got a Swiss army knife that Herb gave me, a little flashlight, a hair tie, my ID card. Why?"

"Get me the bucket and don't scare the rat. I've got an idea."

———

When I remove the Wonder Bar, the door opens a crack, but the noise the hinges make is intense. The two Homies put their shoulders into it and see nothing in the room, but the grate in the floor moved to the side. With the light bulb now broken, their night-vision goggles can only make out Mary's flashlight bobbing around in the room at the bottom of the shaft. They both sling their weapons over their shoulders and start down the ladder. After a minute, one says, "The rest of the ladder is rusted out, they must have jumped down."

"Let's go back up and drop some grenades on them. I don't want to break my ankle for a couple of terrorists," the other replies.

"Hey," I shout down to them. The Homie closest to me looks up, as a brick hits him in the face. He lets go of the ladder and falls, taking his comrade with him. There's a splash, a couple of moans, and then a second later, the rat, with Mary's flashlight still strapped to its back, comes over to see if the Homies are food.

"Good work," Mary says. "Two down, thirty-five thousand to go."

"Three," I say, as we walk through the tunnel. Mary stays close behind me.

"There were only two of them. Nothing either way," she says, as she aims the Snooper down each branch of the tunnel.

"If we're keeping score," I say, stepping a few paces down the right branch, listening, then coming back, "there was the one in the library's basement, too. I can hear a little bit of static down this one." I step into the left branch. "Nothing." We stay to the left, me and the Wonder Bar up front, Mary aiming the Snooper over my shoulder.

We don't get far before my wrist vibrates. I disable the alarm on my L.I.F.E. "We have five minutes until broadcast."

I can't see or hear her response, just feel her guiding me from behind through the dark tunnels.

"Will this work?" Mary says, about a small alcove off the main tunnel. I still can't hear any sort of broadcast from the Homies, not even static. The Gizmos all have full signal strength, the smell isn't too bad, and the floor is dry.

"This is perfect." We sit with our backs to the wall as the receiver scans for Flanery's station. "Do you want to listen?"

She nods.

The Gizmo beams audio to the two of us just as The Flanery Defense airs. "What did this man do to deserve torture by McGewan-X04?" A picture of Mikey appears on the screen as Flanery speaks. "If this citizen wasn't safe, then you aren't either. The Flanery Defense is going hot."

"You did a really good job on Mikey's makeup."

"Thank you," Mary says.

"Shame only Flanery is going to see it."

Guitars scream as chunks of the American flag drop into the shape of a shield, lasers spell out The Flanery Defense. An aerial shot shows Flanery's studio emerge from the top of his building. The shot zooms in, through the bulletproof glass, to a tight close-up of the man himself. As the studio rotates up to speed, I see the jumbo screen on the building opposite, broadcasting the Defense to the people on the street.

"Spin is dead, long live The Flanery Defense. Good evening, I'm Jack Flanery, welcome to night four of The Manhunt for McGewan-X04," he shouts, red-faced and smirking into the camera.

The crawl starts up at the bottom of the screen. "Office of Homeland Security has McGewan-X04 surrounded in his fortified compound..."

"At any moment McGewan-X04 will be brought to justice, fellow citizens. But why does he need to be brought to justice? I know he's committed countless atrocities, that's not in dispute. What is in dispute is why were his parent's licensed to procreate? DNA psychotherapy was a compulsory step in the licensing process. How did this lunatic's genetic material slip through the cracks?"

"Office of Homeland Security has taken six of McGewan-X04's eight lieutenant's into custody...." The crawl starts, but Flanery keeps distracting me.

"Fine, some underpaid government employee was asleep at the switch at DNA harvest and they incubated a sociopath named, McGewan-X04. Forgive and forget, that's my motto. But no one tested McGewan-X04 at the Academy? No one noticed that he was the embodiment of evil growing up?"

"I thought I was a nomad that never went to the Academy?"

"That was yesterday's news."

I nod.

"Is this going to work without Mikey?" Mary asks.

"Sure, it will."

"What about the distraction? Someone will notice that the clip on the monitor in the studio isn't the clip that's being broadcast right outside the window. They can just stop the show until they sort the problem out."

"It would have been a lot better with Mikey, but this will still work. I know it will. Besides, the clip is just another part of the distraction."

"When we come back," Flanery says, "a Flanery Defense exclusive. One of McGewan-X04's own men tortured and killed on video, and only the Defense has it. Stay right there. Your life may depend on it." The camera pulls back from Flanery, then the screen fades to a commercial.

"Why is this taking so long? Just show the damn clip."

"He's just trying to suck more people in," I say. "That's good for us, bad for him."

All the commercials feature me in some way. I have to

smile. *Real Patriots drink our beer, McGewan-Xo4 drinks that other beer. Do thoughts of McGewan-Xo4 keep you awake at night? Then, ask your healthcare technician about this drug. Ten percent of all furniture sales today will go to the families of McGewan-Xo4's victims, so hurry in.*

According to the information on the side of my Gizmo, about two-million people are watching Flanery at home or on their portable devices before the commercials. But the Defenders, Flanery's diehard fans, won't let an exclusive slip by unnoticed. Calls and text messages go out. Customers in coffee shops will demand that the station be changed. Pockets of ten, fifty, a hundred suddenly tune in, jumping the number up. Flanery's ratings will break a record, but that's the idea. Demonize me for a bigger share of the market. Have a big number to go into contract renegotiations with. Get that raise. Get that bigger mansion. Get that newer, tighter, tanner, trophy wife. Get my head on a platter, and get it all, Jack.

Flanery's red, white, and blue shield appears, and then fades to a close-up of Flanery. The crawl starts before he can speak. "Terror Level upgraded to Severe-Severe-High or Red-Orange—McGewan-Xo4 has eluded Homeland Security and is on a rampage in the city. Officials are asking all citizens to stay indoors. Stay tuned for further details."

Flanery's ratings spike even further, jumping thousands at a time now. "Welcome back. I've just been notified that McGewan-Xo4 is loose in the city. We will keep you up to the second when he is spotted, but right now, a horrifying video that was smuggled to us from a source inside McGewan-Xo4's organization."

"Did Sameer use standard mail to send the thumb drives out?" I ask.

"I think he paid for express delivery."

I nod.

"What you are about to see is hard to watch, fellow citizens. This is not special effects. Our experts have told me this is an actual video from inside McGewan-X04's compound. Everything you are about to watch is real."

For a split second, Mikey is on the screen, bloody, beat-up, gun pressed to his temple. I press a button on my Gizmo, and the shot shifts. Inside the chase Mikey was climbing out of the last time I saw him, my laptop receives the signal and hijacks the feed coming from Flanery's studio just before it is broadcast out to the world. Mikey's face is normal, the pistol vanishes, the other video broadcasting to everyone except Flanery and his staff. The crawl changes as well.

"Manhunt for McGewan-X04 memorabilia available for purchase now..."

"Fellow citizens, McGewan-X04 is not a terrorist. He doesn't torture people. He's bombed nothing. This is all a scheme by the government."

"Terror Level downgraded to Elevated or Yellow..."

The screen splits, Flanery on one side, Mikey talking on the other. "Citizens, terrorists are attacking the building I am in right now." The fire sprinklers turn on and douse Flanery. Sirens and flashing lights go off in the background. "McGewan-X04 is trying to stop me from showing this video to you, but I will keep broadcasting, no matter the risk to myself or my crew."

"Did your Gizmo do that?" Mary asks.

"I didn't do anything," I say.

We look at each and back at the screen. "Mikey," we say, in unison.

"The government keeps you afraid, so you'll obey every command, every insane law," the video of Mikey continues. "They want you drugged so you won't be able to think for yourself. They want you to work yourself to death, so they never have to lift a finger. They want you to be consumers so they can stay rich. They won't let you pick a mate. They won't let you have a child without approval. They won't let you be involved in your child's upbringing. All this to keep you, their army of genetically engineered workers, pumping out the products, keeping their stock prices up. They manufacture threats, manufacture the news, so you won't travel and see how citizens in other countries are treated. We aren't at war with the rest of the world, we aren't boycotting the planet. The rest of the world won't have anything to do with us because of how the government treats us."

"Manhunt for McGewan-X04 memorabilia available for purchase now..."

"Stop buying the crap we produce. Stop asking your healthcare technician about every drug that makes it to market. Go on vacation. See the world. Trade your credits in for Euros, and buy a house in Europe. If nothing else, start paying attention. Our forefathers built this country on the principles of freedom of speech, freedom of press, freedom of religion. We hear that every day. Then why do immigrants have to convert to Christianity to become citizens? Why do the five companies that run the country own all the news sources? Why are citizens arrested for having an opinion or assembling peacefully anywhere except in line to buy memorabilia? Stop believing everything that comes on the television and start forming your own opinions. This is the only way we can survive." Mikey smiles into the camera. "Thank you for listening."

"Terror Level downgraded to Elevated or Yellow..."

Flanery comes back on the screen, his suit soaked, his hair matted to his head. The sirens and sprinklers have stopped, but alarm lights still flash in the background. "Hard to watch, I know, citizens." He probably rubbed his hands together and cackled maniacally when the gunshot sprayed Mikey's brain across the monitor in his studio. I can't help but smile, as well.

The tight shot of Flanery pans out and reveals a four-man fire team of Homies surrounding him. Flanery, a veteran live news reporter, barely flinches. "The threat to myself and the rest of my crew is now over as you can see from the arrival of Homeland Security in my studio. Thank you, gentlemen."

"Mr. Flanery," says a Sergeant, trying to ignore the cameras and simply do his job, "we're going to have to ask you, and all your staff, to come with us."

"Is the threat that serious? Is McGewan-X04 in the building?" Flanery asks. "McGewan-X04 is in the building," he says, into the camera, "and coming for me. We will keep broadcasting, citizens, as they spirit us from the clutches of McGewan-X04 and his terrorist cell."

"I'm afraid that's not possible, Mr. Flanery. Shut the cameras off, you're all under arrest for alleged terrorist involvement."

"What? This is an outrage." Flanery is on his feet. A stun gun puts him on the floor before another word comes out of his mouth. The screen goes black, only the crawl remains.

"Manhunt for McGewan-X04 memorabilia available for purchase now..."

"That was quick," Mary says. "I didn't think they would arrest him on the air."

"Terror Level downgraded to Guarded or Blue for the first time in eighty years..."

"Me either." I stand and help Mary up. "We should try to find Mikey and get the hell out of town before the riots start."

"Manhunt for McGewan-X04 memorabilia available for purchase now..."

"That's not the plan," Mary says, as she brushes off her jumpsuit. "We get to the docks, if anyone else is there, they come with us. If not, we sail without them. There's no way we can find Mikey and make it to the ship on time."

"But, he's your brother."

"What would Herb say if he were here?"

I nod. "Be a smart terrorist. All right, let's go."

CHAPTER 18

My clothing looks like I feel. Both boots malfunctioned after my fall into the lake. The right is loose and slides off my heel with each step. When I try to tighten it by hand, the boot sends a charge of electricity into my foot like a rabid animal lashing out at anything within reach. The left boot cuts off the circulation at the ankle and my toes feels like they're submerged in ice. The jumpsuit's breast pocket was torn off. Two long hairs on my right nipple sway in the breeze. As I stumble along, the walls snag more threads and open more holes. The software in the collar can't keep up with all the openings, can't meld the fabric back together fast enough, and it's overheating. This makes the "smart" zipper bulge open at random to expose my stomach when I least expect it. If I grab the zipper around my stomach it seals, then opens elsewhere. Maybe my shoulder is exposed to sunlight or the zipper opens along the inseam with flesh-searing speed toward my groin. Raining punches down on the jumpsuit confuses it, calms it, and adds bruises to the bruises I already acquired.

I have slid so far down the socioeconomic ladder that I now own only what I'm wearing. The important thing, I think, is to protect the boxers. Only my underwear is still acting like clothing and not a portable torture device for the masochist on the go. Exposure to the elements would change that. Fleeing from the law, being separated from the only four people in the country that aren't trying to kill me, being bruised, lost, and tired would pale in comparison to an underwear malfunction at this point. What my unmentionables would do if I angered them is anyone's guess.

Didn't someone say that if you expect a shock to the balls and only get a wedgie, you've come out ahead?

No, probably not.

As far as assets, I still have Herb's Wonder Bar in my left hand. I think of it as borrowed. The alternative is to think I own it because Herb has gone to a place where fancy levers will do him no good. At any moment, I expect him to pop up and demand to know what I have been doing while he's been fighting the good fight.

Just trying to return your crowbar, Herb.

The alleys behind and between buildings get me away from immediate danger. Only robotic service vehicles ever use them, and until a few hours ago, even I treated them as if they didn't exist. No one would ever dream to go into an alley, it just isn't done. Homeland Security and local police have too much on their plate to conduct street-to-street and alley-to-alley searches, and I need it to stay that way.

My edit of Flanery's broadcast turned the city into a storm cloud, mostly protest with a chance of riot. Law enforcement issued an All Hands Alert. Every agency remotely tied to keeping the peace is out on the streets dispersing crowds and deterring looters. They're too disorganized to worry about individuals, namely me, the root of their problems. A hovercar zips down the street when I reach the end of the alley. Sirens blare, lights flash, the recorded mantra repeats itself endlessly.

"Patriots don't loot. Good citizens would go home. Patriots don't loot..."

After the hovercar passes, I limp and stagger in my malfunctioning boots, across the street, into the safety of the next alley.

———

Mary did not go quietly. We zigzagged around the sewers for an hour after the broadcast. The path of least resistance. Voices to the right, take a left. Static that way, let's go this way. With my L.I.F.E. display only partially functioning, the booby-trap doesn't "see" me walk by. Mary is another story. One second, she has her hand on my shoulder, guiding me through turns with the night-vision, telling me to duck when a pipe crosses the roof. The next second she's strapped to the wall, cursing. I have never seen a micromesh net in person, but it looks as bad up close as it does on television. From reruns of Homies I know that it is flexible, won't rust, fray or wear out, and it's tougher than titanium, so cutting through it isn't an option. If the perp struggles, which they usually do, it constricts until they suffocate or cut off a limb. This comforts neither of us.

"Can you breathe? What should I do?" I ask.

"Forget it, I'm fine." Mary's voice is level, her body still, but her face is crimson, headed for purple.

"I can wait until the Homie with the key shows up and crack him one." I wave the Wonder Bar.

"Nah."

"I can try to pry you loose."

"It won't work. Thanks, though."

"What do you want me to do? Tell me what to do, and I'll do it."

She sighs and twitches her nose from side to side. "There's

probably an alarm on that thing, so a squad of Homies is headed this way. You should take off."

"But they're looking for me, not you. I could give myself up and say you're my hostage."

"That's sweet, but like you said, they're looking for you. So—"

"So?"

"Get moving. I won't give the pricks the satisfaction."

"You sure?"

"Yes, go. Take the Snooper and get the hell out of here."

The Snooper in one hand, the Wonder Bar still in the other. "Mary, I..." My ears fill with a swarm of bees, a tidal wave of noise.

"What?"

"They're coming."

"Go, get the fuck out of here. Just do a right-face and walk away."

Fifty yards down the tunnel, two lefts and a right later, someone deactivates the net. The garbled calls for backup pour into my ear. If she had a weapon, they would have just shot her. One to the head, one to the heart, old school double-tap. Kneecaps, elbows, teeth are not considered weapons. Officially, fury is not contraband. The Homies that unlocked Mary probably thought otherwise.

The Homie Pain Network fades as I walk. An occasional burst of static and sewer stretches for as far as the Snooper can see. The floor feels different for a second, then I am falling, sliding down a drain, bits of rotted wood coming with me. Water breaks my fall. It is chest deep and stagnant. Daylight filters through a grate in one wall, which is good because the Snooper is gone. The Wonder Bar has green and black strands of who knows what dangling from it when I lift it out of the water. The thought that it isn't exactly water makes me gag, but

I hold back. Just a few paces through the water and I'll be on dry land. Just ten steps of water between me and the beach.

This is the ocean, that is the beach.

Just water.

The smell is horrendous.

It was two days after my warranty expired on my refrigerator when I noticed all the milk and cheese and eggs had burst through their packaging.

Five paces.

The steak had Brussel sprouts growing out of it.

Three paces.

All the vegetables were black pulp running together in the crisper drawer.

Throw the Wonder Bar up, dig toes in, push out.

Mayonnaise bubbled with green magma while still in the jar. This is that smell, but an Olympic-sized swimming pool of that smell. Once on the beach, clinging to the Wonder Bar, trying to bend it in half with one hand, I add to that smell. Everything leaves my body the wrong way on a one-way street. Snot and vomit burn their way out. Tears join the mix. After a perceived eternity, I choke back one last dry heave, wipe snot and whatever else on my sleeve, and climb the ladder to daylight.

The Wonder Bar does its thing on the grate then just a short crawl through an almost too small pipe, and I reach open air and sunshine. My jumpsuit ripped open in spots on the crawl, but I've got sunshine. If I stand just right, the breeze blows my smell away from my face. This should go on our recruiting poster. We swim through more underground lakes of sewage before ten in the morning, than most people in a lifetime.

Yeah.

Ripped, Rancid, and Ready to Go, Herb's Terror Squad.

That's why there are tens of us, not tens of thousands of us. With Herb and Mikey and Sameer captured, and now Mary, are there even ten left? And where are the others? How do I get in touch?

Please standby, your consumer experience software is calibrating.

The blank wall to my left scrolls through a myriad of images. A cup of coffee, a car, a fit woman. It stops on a picture of a Wonder Bar.

Based on your most recent experience, the rest of your day is brought to you by the makers of The Wonder Bar. Complex problems, simple tool.

I look down. The Wonder Bar is part of my left hand now. Whatever I had just swum out of was dry. My palm and Herb's Wonder Bar are epoxied together, and it feels right.

"I was born with this thing in my hand, officer. Honest."

An alley is a little way off. Sneak through the city, get to the docks, crack any resistance in the skull, can do, easy. Then the breeze shifts and I can smell myself.

Correction. Get a change of clothes and a shower, and then it's me and the Wonder Bar against the world.

The first two blocks of alleys are quiet, no one on the cross streets. The third has a riot in progress about thirty paces to the left. Homies with body length bulletproof shields stand their ground at the far end. Rioters with sticks and rocks surge toward them. The smart rioters listen for the Thunk and run back before the foam mortar detonates. The dumb ones just look up, then everything but their face is immobilized in expanding riot foam. The still mobile rioters run up their foam-encased comrades, a little above the Homies, then Thunk. Everyone separates. The Homies backpedal toward the mortar crew. The citizens back up almost to where I am crouched. A few less rioters, but a few less Homies as well. The dance renews. The riot foam ramp grows and grows until rioters can stomp Homies in the head. Then the line breaks. Rioters charge the mortar crew. With no defense, no batons, no shields, no stun guns, just a mortar, the remaining Homies open fire on everything and anything that moves.

Thunk. Thunk. Thunk.

It freezes everyone on the street. Homies and rioters stuck in a museum diorama of violence.

"This next display is called 'Civil Unrest,' children," the tour guide will say.

A robin flies by overhead. Riot foam stops it mid-chirp, and the encased bird drops to the ground.

"I'm unarmed, an innocent bystander," I shout. "I'm just passing through." I stand and point to the next alley. "I'm just going to cross the street."

"Go ahead," says the officer in charge of the mortar with a wave. "Have a good day, citizen. God bless."

At the end of the next alley, I see my building, three blocks forward, maybe four, and one block to the left.

"Freeze, hands up," says a female voice from behind me. "Turn around very slowly."

My hands rise to shoulder height, as I pray that my jump-suit doesn't take this distraction as an opportunity to expose me in an embarrassing fashion. "I'm sorry, I don't mean to be diffi-cult, but do you want me to freeze or turn around slowly?"

"Don't be smart. Turn around."

I let that comment go and turn as directed.

"I'm Fitness Enforcement Agency Agent Amber, and you're under arrest." The woman's bottle blonde hair is teased up in a hairspray helmet, with just a touch of brown showing along the scalp. Tanned to the point of leather, her cheekbones and brow-ridge stick out of her taut, angular face. The bullet-proof sports bra and sequined short-shorts are a mere nod to clothing. The knee-high wrestling shoes with a six-inch heel make her leg muscles stand out like a medical diagram, certain parts blown up for instructional purposes. Her fingers, each tip Freedom Manicured, are curled like claws, ready to scratch my eyes out or put me in a submission hold. It takes my eyes a second to travel across her taut and lightly oiled body. She isn't armed. FEA Agents rarely are. She could rip my arm out of the socket and beat me to death with it, but she doesn't have a pistol or even a set of handcuffs that I can see.

"Ma'am..."

"Call me Amber," she says, her face serious, but her voice bubbly and chipper out of habit.

"Amber, I just fell into a pool of unbelievably filthy water, and I need to go home and shower before I vomit again." I am not sure if I can give a woman, even this overly developed example of the female of the species, the Wonder Bar treatment. However, it has been the roughest day of all-time roughest days and I can smell myself, again. It is either knock her out or vomit on her. "I don't want any trouble, but I will mess up your pretty face, if you slow me down."

She stands ramrod straight, her hands at her sides. "Is that supposed to be a joke?"

The Wonder Bar is making my shoulder burn from keeping it aloft, so I lower it, but she snaps her fingers.

"Keep that up. This is a one-on-one Isometric Fitness Audit."

I push my arm up.

"Answer my question. Is that supposed to be funny? Are you making jokes?"

"I don't understand."

"I am a member of the Fitness Enforcement Agency attached to the Department of Homeland Fitness. I am required to be the apex of physical fitness to keep people, like you, away from obesity. I have to lead dozens of fitness audits every day with a smile on my face and with the appearance that it is easy to motivate the citizenry."

"This is getting heavy," I say, glancing at the Wonder Bar.

"Grab it with both hands and hold it at eye level."

I comply. It is better, but not great.

"The only way I can do my job is to be strong. I workout in my free time. Women don't produce as much testosterone as men, so I take supplements. I move heavy weights. I hold the Agency record for squat and deadlift. Not for women, for all Agents because I work twice as hard as everyone else. My femininity is not my chief priority. I don't look like the porn stars you prefer because I am not a porn star. I am an Agent and I will be the first female Fat Czar. That's my goal. But I work for an organization that has the unfortunate acronym of FEA. That's the feminine conjugation of 'ugly' in Spanish. I get it. You think I'm hideous, so you make a crack about my face, like everything I do is so laughable. I am powerful. Not a powerful woman. Powerful period. You will not make me feel bad about my life choices."

My heartbeat throbs in my face as I try to keep the Wonder Bar at eye level. Even with shifting the weight from arm to arm, both my shoulders are on fire.

"Rest," she says.

I drop my arms and sag into a hunch.

"You want to make another joke before I run you in for Fitness Unbecoming a Patriot?"

The combination of my stench and the isometric exercise makes me swallow a handful of times before I feel comfortable speaking without the threat of vomiting. The smart thing would be to apologize, beg her forgiveness, but the day had caught up with me.

"So, anytime someone mentions your looks, they're

mocking you?" I say, still hunched over, talking more to my knees than to her. "I didn't compare you to a porn star, and I never said you had to look like one. I have had a very long, horrible day, which includes, if you were listening, falling into a pool of filth. I'm calling it 'filth,' because if I say out loud what I think it was, I will definitely vomit. Again. I want to go home. I want to shower. I want to burn the remains of this jumpsuit and shoot it into space. I want to sleep. Not rest. Sleep like it's a competitive sport. And now, you want to arrest me because I made a stupid phrasing choice?" I stand and face her without ejecting anything other than a foul smell. "If that's how today is supposed to end, so be it. But I think both of us would rather be doing something else right now."

She tilts her head to the side and considers me. Finally, she points at my exposed chest. "Five minutes a day on a chest machine would firm you up nicely. And a little tanning would make you look leaner and healthier. Go about your business, citizen. I have more important things to deal with right now."

She turns and, with arms and thighs too muscular for normal movement, ambles off down the alley. I replay the conversation in my head, still not understanding why I wasn't in custody. She turns the corner and is gone.

A minute passes.

No reinforcements.

No squad of Homies.

I shake my head and, as ordered, go about my business.

Fifteen minutes later, I am behind my building. The streets had gone quiet, not even the hovercars for looter deterrence zip through the neighborhood. The back door has a flap in the bottom for service robots, none of which gave me a second look when I crawl inside. Bags of groceries, hangers of dry cleaning, bundles of mail swirl around me in a robot-induced maelstrom. I follow a grocery-bearing 'bot into the corridor and join it on the service elevator. For the first time all day, I am in a room that doesn't contain someone trying to kill or arrest me. My mouth opens, but I catch myself before I initiate small talk with the metallic gentleman's gentleman. There is probably a fine for talking to someone else's service robot, and it would ruin my credibility to have such a measly charge brought against me. Without a word, not that I expected one, the robot got off five floors below my apartment, deactivating the elevator.

My building is equipped with stairs, unbeknownst to me, and they are operational. The turns jar me. The step flattens, whips around the corner, and rises. The point of the step always coming up just ahead of where it had been before, unbalancing me each time.

There is nothing remarkable about my floor in the apartment building. That is, everything is as it has always been. Unremarkable. Hallway, precisely straight. Doors, identical, evenly spaced, no uniqueness other than the increasing apartment numbers. No plants. No paintings. Stark light from recessed fixtures to approximate daylight. Clean. Sterile. Drab. My home is a locked ward in the mental institution, and for the first time, I see it for what it is.

The door. The door of the former citizen known as P. McGewan-X04. Not my door any longer. A prisoner lives here, has the credentials to pass in and out of this door imbedded in his handprint.

I have no such credentials and have no need for them. I am that most dangerous of criminals, the terrorist. My chief weapon is the Wonder Bar stuck to my left hand.

The Wonder Bar and utter contempt for the law are my two terrorist tools.

The Wonder Bar, utter contempt for the law, and the knowledge that no modern weapon can hurt me.

Contained in my terrorist arsenal are weapons such as a

Wonder Bar, utter and complete contempt for the law, and the knowledge that no modern weapon can hurt me. And a smell that can —

The door slides to the side before I can order my thoughts. A chrome, shiny, and above all, antiquated weapon points at my forehead from inside my former apartment.

"Do you know what this is?" the voice asks.

I nod.

"Good. Get in here before you scare the neighbors."

"Damn," I say under my breath, as the door seals me into the apartment with the Black Coat.

CHAPTER 19

"Come in," says the Black Coat. He looks like every other Inquisitor, but with his thick accent, I know he is the Black Coat from the factory, my Black Coat. "Make yourself at home." He walks into the living room and places the chrome revolver on the mantle then turns, hands clasped in front, his body relaxed. The mirrored lenses of his sunglasses reflect me standing in front of my couch. "Have a seat."

"I'd rather stand. What can I do for you? Why are you in my home?" I ask.

"Your home?" His laugh is mechanical and quick. "You're a terrorist. This is more my home than yours now. And you came to me. That saves me the trouble of dragging your body in here and staging your death, so you've done more than enough for me already. Please, sit."

"No, thank you." My fingers flex around the Wonder Bar. Just move a little farther from the revolver and I can...

He is so quick I can't see his actions, only their results. The lapel of his coat rustles after his hand emerges. My eyes shift to see his arm straight, the wrist snaps back. My lungs deflate. The concussion throws me back like a rag doll onto the couch. His lapel twitches to the side again, and then his hands are clasped together. His service sidearm was never visible. I don't realize that it had even made an appearance until my L.I.F.E. sensor told me about the four broken ribs and reminded me that it had been manually overridden.

L.I.F.E. is currently unable to dispense pain medication at this time, sorry for the inconvenience.

"Are you dead?" He takes a step forward.

My breath comes short and quick. Rips in the front of my jumpsuit aren't pumping blood. "No," I say, when I had enough air inside to speak, "I don't think so."

"If you don't mind me asking, how are you doing that?"

"Doing what?"

"Not dying when people shoot you. Several of my underlings told me that someone disabled their weapons when they tried to apprehend you."

"Apprehend?" I half-shout, but the pain in my ribs lowers my voice to a whimper. "They were trying to kill me."

He gives me a dismissive wave. "This is no time to argue semantics. You are the most wanted man in America, but that round self-destructed. Of all the things we need to talk about, that intrigues me the most."

A grimace pulls my face tight as I sit up.

"I will allow you to take pain medication. I'm not a monster." The mirrored sunglasses come off and are place on the mantle with the revolver. He is menacing with the glasses. Without, he is a bald kid with vibrant blue eyes, ten years too young to do this sort of thing full-time. He is young enough that he probably should have just graduated from the Police Academy, and then after a few years on a tough beat, maybe an offer from Homeland Security. I could tell he was in good shape, even under the shape-obscuring trench coat. He is handsome enough to be on the local news, possibly good looking enough to be a national talking head. He could have really shone on

Homies, come into people's living rooms nightly via the television, tracking terrorists, arresting terrorists, demonstrating how futile it is to be a terrorist. Instead, he is an Inquisitor, a Black Coat. He's probably only three years older than my son.

My son. My wife. They sound like titles for people I don't know. At least, they are safe. Two fewer people that could be hurt by this mess.

He has a stylus poised over his wrist display. "In your own time."

There is no foreseeable way to escape the city now, let alone my own apartment. With a sigh of resignation, I decide to tell him everything and be done with it. "My L.I.F.E. is partially disabled."

"Really? How did you disable it?" He takes notes on his wrist as I speak.

"You have my record?"

"I know everything that you've done since leaving the Academy. A call to a judge will get me everything before that point."

"The car accident from a few days ago."

"Yes, what about it?" He glances through my file on his wrist display. "They ran a diagnostic battery. Your L.I.F.E. was fine."

"It has something to do with lead."

"Nobody can get a target lock on you because of lead? Interesting," he says, as he wrote. "What else?"

"It won't dispense drugs." Even if Mikey is headed for the gallows, I will not add to his list of charges by admitting that he fiddled with my L.I.F.E. "It stopped asking if I wanted to talk to my personal counselor. Some of my Gizmos still work, but my ID is disabled. I'm not sure if that has anything to do with it."

"I disabled your ID. Anything else?"

I thought for a moment. "That's everything."

Commander.

"Excuse me," says the Black Coat to me. "This is Commander Lemarck...," he says, his gaze locked on the wall above and to the left of where I'm sitting.

I hear the voices in other people's heads. That's what I forgot.

They've escaped, Commander.

The Black Coat, Lemarck, looks at me, his face impassive. "Clarify."

The old man in the library, the man and woman in the sewer, they were in transit to the Hall of Justice, and they disappeared. We're looking into how they got out of their restraints and how they affected their escape. The manhunt is still in full force.

"Carry on."

There is an almost too lengthy pause.

We have no news on McGewan-X04, commander. I take full responsibility.

"Calm yourself. I have him in custody. Keep me informed. Lemarck out." He turns back to me. "There is not an easy way to say this, so I will just say it. All your friends have been executed. They resisted arrest and were, shall we say, apprehended with extreme prejudice. My condolences."

I am elated that someone might still make it out of this mess, but shift until my ribs put some real pain into my voice. "That's horrible."

We stare at each other for a few moments. "Do you know why this happened to you?"

I shrug.

"Did you commit any crimes as a child?"

"What? No," I reply, quickly. "Everything on the news is bullshit, and you know it."

"Not that. Think before you answer. Any crimes? Perhaps

210

you got away with something because they blamed someone else?"

"I don't know what you're talking about."

"Do you know any German?"

His questions seem random, and my confession drained what little strength I have left. Besides, my ribs hurt, and I reek. "I knew a little German, but apparently you executed him."

"I didn't execute him. They cleansed him from the roster for the good of the collective."

"So, there is no accountability?"

A smile cracks his lips for an instant and then vanishes. "Regardless, my boss wanted me to define a word for you. Schadenfreude. Have you heard the word?"

I shrug, again. "Perhaps."

"It is the joy obtained from the trouble of others."

I nod. "Okay, and?"

"That's all. Now my boss would like to talk to you." He types a brief message into his wrist.

"Your boss? The Terror Czar?"

He shakes his head. "Someone even more powerful."

I look at the state of my clothes and smooth my hair down with my right hand. "The President?"

The smile returns, then vanishes. "Just between you and me, President Jackson is so terrified about what he sees on the news, that he's been circling above the country in Air Force One for years. How can a man be powerful if he's afraid to step foot in his own country?" He glances down at his wrist. "He'll be with us in a moment."

Who could be more powerful than the Head of Homeland Security and the President? Who else has the authority to sic a Black Coat on me? Who did I manage to piss off?

The living room wall flickers, and a floor-to-ceiling face

stares at me with a smirk. This is the Black Coat's boss? It can't be.

"Mr. McGewan," Jack Flanery says, "we meet again."

I clear my throat. "Again? We've met before?"

"It disappoints me that you don't remember me. Because I remember you."

Flanery's voice makes my fists itch. "What the fuck are you talking about?"

The Black Coat takes two long strides toward me, and the force of the slap pushes me back into the couch. "Monsieur Flanery doesn't like that sort of language."

I rub my jaw. "I saw you arrested on national television. How could you be back in your studio already?"

"Your hack job was easy to find, and my lawyer spits ancient Latin phrases, like a camel spits," he says with a grin.

I cock my head. "Like a camel spits what?"

"Like a camel," he says, "never mind. Are you afraid?"

"Afraid? No, I'm afraid not," I say, apparently not reading off the same script as Flanery, "but I don't understand why you're trying to ruin my life."

"Ruin your life? Trying?" Flanery chuckles. "I believe I've successfully ruined your life, because you ruined mine. You look confused. The Academy? You got me expelled."

It takes me a second, but it's him. The kid from the Academy. The one that modified his L.I.F.E. I never knew his name, never learned what he had done. He probably tried to install a bootleg version of solitaire, thinking he was clever, while I was changing grades in the database. I only saw him that one time. Robotic proctors led him out of the Dean's office past me in the waiting room, never to be seen again, right before I was led into the same office and permanently lodged in the X-class. The look of terror I saw that day is gone, replaced by rage and smug satisfaction.

"Let me catch you up a little," Flanery says, "tell you what I had to suffer because of you. My parents, in their infinite wisdom," his face is headed from red to purple, spittle flecks the screen, "sent me to live with a distant cousin after they expelled me. I... you shamed my family so much that they banished me to the most backward country in the world. They sent me to France." He pauses as if he expects ominous music or a horrified gasp. "France," he continues as I stare at him blankly, "where I was ridiculed because no one there was smart enough to learn American. Where they claim to be the inventors of modern cuisine but insist on eating sea bugs and can't master the art of making hard cheese. Where they took football and stripped away all the strategy, all the skill and turned it into a bunch of sissies in running shorts playing grab ass, then watched it like it mattered. Get a helmet, learn to use your fucking hands, and then we'll see which country has better athletes."

"Hold on a second," I say. "Who slaps your mouth when you fucking swear?"

Lemarck swings, but he is too close for me to bring the Wonder Bar up. I catch his arm with my empty right hand before the backhand connects. "Son, if you're going to beat me up, it will be with a closed fist, like a man. I'm sick of you slapping like a schoolgirl." He wrenches his arm free, and I don't see the other hand until the heel of his palm pulls back from between my eyes. My vision turns to static and stars for a moment.

Now dispensing stool softeners.

"Was that me?" I ask. Lemarck and Flanery stare in silence. Suddenly, from the bottom of my ribcage to the top of my thighs, I feel warm and relaxed.

Lemarck's face wrinkles in disgust. "Monsieur Flanery, I hit him so hard he pooped."

No, I thought, you hit me so hard the button in my mouth got stuck and dispensed a laxative, you French piece of —

"Hold it," I say. "If you hate the French so much, why do you have one as a henchman, Jack?"

"It's Mr. Flanery, and I was getting to that." He rolls his head from side to side and readjusts his smirk. "The Lemarck family was my salvation, you see. Despite their racial handicap, they were better Americans than you ever were. They wanted to learn American. They wanted to understand baseball. I taught them about French fries and French toast, things that whole God forsaken country had forgotten about. When I came back to the States with a journalism degree, most of the family had passed away, all but Inquisitor Lemarck. They had suspended him from the French police for excessive force. Excessive force? Only the French would want police officers with their balls cut off, just like the rest of the citizenry."

"So, you got him a job as an Inquisitor and sent him after me. Yeah, yeah, yeah. Can we speed this up? I need a shower."

Flanery laughs. "I didn't get him a job as an Inquisitor. I created the Inquisitor Branch of Homeland Security so he could have a job that suited his talents."

I nod in disbelief. "You created the Black Coats? Riiiiiight."

"America was soft when I got to the national news after the Collapse. No one had any fear of the American way of life being sold out and diluted. Our uniqueness, our exceptionalism, was bleeding away from too many foreigners acting like this was their home, like they had a right to be here as much as anyone else. Christian values needed to be re-established, the real American way of life needed to be resurrected." His smirk turns to a full smile.

"So you lied to the American people," I say.

His smile falters, and the smirk returns. "I gave America the stories it needed to hear. Did you ever ask your son what happened to the Dean of the Academy? The one that expelled me? No? He was my first foray into editorialized journalism."

"You mean, fictionalized journalism."

"Shut up. Shut your damn mouth." Surround-sound speakers fill the room with his teeth grinding. "To avenge my family's shame, I told all of America that he was a non-practicing homosexual, a threat to our future, the children of this country. He had never married, never had children of his own, and had never once, not once, donated to the sperm bank for the growth of the collective."

Vomit rises in my throat. My voice hoarse. "He was wounded in the military. He didn't donate, didn't have children because he wasn't physically able, that's why he wasn't granted a marriage license. Non-breeders aren't allowed. He was a national hero injured in the service of his country, not a non-practicing homosexual."

"Well, you're right about one thing. He gets a lot of practice, now."

"Oh my God, what did you do?" My vision narrows, my personal pain forgotten at the thought of what he might say.

"He's in the Leadville Molybdenum Mine and Prison slowly dying of radiation sickness and getting sodomized by any convict that wants an autographed pack of cigarettes from yours truly." His finger jabs the camera. "That's what justice should look like."

I sway on the couch, unable to hold my head up. "Oh, my God." How could anyone be this cruel, this evil, in the name of his, mine, anyone's God?

"That was just the start," he goes on, not caring if I pay attention. "The law enforcement apparatus was too slow, too concerned about the rights of the accused. So, I hinted about a brand new, secret branch of Homeland Security. Men who went where angels feared to tread. Fearless men, Patriots that would march into a den of ragheads with their..."

"... heads in rags?" I moan. "Is that a crime now?"

"Shut your mouth... with their sheep-eye soup and their jihads and their mumbo-jumbo prayers five times a day that mock the true God. But these Patriots would make them accept Jesus Christ into their hearts or else they died by the sword they lived by."

I whisper more to myself than anyone. "I don't like hummus, but I never killed anyone over it. You can't use your right to free speech to take away someone's freedom of religion."

"Who said you could have an opinion? You're just as bad as they are. Worse, because you had every opportunity to be a Patriot, and you chose to be a terrorist. Chose to believe the press that I manufactured for you. And so help me, Jesus, I will have Lemarck break your jaw if you interrupt me again. Where was I?"

"Die by the sword they lived by," I say with a groan.

"Shut up," he says, clearing his throat. "Ah, yes. The response to my little experiment was better than I could have imagined. This is what America wanted. This is what America needed. I designed the uniforms. Lemarck found recruits who had the same thirst for justice that the French had punished him for. The government went along with it, either because they thought we needed the Inquisitors, or they were dumb enough to believe they already existed. Then it was just a matter of research. I'd find an undesirable element, write up a script, and my Inquisitors meted out justice with my cameras close on their heels. My ratings went through the roof. I am the cure for all that ails America, not a journalist that tells it like it is, but a journalist that tells it like it should be. Did you know that Americans can identify my picture easier than they can identify a picture of the Lord? No? If that weren't enough, at the height of my success, you came back into my life."

"When you found me, your little bald executioner dropped a forty-ton box on my car, but it didn't kill me. Yippee," I say with sarcasm. "I know everything. Can Lemarck kill me now? I don't think I can listen to you for another minute."

"Actually, did we have anything to do with that?" Flanery asks Lemarck.

Lemarck shakes his head. "Every investigator said it was an accident. Just some peasant that worked too many consecutive eighteens."

"See, just an accident, or as I like to call them, divine intervention events." He raises his arms in benediction, and his eyes looks up to the ceiling as if he is reading God's teleprompter. "When your name came up on the crawl, I felt the hand of God on my shoulder. The Lord wanted me to find you now, at the height of my power, so I could destroy you, your family, and your friends. Leading us to an actual terrorist cell was just a bonus." He sighs and looks at me, a grin on his face. "Now, I get to watch Lemarck kill you."

The chrome revolver is off the mantle and pointed at my face.

"I think a suicide makes the best story," Flanery says. "He's left-handed." Lemarck moves to my left and presses cold steel to my temple. "'Guilt-ridden from all the tragedy he wrought, the Super Terrorist takes his own life.' I like that. For giving me such good ratings, I thank you, my sponsors thank you, and my bank account thanks you." He chuckles. "When you're ready, Lemarck."

"Wait," I say, "don't you want to hear my last words?"

Flanery snaps his fingers. "Good thinking, let me make sure I'm still recording." He checks the display on his end, then says, "Ready. Go ahead."

There was no fear, no pain left in my body. My own putrid smell didn't even register. When the revolver touches me, every moment since the accident plays through my mind.

"This was all a divine intervention event, like you said." Flanery nods. "The accident, my L.I.F.E. going haywire, meeting the terrorists, messing with your broadcast, all of it."

"You're stalling. Kill him."

"Wait, I'm getting to my point."

"Make it quick."

"Where was I? Oh, yeah. It was divine intervention, but the Lord didn't want you to find me at the height of your power," a smile pulls my lips back to expose all my teeth. "He wanted me to find you."

"What? Blasphemy!"

"I know you've figured out how I messed with your broadcast, that's how your lawyer got you out of jail so quickly, but that was just a diversion. You see, your fans have always wanted you to sell memorabilia on your show, but for whatever reason you refuse. So, I had memorabilia made and sold it through a dummy page on your Website. Order one, I'll wait."

A range of emotions cross Flanery's face. It settles on a disgusted sneer as he types into his keyboard, and a moment later the vacuum tube pops up on his desk. He inspects the bracelet. "I wouldn't have chosen yellow, personally. 'Manhunt for McGewan-X04,'" he read, "and my logo. It's nice, I like it. Other than your infringement of my copyrighted logo, I don't see what the big deal is."

"Try it on."

"Does it go here, over my L.I.F.E. display?"

I nod.

The Technicolor drains from his face as soon as the bracelet touches his wrist. "Oh my God."

"That's a rare Earth magnet, Jack. It holds the bracelet on, and the bonus is, it stops THAW from dripping into your bloodstream."

"Oh my God."

"THAW withdrawal sucks, let me tell you. You'll have a screaming headache in a few minutes, but the immediate symptom is clarity. Self-tying shoes and your dead-end job and all the bullshit they tell you on the news doesn't matter anymore. Your mind will be flooded with questions, and you get angry that everyone is lying to you. Is there a number on the inside of your wrist, Jack?"

He looks down at his arm and nods. "Eleven, five eighty-five, three forty-six. What's it for?"

"I had to prepay for the first two million bracelets, but the company agreed to make anything after that on an on-demand basis."

"Oh my God."

A little more color drains from his face when he realizes what the number means, but I rub his nose in it anyway. "There are almost twelve million of those on the street now, Jack, and every one of them is on the wrist of your Defenders, your nightly fans, the middle of the road people you suck in for the big stories, and probably a bunch of memorabilia collectors. All of them are your worst enemies now. They are tearing up this city and every major city in America. Those aren't my terrorists on the streets, those are your fans."

"I can fix this, I can spin it back to the positive," he mumbles.

"How?" I ask. "Go on the air and tell everyone the government is feeding them drugs to keep them docile and that your bracelet stops it? You'd be dead before the second sentence left your mouth."

"I could say nothing, blame this all on you when the authorities ask. Wait, I could get my fans to take off the bracelets and return them."

"All your fans are tearing the city apart because you and the government were persecuting me. They won't listen to you now, not as long as they have the bracelets."

"We could forcibly remove the bracelets..." his voice fades to a murmur.

"Jack, the intrinsic problem with a police state is keeping the people unaware that they outnumber the police. Even if you manufacture a dozen new police agencies, you still won't have enough manpower. And, if you tell the law to remove the bracelets, they'll know you had something to do with this, and your fans will be killed, arrested, or they're just never going to want to see your face again. You won't have enough viewers to get a donkey show on public access."

"Excuse me for one second," Flanery says, then cuts his microphone.

Lemarck, don't make a sound. Flanery's voice comes into my head. We need to—

"Jack," I say, "I can still hear you. That's the one thing I forgot to tell your boy. One thing he forgot to tell you is that he hasn't caught a terrorist all day."

What?

Lemarck and I both jerk when he yells into our heads.

"Turn your microphone back on, Jack. All my terrorist buddies escaped from the Homies. My family is safe in Europe. Your career is a pile of smoking rubble. What else? Oh yeah, the only profit on the day is you get to kill me over an eighth-grade grudge."

"So, I still win," he says through my surround-sound speakers.

"I'm a free man now, Jack. A week ago, you could have led me around by the nose with very little effort, but now the sleeper has awoken. I make the decisions now without your guidance, without anyone's guidance, without your or anyone else's spin, and I take full responsibility for my actions. You won't win, you won't conquer me. The most you can do is kill me. I'm the most powerful man in America, right now. Want to bet I'll be more powerful as a martyr?"

Flanery pries the bracelet off. His face goes from putty gray back to borderline furious. "I'll take that chance. Lemarck."

"Sir."

"Kill him."

"And then..."

"Find his friends and kill them yourself. I need to start spinning this clusterfuck."

"Jack," I say, "if I see the Devil, I'll tell him you're coming."

Flanery's teeth grind together. "Take all the time you need, Lemarck." The wall went blank, and it was just me and the Black Coat, again.

"On your feet," Lemarck says, as he jabs the barrel of the pistol into my temple.

CHAPTER 20

Two nights ago, maybe three, I sat on this very couch deciding how to commit suicide, but couldn't bring myself to do it. Now I want to live again, but that is about to be taken from me.

"Get up," Lemarck says, the gun in my face.

As I stand, I bring the Wonder Bar up and around, aiming at Lemarck's head. He catches my wrist and twists me to the ground. My entire body cries out in pain as the Wonder Bar falls away with bits of skin still attached. He gives me a kick to my already abused and broken ribs. "Stand up."

He pulls his leg back for a second shot, but I wave him off. "I'll get up, I'm getting up." As I stand, Sklrda comes out of its cubbyhole and examines the Wonder Bar.

If you have no objections, sir, I'll just clean this up for you.

The butler grabs the Wonder Bar with a metallic tentacle.

"Sklrda, no, leave it there." I say, but my robot butler ignores me and heads to the kitchen. "Damn thing never listens to me."

"You are probably saying its name wrong," Lemarck says. "I had the same problem, so I got rid of mine."

Sklrda is whistling, or playing a recording of someone whistling, while it scrubs the muck and blood and skin off my only weapon. I should have gotten rid of that annoying little robotic football. Defenseless now, I know that after my death, the stupid thing will spend its days scrubbing blood out of the upholstery while quoting Bible verses to my rotting corpse.

"Hey, focus," Lemarck says, snapping his fingers. "What is going on with you and that stick? I saw how you held it. You would think it was magical or something."

I look at the Black Coat. "It is. It's the Enchanted Wonder Bar of the Chosen One. You got a problem with that?"

"The Chosen One?" He chuckles. "Is Herb still feeding people that line?"

"You know Herb?"

"I trained him," he says with a shrug, as if this were common knowledge.

"Herb's an Inquisitor?"

Lemarck shakes his head. "He is an undercover agent attached to Homeland Security. We lost track of him several years ago, but you helped us out there. Thanks for that."

"You're lying," I say, "just like you lied about them being dead."

"Is he still feeding people that same tired speech? How does it go? 'There is no room for superstition, good luck charms, or prophecies in my life. But you are who we have been waiting for all these years.' Did he tell you that?"

"That proves nothing."

He ignores me. "It surprises me that with all Herb's training as a counter-revolutionary, he didn't plan his own revolution very well."

I look around for another weapon. "How so?" I need something, anything that I can use to bash this guy, but I have nothing. Nothing heavy. Nothing metal. Nothing even has a sharp corner.

"Everyone knows there are three factors required for a large populace to turn on its handlers. When the people recognize their chains of bondage," he says, holding up his thumb, then the index finger of his free hand, "and when they perceive a hope of escape from bondage. You did those two perfectly with the bracelets and explanation of THAW. I must commend you. But you forgot the most important one. You didn't give the people a leader. They don't know that you freed them from bondage. In years to come, they may understand, but a figurehead that people could rally around did not instantly appear. Salvation with no messiah." He shakes his head. "Herb is old and has been undercover so long, he forgets things. He long ago forgot there was a wolf under his cheap clothes."

I raise an eyebrow. "Is that a French saying? I don't get it. What does cheap clothing have to do with wolves?"

"Not cheap," he says with a groan, "cheap. 'Bah, bah, black cheap, have you any wool?'"

"Oh, sheep's clothing."

"That is what I said. I do not like when people make fun of my accent."

Lemarck bares his teeth, and I know why the French police had suspended him. My hands go up to block the punch, but he brings the pistol around when I flinch for his feint. The pistol's butt connects with my jaw and the grid comes up in my vision.

Five teeth broken.

A graphic painted on my eye shows which teeth are damaged.

Please contact your dental healthcare provider for assistance.

"Yeah, yeah, yeah," I say. Lemarck takes this as a taunt and rains down punches and kicks. The voice in my head rambles on, like the color commentator for the World Series of Pain.

The Black Coat brings his leg up to his ear, then straight down on my shoulder, taking me to my knees.

Dislocated shoulder.

He yanks me back to my feet and bashes the side of my face with the flat of the pistol.

Broken molar... Chipped tooth... Chipped tooth... Crown dislodged...

He snaps me in the face with a head butt.

Broken nose... Would you like to dispense... Please select dosage... Are you sure you want to continue?

"What?" I say.

Lemarck backs off for a second, confused, and the voice in my head finishes a sentence.

If you continue you may receive a potentially lethal dose of the selected medication. Continue?

A box appears with 'Yes' and 'No' buttons.

"On your knees," Lemarck says.

The button in my mouth is stuck and I can't cancel the selected drug.

"No," I shout.

Lemarck punches me in the throat.

I sag to my knees with a burble. "Skur-lah-dray," is all I can get out.

The pistol aimed at my face, Lemarck pulls the hammer back.

Approved, now dispensing painkillers.

My butler appears at Lemarck's feet.

You called, sir?

Lemarck jumps back. "What the — ?"

It is the first time Sklrda ever listened to me. I celebrate by grabbing the robotic gentleman's gentleman and bring it up under the Black Coat's chin.

Dislocated jaw. This is Lemarck's L.I.F.E. talking for a change. *Four broken teeth.*

He stumbles and drops the pistol. I bring Sklrda down on Lemarck's head.

Laceration. You are currently losing blood. Avulsion. Possible concussion. Skull fracture. Broken nose. Broken cheekbone.

I don't have much time. My body is about to be full of drugs, and I can't let the Black Coat get up.

Laceration. Five broken teeth. Broken jaw.

Sklrda slams into his head five, ten, thirty times before the Black Coat and my butler are quiet and still. Lemarck's L.I.F.E. had shut down and stopped talking. Sklrda wasn't asking if it should clean up all the blood on the floor. I leave them in a mangled heap and crawl to the couch.

The painkillers take hold, and my muscles are too numb to hold my head up. I slip onto my side.

You are currently experiencing an overdose.

"No shit," I mumble.

Would you like to dispense adrenaline?

The buttons are too damaged to be functional, just shards of jagged plastic in the roof of my mouth, and my tongue is too swollen to operate them, even if they weren't. Too drugged to move, my vision narrows. I hear, or hallucinate, the sounds of explosions, car alarms screaming in protest.

My thoughts are a jumble, a hundred different voices in my head.

Is that the door?

Sklrda, would you get that? Oh, you've killed someone.

I bet Herb would know what to do.

Could someone get the door?

I should ask Mary out on a date. Would my wife mind?

Who's at the door?

Dinner and a movie? No, that's too cliché.

Your heart rate is dangerously low, and we'd like to take this opportunity to thank you for your continued patronage.

A fuzzy version of the L.I.F.E. logo hovers on the wall. Or was that in my head?

If reincarnation is a tenet of your belief structure, please choose Life-force Input and Feedback Equipment in the future. If not, thank you again, and have a nice day.

The L.I.F.E. logo fades, and my eyes close.

———

"Pat?" a voice, like Herb's, asks. "Pat?"

"I think he overdosed. Let me get my tools," Mikey says. "His L.I.F.E. is totally shut down. Get the battery out of the butler, and I might be able to jump it."

I open my eyes a crack and make out familiar shapes. "Herb, tell them I don't want to be cremated."

"I'll tell them," Herb says.

"It's too bad Sameer is Muslim," I say.

"Keep him talking," Mary says, as she pries the battery out of my butler.

"Mary's here. That's good. We're all here. It's too bad about Sameer, though."

"What about Sameer?" Herb asks.

"He's Muslim. I mean Hindu. Hindus go to a different heaven than Christians. That's too bad. Herb's Terror Squad could have been together for all eternity. Did I tell you I had an idea for a recruiting poster?"

"No," Herb chuckles, "tell me about it."

"It doesn't matter. We can't use it now that we're dead."

"We're not really dead," Herb says, as he pats my forehead.

"I know, life eternal at the right hand of the Father, along

227

with all the other good Patriots. Do you think we could get a day pass to go visit Sameer in Hindu heaven?"

"I'm right here, Pat," Sameer says. "Why is he talking like we're all dead?"

"Sameer, they put you in the wrong heaven. Are all bureaucracies completely inept?"

"Yes," Herb says, "yes they are."

"This might sting a little," Mikey says. "I'm sorry."

With much pain and gnashing of mostly broken teeth, from the ashes of the once good citizen turned terrorist known as McGewan-X04, a free man rises. He is not a superhero, not without fault, just a man that did what he thought was right for his friends and family, not for Patriotism. The rumor of his death is far more powerful than the facts of his life. By and by, the whole world changed a little at a time because of him.

But that is another story.

A man came out of the ocean for me today...

We have been on The Island for three months. This is Herb's hideaway, and I am reluctant to put a name to our sanctuary. Even in my journal, I choose not to use the name or location. We are simply on The Island and live in The Village, long ago abandoned by tourists and locals alike. The journal was a present from Herb, but this is the first day that anything warranted me cracking it open and putting pen to paper. Every entry that I neglected to write would have started with "Weather continues warm..." and then faltered for lack of anything else to report.

Our flight from civilization was uneventful, at least for me. After being cleaned up, Sameer carried me most of the way over his shoulder, like a sack of bloody and bruised potatoes. My bouts of consciousness were full of ravings of a man believing himself to be dead, but content to spend the rest of eternity with his likewise deceased friends. There were the docks, bribes paid by Herb, then innumerable hours inside a container within the hold of a ship. The ship's doctor removed the now useless L.I.F.E. from my wrist and broken mouse from my mouth. The ship's dentist fixed the repairable teeth, gave me a fake bridge for the ones that were gone for good.

Herb answered my questions when I was coherent enough to speak. Yes, he worked for Homeland Security. Yes, he was an undercover agent. Yes, he switched sides. No, there aren't any terrorists remaining.

I didn't understand most of Herb's answers at the time — he has since repeated himself — but felt more at ease each time unconsciousness wrapped its tendrils around me. My body slowly healed, and within a few days, I slept soundly instead of passing out from the pain. By the time we reached The Island, I was strong enough to lower myself to the lifeboat, but Sameer would not allow me to help him row to the beach.

Herb plans to wait until we are sure no one is looking for us, then leave. To where hasn't been decided. Sameer wants to return to Nepal. Herb wants to go to Germany again before he dies. Mary and Mikey can't agree on where in Europe they want to go. I try to focus on today and not worry about tomorrow.

There is not much to do in The Village, just time sitting around waiting to be whiled away. We have living quarters, tourist bungalows that were sealed at the end of tourist season, never to see the season come back. Clothes and knick-knacks in the souvenir shops, postcards that will never be signed and delivered, day-glow T-shirts and hats advertising where they are from. There is fruit to be picked on the edge of The Village, where the jungle crept back to reclaim what was cleared away for the tourists. The protected cove is crystal clear down to twenty feet, and fish are easily plucked from their home on the end of a homemade spear.

When Herb was still an undercover agent working for Homeland Security, he had heard 'terrorists' talk about The Island as their fallback position. Herb never reported its whereabouts, and no one in America who knew of its existence is still alive.

Shortly after our arrival, Herb found a key that kept him busy for days. He said it was important. "Who would put a key on a gold chain if it wasn't important?"

"Who would leave a key on the beach if it was important?" we all asked. Herb dismissed us and put the key around his neck. Whenever we found a new door, he tried the key, but the doorframe was usually so rotted that the door pushed in with ease, key or not. This became Herb's hobby.

Mary took the first bungalow we came to when we arrived and declared it hers. She gathered trinkets and shells and gave the one-room house a thorough cleaning. Two days later, she sealed the bungalow up again and moved closer to the center of The Village. She moved all her personal touches from one house to the other, saying the first was too drafty. A few days passed before she moved again, this time because of Sameer's snoring. A little while later she relocated for some other reason, the surf beating against the pier or something. Again and again, never staying in one place for more than a few days. This was Mary's pastime.

One of the locked doors that Herb's key did not work on, we opened the old-fashioned way via Sameer's boot. On the other side was a workshop with dusty, but well-preserved tools. Boxes under the workbenches held ancient electronics that seemed to work by witchcraft. Mary dropped one television into the ocean after Herb's explanation that a pair of rabbit's ears, once installed, might allow us to pick up a signal. She had no similar aversion to needles, transistors, or vacuum tubes, but she put her foot down against animal cruelty for our entertainment. Also, there was a tattered and dog-eared book titled "Basic Electronics Repair for the Total Shithead."

The Librarian in Herb came out when there were threats

that our one book would join our one television in its watery grave.

"Total Shithead," Herb explained, "is an antiquated euphemism that means 'beginner' or 'novice.'" When this didn't register with Sameer, who dangled the volume over the water at the end of the pier, Herb continued, "It's like 'The Utter Schmuck's Guide to Home Tattooing' or 'Mechanoid Foreplay for Ginormous Wankers.'"

Explained that way, Sameer kept the book, and, upon returning to the workshop, volunteered to be the shithead that would fix "whatever that is" indicating a large wooden box with fabric on the front. This was how Sameer spent his time.

Mikey, with all his re-engineering experience, was no help to Sameer for several reasons. First, he did not agree with Mary on much of anything since landfall on The Island, but he conceded that Sameer's "whatever that is" probably was demonically powered. Second, he pointed out that none of us had picked up our old jobs, so why should he.

"It's not like you're running the souvenir shop," Mikey says, when Sameer asked him for help. "Pat's not building cubicles, Mary's not acting like a receptionist, Herb's not sorting books. Why should I go back to electronics? I'm going fishing."

There was a freshwater spring and enough alcohol to drown a platoon of Homies a hundred times over, but for the first few days, we ate only fruit, as all the stored food had rotted. Once Mikey declared that he would fish, we had more meat than we knew what to do with. He was still a bundle of energy on land, but once he was ankle-deep in water atop a sandbar, his demeanor changed. He would stand for hours, his homemade spear poised overhead, perfectly still, waiting for acceptable quarry to pass by. He was the calm center of the universe until he saw his prey, then his spear launched with laser-like precision and speed. This became Mikey's hobby.

Herb helped gut and fillet the first few catches, being the only one of us that had ever turned a live animal into food before. Mikey caught on quickly, and Herb resumed his quest for a door that his key would fit in.

I toyed with opening a coffee shop, my dream job, but there was no sense... no currency, no customers. There was also a complete lack of coffee and a coffeemaker. I found a fishing rod one day, Herb said it's for sport fishing, marlins and sharks, and that I need to be on a boat for it to work properly. I didn't care. I went to the edge of the pier and with all my might, cast my line out into the cove. Then I'd sit and slowly reel the line in. Once the lure was back to me, I would get up and do it all over again.

It was at the beginning of the second week that we all heard Herb shouting, whooping, and hollering. We dropped what we were doing and ran inland to find him, but by the time we left The Village proper, he had gone quiet. It took a few minutes of circling through the denser parts of the jungle before we came upon him, sitting on a log reading a book.

"What the hell were you shouting for?" Mary asked.

"Oh, hello," he says, looking up. "I found the lock for my key, finally. It goes to that house." He pointed over his shoulder and went back to his book.

We stared at the jungle behind him and saw just, well, jungle. A little light filtered in through the canopy above, making the noon-day sun into a dusky shadow world, with an occasional burst of colorful vegetation basking in a gap in the foliage overhead. Mary took a step forward, then another, then, foot frozen in midair, she gasped. I stepped up to her and tilted my head to the side. An unnaturally straight line resolved itself amongst the tree trunks and vines. The four of us left Herb on his log and walked shoulder to shoulder to the group of trees. As we neared, the outline of the shack got clearer and clearer, until we could separate the overgrown thatch and wood from the surrounding jungle. A heartfelt sneeze might topple the little building, but with the trees as a windbreak, this had never been a problem. Theft was more of a threat from the look of the deadbolt and solid door. Inside, there was a cot in one corner, a pitcher and basin for water on the table, with its sole chair, and that was all in the way of amenities. The former occupant must have gotten food daily and cooked outside in a long-since overgrown fire pit. The only other thing in the building was bookshelves. They went from floor to ceiling on all four walls, the only gap being the door we had entered through. Even the cot and table stood blocking parts of the shelves. Had the driftwood blown away on the outside, the packed shelves would have kept the roof up. We left quietly, all of us chilled to see a building with an actual lived-in feel, not the sterile but dusty quarters for the tourists. Someone had built this place, someone had found or sent away for these books, and someone had cared enough about them that they locked the door when they left. Whether they lost the key when they left or left the key to be found for the next visitors was anyone's guess. Herb left the key inside but trekked out into the jungle every couple of days to return the finished book and borrow another.

And nothing exciting has happened since then until...

———

Today, I sat on the end of the pier casting my line on my too-long rod out into the cove. Herb sat next to me, a broad-brimmed straw hat shaded his face and neck. My line came in to the rhythm of the waves. Every third wave hit the pier's pilings hard enough to splash our dangling feet. In all my time fishing, I had caught several hundred pounds of seaweed and one boot. The others laughed at me, a little, at my utter lack of angling prowess, but when I pulled the boot onto the pier, there was no end to the jokes.

How do you prepare one of those?

Fillet of sole, again?

What sort of wine do you recommend for old leather?

Etcetera.

Etcetera.

I didn't mind. I was there for the fishing, not for the fish.

Mary and Mikey were nowhere to be seen, probably sunbathing and catching fish, respectively. Sameer was working on his "whatever that is" which had turned out to be a radio. Due to its age, the only station it picked up played a loop of old, tinny regimental marching songs without interruption. Herb named most of the songs in the loop, and the rest of us played a game where we tried to name the song the quickest. Sameer was currently trying to hook the radio up to the public address system with its speakers scattered among the cabanas on the beach. As it was, I could just make out the sound of Ruffles and Flourishes over the sound of the ocean.

"That's odd," I mumble.

"What?" Herb asks without looking up from his book. "Did a blind fish bump into your hook?"

"I just saw this enormous bubble out by the reef."

Herb marks his place with his finger and squints into the cove. "In all recorded time, you must be the first person ever to see a bubble on the ocean. Congratulations." He reopens his book with a chuckle.

The squeak of my reel stops. "There's a person out there."

With a sigh, he closes the book again. "You aren't going to let me read, are you?" He looks up, but the figure is gone. "Where? I don't see anyone."

"I swear someone was standing out there."

"How? Just some guy strolling across the ocean?" A grin

spread across his face. "Better confess your sins, it's Jesus come to take you home." The chuckle catches in his throat when a man struggles up out of the water and waves at us. "Is that the fellow you saw?"

"That would be a tremendous coincidence if it wasn't."

"I wonder what he wants?"

I shrug as Ruffles and Flourishes ended. In unison, we mumble, "Pomp and Circumstance," as the next song plays. The waves slap harder and harder against the pier.

"Oh shit," I say, "Pomp and Circumstance. The tide's coming in." I jump up and my pole slides off the pier and with a plop, sinks to the bottom of the cove. "The tide, Herb, what are we going to do? He'll get torn apart on the reef. We have to do something."

"I intend to sit here and watch the show."

"He'll be killed."

"Precisely," Herb says. "Don't look at me like that. He either knows who we are and intends us harm or he's lost and will want to call in a rescue ship to get himself back to civilization. Either way, letting the sea claim him saves me the trouble of drowning him myself." He squints up at me with the cold, calculating eye. "Be a smart terrorist again, Pat."

"I'm retired," I say, then cup my hands around my mouth and shout. "The tide is coming in. Hurry."

The man's response is absorbed by the sound of the ocean.

I do my best pantomime of swimming, gesture for him to come to me, run in place, shout, wave, but nothing clicks with him. The waves unbalancing him on the head of coral that he stands on makes him look over his shoulder, but too late. He dives in and swims toward us. But even an Olympic-caliber athlete couldn't have swum the hundred yards fast enough. The first few waves push him under, and he struggles to the surface each time to restart his stroke, but it is no good.

Herb whistles through his teeth. "Here it comes."

The wave picks the stranger up. The crest carries him, weightless for a moment, his arms and legs still flailing for the beach, then the bottom of the wave catches the reef and the crest slams him into the bottom. I dive off the side of the pier and swim towards where I last saw him. I stay close to the shallows, swim under the waves as they come at me. I use a sandbar to stand and try to spot him.

"Hey, Pat," Sameer shouts from under a nearby palm tree, "it's high tide. You shouldn't be swimming right now."

"There's someone out here," I shout back.

He seems to ignore me. "Why don't you help me with these speakers?"

"There's a stranger out here."

"Really? Do you think he knows anything about speakers?"

"I'll ask when I find him." I dive towards a dark spot, catch the collar of his wetsuit, and haul him toward the shore. He is conscious and struggles as I swim, eventually getting out of my grip as a wave takes me under. The water is chest-deep, and I stand again to spot him. The riptide carried him away from me, but thankfully not out into the deeps. He is twenty feet away, walking on unsteady legs toward me, fighting his way against the surf. He has a full beard, streaked with blood. His hair sticks out at odd angles. The reef has shredded his wetsuit and the business suit underneath. He pulls a black pouch off his belt and waves it at me.

"What is it?" I shout. It is the wrong shape to be a weapon, but I am ready to dive under if he threatened me with it.

He is in knee-deep water now, five feet away. He sways, his breathing labored. When he has enough air inside, he points at the pouch, and says, "It's—"

Sameer figures out his speaker problem at that moment, and the Liberty Bell March blasts from all around us, too loud for either of us to be heard. I can see his lips moving but don't hear a word of it. Just as the song ends, a wave slams us both underwater, like the foot of a giant.

Somehow, I catch his collar again and drag his limp body out of the water, his pouch dragging along behind him on a tether. Once on dry sand, I collapse next to him and try to catch my breath. A shadow passes across my face, and I look up at Sameer.

"What's going on, Pat?"

"Nothing."

"I got the speakers working."

"Good."

"Who's that?"

"I don't know. The surf knocked him out before I could find out."

Sameer looks around the horizon. "Where'd he come from?"

"I don't know."

Sameer nods. "What's he doing here?"

"How the fuck should I know? I saw him standing on the reef, he swam in, the tide knocked him unconscious, and I dragged him out of the water. You officially know everything I know." Standing is difficult, and Sameer doesn't offer to help. Our visitor is still breathing, which is good, as my CPR certification had lapsed. Blood and saltwater muddy the sand around his body. I am about to ask Sameer to help me get him to The Village when Mary and Mikey walk up. Mary's wearing a two-piece bikini with a sarong around her hips. Mikey has his fishing spear in one hand, and a chain that held fish off his belt, like the least pleasant watch fob ever.

"Who's this?" Mary asks.

"I don't know," I say.

"Some guy Pat dragged out of the cove," Sameer says.

"Why is he all beat up?" Mikey asks.

"He got caught in high tide," I say.

"The reef knocked him out," Sameer adds.

Mary and Mikey mull this over. "So, what's he doing here?"

I growl at the question, pick the visitor up in a fireman's carry, and stomp toward The Village.

"What's his problem?" Mary asks.

———

Herb is waiting for me in The Village's clinic, the first-aid kit open next to the exam table. He raises his hand before I can speak. "I'll fix him up, find out what he wants, then I'll worry about drowning him." I nod and put my charge on the table. Mary comes in and shaves his beard while I cut off the remains of his clothing. There is one cut along his right eyebrow that Herb stitches, the rest are just cleaned out and bandaged. Sameer holds a flashlight during the stitching but mostly stands out of the way for the rest of it. Mikey comes in with a pile of clothing out of the gift shop, and we dress him in a dark sweat-suit and T-shirt, both commemorating the island's sixth annual bicycle race. When we have done as much as we can, Mary opens doors, while the four of us carry the patient to a clean bungalow that she had lived in for a while.

We get him into bed, his black pouch on the nightstand. The others leave Herb and me standing over him and go work on dinner.

"All kidding aside," I say, "what do you think he's doing here?"

Herb shakes his head. "We'll have to wait and see."

"Should we open his pouch?"

He shakes his head, again. "It's not a weapon, not heavy enough. Everything in its own time." He tilts his head to the music outside. "A Toast to the Host, it's Happy Hour. We'll let him rest."

————

We find the others in the shaded section of the square, the catch of the day grilling, the cocktails being passed around. If it wasn't for the radio coming out of speakers all over The Village, it would have been completely silent. We all have questions about our guest, the man the ocean had coughed up onto our beach, but no one wants to be the first to ask.

After a while, Sameer leans forward and refills his drink. "Is it just me, or is it really weird that we don't even know the guy's name, let alone how he got here or what he wants?"

We all nod.

"I've been calling him 'the visitor' in my head," Mary says.

"I think we should call him Number Six," Mikey says.

"Why?" I ask.

"That's the number on the front of the shirt. It's like he's a random athlete that I'm cheering on. Get him, Number Six. Go, go Number Six. Wonderful shot, Number Six." Mikey's face reddens. "That sounds kind of dumb saying it out loud."

Herb raises his glass. "That works for me. A toast," we clink glasses, "to Number Six and whatever it is that brought him here."

————

Dinner finished, sun down, we sit and laugh over cocktails at ridiculous possibilities for Number Six's presence.

"Maybe," I say as I try to take a drink, spilling it onto my chest, "maybe, no listen, maybe he's with Fish and Game, and

240

he's going to take Mikey away for fishing without a license."
The drinks make us all laugh a lot louder than was necessary.

"Well then," Mary says, "you've got nothing to worry
about."

Sameer coughs up his drink. Mikey slaps him on the back
as he laughs. Herb pounds himself on the thigh as he howls. I
throw a lime wedge at Mary, which she dodges, then sticks her
tongue out at me.

As the laughter dies down, Mikey says, "Maybe Number
Six is a spy who tried to retire, but he knew too many secrets, so
they sent him here as punishment."

Herb and I laugh but stop when Sameer jumps to his feet.

"What's wrong?" I ask.

"Who is Number Six?" asks a voice from behind me.

We turn to look at our guest. He has one hand on a palm
tree for support, the pouch is in the other hand. He looks dazed,
doped up, but fights it, trying hard to maintain his composure.

"Come and sit," Herb says. "We'll get you some dinner."

Sameer helps him to the table. Mikey pours him a cocktail
after he is seated.

"Who is Number Six?" he asks, again.

"The shirt," Mikey says, pointing. "We didn't know your
name, so we've been calling you Number Six."

He looks down at the logo of a bicycle tire with a six inside
of it and nods. "I'm not a number. I'm a free man."

"Excuse me?" Herb says.

"I'm A. Freeman, Alexander Freeman, and I'm looking for
someone. Thanks for the shave, by the way."

"You're welcome," Mary says.

"Someone else packed my little submersible for me, and
I've gone almost three months without a razor. Of course, no
one realized, not even me, that I would be out here this long."
He sips his drink. "Strong. Just what I needed. Thank you."

"Who are you looking for?" I ask.

"It's a snipe hunt at this point. Fellow probably died of his wounds or was shot trying to leave the country. The upside is that I'm getting paid to visit every rinky-dink island in the Pacific. That is, it's an upside, as long as the locals don't try to kill me when I stroll up onto their beach."

We all lean forward and hang on his every word, while he sips his cocktail.

"What did you say this fellow's name was?" Herb asks, though it is on the tip of everyone's tongue.

"I didn't, I don't believe. It's McGewan-X04."

Sameer and Mikey drag him out of his chair backward, his drink shatters on the paving stones. Mary grabs her brother's fishing spear and follows them as they pull Freeman toward the beach.

"Herb — ," I say, but he cut me off.

"I told you, Pat. We find out what he wants, then we drown him. It's the only way to stay safe."

"Pat?" Freeman shouts, as his heels dig tracks in the sand. "You're Pat? Pat McGewan? You're X04?"

"I am, I was X04," I say, as I walk beside him. "I'm a little worse for the wear and I'm retired, so it's just Pat, now."

"But I've come all this way," he says.

"Should have stayed home," Sameer says. They had him at the end of the pier. Without a word, Sameer holds Freeman while Mikey ties the prisoner's hands behind his back. Mary goes down on one knee and lashes his ankles together. This is one-half Herb's German preparedness gene and one-half his Librarian attention to detail.

"At least let me give you the package," Freeman says. Herb shakes his head, and Mikey and Sameer lift our bound visitor off the pier.

"Herb, wait," I say. They put Freeman down. "At least let me open the package."

"We can just as easily open it when he's dead," Herb replies. Freeman's feet leave the ground.

"Wait," I say, and they put him down, "he's come all this way."

"That's right, I've come a long way."

"What if I have questions about the package?"

"Right, questions, I can answer questions."

"There could be a combination or a password to open it."

"Right, right, a combination."

"We should at least find that out before we kill him."

"Right, you should, well the first part at least. The second part, maybe not so much."

Herb scratches his chin for a second on my side of the pier, for a day and a half on Freeman's end. "All right, go get the package."

I turn, then spin back around. Freeman's feet dangle over the water. "Herb?"

"Fine, set him down. Mary, would you kindly run back to the table and get Mr. Freeman's package?"

Mary rolls her eyes and walks back up the beach.

"So," Herb says, "why don't you tell us about this package while we wait."

"It would be better if I showed you, because, you see..."

"If you wait, you might live longer?"

"That pretty much sums it up."

Mary returns and hands the pouch to Herb.

"Do I need to worry about booby-traps?" Herb asks.

"It will go very badly for you if there's a booby-trap," Sameer growls in his charge's ear.

"Really? Worse than being drowned?"

"No one said you had to drown quickly."

After traveling around the entire Pacific in a one-man sub, Freeman's worst possible fear is probably drowning slowly. "I assure you there are no booby-traps, but there are documents inside, so please watch out for paper cuts."

Herb pulls out a black rubberized cube the size of his fist and a sheaf of papers in a waterproof bag. "You represent Anderson and Goldberg?" Herb asks as he leafs through the pages.

Freeman nods.

"Why does that sound familiar?" I ask.

"They're your landlords," Herb says.

"Property management specialists," Freeman corrects.

"Argue semantics with Herb again and see what happens," Sameer spits.

"Sameer," Herb says with a raised eyebrow.

He nods. "I'll take it down a notch. Sorry."

"What do they want?" I ask.

"It's a copy of your lease," Herb says.

"You've got to be kidding," I say. "You came all this way because I skipped out on my lease? Or, are you here to hit me up for damages?"

"Actually, neither," Freeman says.

"Did you read this thing before you signed it?" Herb asked.

"It's a lease. Who reads leases?"

"Did you ever wonder why your rent was so cheap?"

"I didn't have a lot of credits, so I looked until I found something I could afford."

"One of your landlords apparently dabbles in television production."

"Who? Goldberg?"

"That's racial profiling," Freeman says. "Just because he has a Jewish surname doesn't automatically mean he's the one in show business." Herb cocks his eyebrow. "It is Goldberg, but it could have just as easily been Anderson."

"It says here that you are under constant surveillance while in the building," Herb read.

"That's pretty standard," I say. "If I take a crap in Ishmael's, then I'm on video so they can give me a ticket for not flushing. So what?"

"The next part isn't so standard. Do you want to tell him?" he asks Freeman. "I'm assuming that's why you're here."

"Section 129, Paragraph D, Clause 243, Sub-Section j, states that the aforementioned surveillance recordings may be released without notification or compensation of the tenant as the management sees fit."

"Okay," I say, not understanding. "You don't need my permission, so what do you need me for?"

"Section 129, Paragraph — ," he starts.

"He wants the rest," Herb cuts him off. "He wants you to sign a release, so they can subpoena every other surveillance recording from around the city and have the complete story. Or did I misread that?"

"That's exactly right. We leaked a clip of you arguing with Flanery and fighting with the Inquisitor, and people are clamoring for the rest."

"How can you leak something that is your property?" I ask. "I always thought you needed another party for that."

"It's standard practice now," Mikey says. "It does away with the high cost and abysmal payoffs of pilot episodes and test audiences." We all stare at him. "I worked in a broadcasting supercenter. You pick things up."

"Clamoring, you say?" I reply.

"Full-blown, epidemic-level clamor. Flanery's gone. Wait. I don't want to give away the ending."

"The ending?" I shout. "It's my life. How can you know the ending?"

"Are you sure you want me to spoil it for you?" he asks. Mikey and Sameer lift him off the ground. "Fine, I'll spill. Flanery's off the air and is serving time in the molybdenum mine. We saw to it that the Dean was released. We tested, small scale, Flanery getting buggered by the Dean before the Dean's release, but it seemed trite. A little too matchy-matchy, eye for an eye, if you know what I mean."

"And?" I say. "What about the other stuff?"

"What other stuff?"

"What about the government, the fear of mythical terrorists, the bullshit commemorative cups at Ishmael's? All of it."

"We refer to your fight with Flanery as The Protest. Capital 'P', like The Collapse. You have no idea how much you've changed everything. The riots caused enough stress in the big cities on the computerized infrastructure that only essential services were available. Water and power, nothing else. This caused the cars to stop self-driving on the streets, which caused accidents, which caused more stress on the network. Everything computerized suffered. This branched out in cascading concentric circles until it went nationwide. Flights were grounded. Highways were closed. And most importantly, everyone's L.I.F.E. went offline within twenty-four hours of you leaving the country."

"No more THAW?" I ask.

He shakes his head. "Let me tell you, the buzz on this is ginormous. The citizenry has spoken with a flood of emails and non-stop text messages to their state and federal representatives. People are protesting in the streets for the first time in decades. The first day we leaked that clip, so much digital feedback went through that the government's network shut down again. They had to postpone Congress for a day because the

Las Vegas Two Space Station couldn't vote until the network was re-established. This is bigger than the Great Wall of China magically appearing around Washington, D.C. and the Mongol Horde raping and pillaging through central Nebraska."

"That big, huh?" I say with sarcasm.

"I've got the numbers if you'd like to see them."

I shake my head.

"The government has reopened talks with the European Union. The President did the State of the Union from the Senate floor instead of from Air Force One. That hasn't happened for the last four Presidents. The networks have gutted the news apparatus to avoid being shit-hammered by new federal laws that are in the works. It will seem like a different place when you come back."

"Back?" I say.

"Of course, you have to come back. There are parts of your story that the cameras didn't get. We need you, all of you, to come back and reenact some of the scenes and fill in the holes."

"Do you have sponsors and endorsement deals lined up already?" I ask.

"Companies couldn't get in line fast enough. Your style, your face, your ideas will be everywhere."

"Instead of 'If you don't use our product the terrorists have already won' it will be 'Drink this, eat this, wear this because Xo4 does?'"

"Yes, indeed."

"'What would Xo4 do?' bumper stickers and buttons?"

"Definitely."

Herb looks at me, a half-smile on his lips.

"Fuck that," I say, "I'm not going back, not like that."

"What? Why not?" Freeman asks.

"I'm not going to risk my life fighting a corrupt, fear-based system so I can go back to a new corrupt, fear-based system. It's great that people know the truth now and they aren't afraid of fictional terrorists anymore. But I am not going to fill that void by being the friendly terrorist they're afraid to anger. Thanks, but no thanks."

"What's in the cube?" Herb asks, weighing it in his hand.

"It's the first payment on the contract," Freeman says. "Goldberg wanted me to tell you that it was your damage deposit with a little extra. It's keyed to X04's fingerprint."

I take the cube and press my thumb into the lid. When it swings open, Mary gasps.

"They didn't know where you were or what currency you'd like, so they sent diamonds."

"A lot of good could come out of that kind of money," Mikey says.

"Good food, good clothes, good cars, good houses," I say. They all nod. "Good people bowing and scraping to me for their grocery money. I don't want it." I close the lid and hand the cube back to Herb.

"You're thinking about this one-dimensionally," Herb says.

"That's funny coming from you."

"We need to discuss this."

"I'm not going back."

"So, it's a monarchy?" Mary shouts. "What you say goes? None of our opinions matter?"

"No," I say. "It's exactly the opposite. One person, one vote. My vote is that I'm not ready to go back, but you can do whatever you want."

I look at my friends. Mikey leaning on his spear. Sameer, his face skinnier, but his beard growing wild to cover that fact. Herb in his floppy hat, a book in his hand. Mary, too many years in a drab jumpsuit to everyday in a bikini, laughing over cocktails. My fishing pole that I'll never catch a fish with, resting at the bottom of the cove.

There isn't a great philosophical reason for not wanting to leave. I don't want to become the new Flanery, but edgier. Granted. But there is a simpler reason.

I want to spend the rest of my life in safety with the only friends I ever had.

We walk along the dock, back to The Village.

"Are we forgetting something?" I ask.

"Hey," shouts Freeman, as he hops after us. "Are you just going to leave me here?"

Sameer and Mary laugh.

"If you hurry," Herb says, "you can come with us."

We wait at the end of the dock and watch him try to keep upright.

A thought occurs to me. "You said you were in a one-man submarine, right?"

"Yeah," he says. One-word answers seem the best course with how hard he is working to catch up to us.

"What was your plan, if we decided to come back with you?"

A shadow crosses the ground between us. Everyone reflexively looks up. The ground shakes, and when we look down, Freeman is gone, crushed under a metal box. Not a forty-ton Conex box, but big enough to make him disappear. Everything but his bound feet.

I look to Herb and shake my head. "Where do you suppose that came from?"

Wind tousles our hair. Herb grips his hat. On the beach, silent as a whisper, an aircraft, military issue gray, is landing vertically.

"Check this out," Mikey says, poking around the box that had killed Freeman.

"Get away from there," Mary says, not looking away from the plane.

"It's full of diamonds and gold," Mikey says.

"What?" Sameer says.

That got everyone's attention. The plane seems to be doing nothing, so we risk a glance. Mikey is holding a handful of diamonds and gold coins.

"First, lead paint," I say, "now gold and diamonds."

"You're an alchemist, Pat," Herb says.

"I spent so much time rescuing that guy, and he gets crushed by a box of treasure. Someone's getting a strongly worded letter. Shall we meet who I'm addressing that letter to?"

"Let's shall," Herb says.

The five of us walk down the beach toward the aircraft, its engines spooling down. A ramp descends as we approach.

"Right there will be fine," says a voice from a hidden speaker.

We stop.

"Mr. McGewan, I have been looking for you for quite some time," the voice says.

"I'm getting a lot of that recently," I shout. "Who are you?"

"Why don't you come out where we can see you?" Sameer says.

"I will, but I have to warn you, I am a very old man."

I look at Herb. He shrugs.

"Doesn't matter to us," I say. "We're equal opportunity here on The Island."

"I don't say it out of fear of ageism," the voice says. "I just don't want my appearance to startle you."

"Do we need to help you?" I ask.

"No, I'm more than capable."

There is a grating of metal on metal. The plane rocks slightly on the sand, and a figure emerges. It isn't a man, not by any definition I know. The figure is a bipedal robot, all torso, no neck or head. Hydraulic tubing courses down each leg and along each arm. It comes down the ramp and stops at the edge.

"I don't mean to be rude, but I'll stand right here if you don't mind," the robot says. "Sand plays merry hell with my gears."

"Who... what are you?" Mary asks.

"'Who' would be more correct." A section of the torso, where the stomach would be in a person, slides open. Under the metal is a glass tank, full of liquid. A brain with eyes still attached floats in the liquid. "I am still a who and not a what, despite appearances."

"Okay," I say, "who are you?"

"You've never heard of me, so telling you my name would be pointless."

"I assume you aren't Goldberg or Anderson," Herb says.

"That is correct. You can call me, Charles." The front of the glass flickers and a picture of an old, white-haired man appears. "Is that better? Some people find the image more disturbing than looking directly at my brain."

"What brings you here, Charles?" Sameer says.

"I have a business proposition for you, Mr. McGewan," Charles says.

"You just killed a bound man with a box of treasure," I say. "I'm not sure I approve of your negotiating tactics."

"Who? Freeman?" He makes a gurgling sound that might be a laugh. "I assumed he had died ages ago. There's fifty more where he came from. Don't lose sleep over it. It shocked me when he activated his locator beacon, truth be told. And pleasantly surprised that you didn't kill him outright. I played the tape back on my flight. Either he was a better attorney than I thought, or the lot of you aren't that smart."

"Murder. Insults," Herb says. "You are an exceptional negotiator, Charles."

"I am," Charles says, "and I'll tell you why. I have something that no one else has. Money."

"We all had money," I say.

"No, you had credits," Charles says. "Credits don't spend anywhere but in America. You had millions of credits, but that wouldn't be enough to buy you a loaf of day-old bread anywhere in the world. Your grandparents complained about all the millionaires and billionaires in the country, ruining the world. Fine. Throw a couple zeroes on the back of every number and you're all millionaires. I have more money lost in the cushions of this plane than you ever controlled in your entire life."

"Now you are arguing economics with us," Herb says. "Can you get to the proposal so we can say 'no' and go about our business?"

"You're so hasty, Herb," Charles says. "Can't we chat a bit before we get to the business? Besides, the proposal is not for you. Only Mr. McGewan."

"Fine," I say. "Can you speed this up? You're rich beyond our wildest dreams. You have a business proposal. I assume you are one of The Five."

"The Five?" The gurgling noise comes out of the speaker again. "Yes, there are five men that run the five biggest companies in America. They take turns as President. They all played grab-ass in college and made out with each other's drunken wives at parties. But they run the companies. They are the Chief Executive Officers. They aren't the owners."

"So, you're an owner," I say.

"No, I'm the owner. I own them all. I own everything," Charles says. "I own the building you lived in and the factory you worked at and the company that bought cubicles from you and the shipping company that dropped the box on your car and the hospital that put you back together and the television station that Flanery worked for and the company that made your bogus memorabilia. Everything but the air you breathe. I assure you, I'm working on that as well."

Charles pushes a button where his right hip should be and six boxes drop from the plane. The boxes are identical to the one that crushed Freeman. The lids open on their own, after a moment. From ten feet, we can all see the gold and uncut gems.

"I am without a body," Charles says. "My doctors believe I will live for hundreds of years as long as I recharge every few hours. They cannot give me pleasure though."

The five of us exchange a look.

"I'm not sure I like where this is going," I say.

"It's nothing base," Charles says. "When you are without a body, pleasures of the flesh do nothing for you. Food. Women. Hunting. All the things I enjoyed with my brother before he died have paled in the form you see here. But there is one thing that still excites me."

"We can't wait to hear what that is," Mary says, her hands bunched into fists.

"Money," Charles says. "Wealth."

"Greed," I say.

"You say it as if it were a bad thing."

"Where I grew up, it is," I say. "A mortal sin, in fact."

"I am not burdened with your notion of sin," Charles says. "I am only concerned with profit and growth. Flanery is in prison, and he was a reliable revenue stream. You will replace him and become my new revenue stream. That's my proposal. These six boxes and the one on Mr. Freeman will make you the only wealthy person in the country besides me."

"I don't know if you watch the news," I say, "but Flanery and I didn't exactly see eye to eye."

"Your show will be whatever you wish it to be," Charles says. "Rail against The Five. Replace the Inquisitors with the

Fairness Police. Root out corruption. Hand out cupcakes and unicorn stickers. Do whatever you like. I'll make money either way. Anything you choose, the money will filter up to me. Be worse than Flanery, be better than Flanery, it's more money for me."

Arms snake down from the plane and retrieve the boxes.

"Shall we go? Or did you need a moment to say goodbye to your friends?" Charles asks.

"Mikey?" I say.

Mikey's spear leaps from his hand and severs the hydraulic line on Charles's leg.

"What are you doing?" Charles shouts, as his mechanical suit wobbles and falls in the sand. Sameer rolls him over. Mary smashes the antenna housing on the back of Charles's suit with a rock.

"I need my tools," Mikey says.

Mary sprints to The Village and comes back with her brother's tool-kit. Mikey pries the smashed antenna housing out of the suit and throws it into the ocean. Charles struggles to right himself, but the hydraulic pressure is dropping too fast for his appendages to be effective.

"What are you doing?" Charles shout.

"I think we're good," Mikey says.

Sameer rolls Charles over so he could see all of us.

"We disabled the beacon in the back of your suit, Charles," I say.

"How did you know about the beacon? What are you trying to do?"

Mikey squats in front of Charles, the suit's arms flopping uselessly. "Recognize me?" Mikey asks. "People say I look a lot like my father."

"I don't know you or your father," Charles says.

"You sent a squad of soldiers to bust up some workers

attempting to organize a union, to demand better wages and safer work conditions," Mikey says. "Herb was there. There was no talking, no arrests. Your men murdered everyone. My father wasn't involved with the union, he was just another employee that happened to get caught in the crossfire. Herb tried to save him, but all he could do was save his eye. My dad made Herb swear to protect his children, to see this never happened to Mary and me. So, we've been sitting here waiting for you to show yourself."

"You couldn't know about me or my suit," Charles says.

"I worked in the same building as Flanery. You would have the building evacuated when you wanted to talk to your pet revenue stream. I hid in the chases over Flanery's office every time you visited. Herb wanted to keep Mary and me out of trouble, but I convinced him that we would always be in danger, as long as you were walking the Earth."

"But the suit," Charles says.

"Mikey knew you had to be someone important to get a building cleared just to talk to Flanery," Herb says. "Mary backtracked the building's lease through all the dummy corporations and think tanks and found your name along with everything else you owned. Sameer followed the threads through all the companies. He's the one who found that Kinetic Rehabilitation made a prosthetic for your brother when he lost his leg in a boating accident. Then, you bought them out, and they filed for one patent before you dismantled the company and laid off all the workers. Kinetic Rehabilitation's Autonomous Nucleoplasmic Garment, what you're wearing now, what Mikey described when he told us about your visit. You may keep yourself hidden, but I only had to fill out one form to get a copy of the patent."

"You are throwing untold wealth away," Charles says.

"Yes, untold wealth," Mary says. "Immortality. The chance

to be just like you, rotting away on top of a pile of gold while the world shudders and moans beneath your feet. We're really missing out."

Sameer and I grab the chest that killed Freeman and set it next to Charles on the sand.

Mikey and Mary walk up the ramp into the aircraft. The engines begin to spool up a moment later.

"How about now, Pat?" Sameer says.

The three of us stand, looking down at Charles.

"I think I'm ready to leave now," I say. "The neighborhood has really gone downhill."

Herb and Sameer walk up the ramp.

"It took Freeman months to find us," I told Charles, once we are alone. "Without your beacon, I'm not sure if anyone will ever find you."

"I need to recharge," Charles says. "I need you to help me into the plane. There are machines inside that will repair me."

"You could have made the world a better place, but you chose not to. Why?" I ask.

"There is no profit in happiness. Fear is the fuel that brought me all of my wealth."

I consider this as I look at the ocean. "I'd say, 'I'll be seeing you,' but that would be a lie."

"You can't leave me here with nothing."

I point at the chest that killed Freeman. "You have wealth. Isn't that all you've ever wanted?"

I walk into the plane, leaving Charles and his bloody box of treasure on the sand. Mikey retracts the ramp and readies the plane for takeoff. The plane surges into the night sky, away from The Island with my friends beside me.

The Island.

The one I am still reluctant to name, even now, years later.

END

Jason R. Richter is a perennial runner-up in Jason R. Richter look-alike contests. The orphaned love child of Kilgore Trout and Margaret Dumont, he was raised by marauding gypsy accountants. When the bottom fell out of the interplanetary death ray market at the dawn of the new millennium, he turned his hobby (a game he calls "Lies to Strangers") into a career. He currently lives.

To stay up to date with whatever nonsense Jason is up to, visit DiskordianPress.com/Newsletter

If you find typos or errors of any sort, please email us at:
Trouble@DiskordianPress.com

Otherwise, thanks for reading. A review on Goodreads, Amazon, or wherever you read book reviews goes a long way to support independent authors. Cheers!

Made in United States
Troutdale, OR
09/09/2023

12769268R00166